# Warrior

A collection of short stories

WARRIOR © 2017 by Ink & Locket Press

Cover design © Thought Library Media

All rights reserved. No part of this publication may be reproduced, distributed or transmitted in any form or by any means, including photocopying, recording, or other electronic or mechanical methods, without the prior written permission of the publisher, except in the case of brief quotations in critical reviews and certain other noncommercial uses permitted by copyright law. For permission requests, write to the publisher, addressed "Attention: Permissions Coordinator" at the address below.

The authors within this publication retain copyright for their work.

These Bodies are Battlefields © 2017 Tash McAdam
Sole Survivor © 2017 Lewis Bright Rees
The Seeing Hands of Captain Zerach © 2017 Kayla Bashe
Seida the Fairy-Troll © 2017 Claudie Arseneault
Colossus of Ephesus © 2017 Tyler Gates
The Metal Mermaid © 2017 Kelly Matsuura
Howl © 2017 Natalie Cannon
Things We'll Never Know © 2017 B R Sanders
Glass Bones © 2017 Kirstie Olley
Unnecessary Risks © 2017 Abigail Rosenhart
Nothing Good To Say © 2017 E H Timms
From Dust 'til Dawn © 2017 Helle Reiersen

Ink & Locket Press
MacLaurin Building, Bishops Square
Hatfield, UK, AL10 9NE
www.inkandlocket.com

First edition printed by CreateSpace

ISBN 978-1-912159-00-0

# WARRIOR

## A COLLECTION OF SHORT STORIES

Edited by Antonica Jones

Written by Claudie Arseneault, Kayla Bashe, Lewis Bright Rees, Natalie Cannon, Tyler Gates, Kelly Matsuura, Tash McAdam, Kirstie Olley, Helle Reiersen, Abigail Rosenhart, B R Sanders and E H Timms

# Contents

# Trigger Warnings

You are about to dive into twelve thrilling short stories about warriors, some light and exciting, some dark and dangerous, and some a bit of both. We want all our readers to enjoy them as much as possible, so we have chosen to include a list of trigger warnings for each story within the anthology.

At Ink & Locket Press, we support readers actively engaging with literature and discussion they are both comfortable and uncomfortable with. After all, when we ask people to read more diversely, we are often asking them to engage with topics they may find foreign, strange and, yes, uncomfortable.

But some readers may find certain topics more difficult to confront than others. Painful memories might be stirred up by the mention of distressing events and trigger physical illness or panic attacks. In theory, any subject can become a "trigger", but there are a few culprits that often lead the pack, such as mentions of violence, abuse, blood, war, eating disorders or self-harm.

What follows is a list of core trigger warnings applicable to each story in this anthology. These trigger warnings are not intended as signs to those who find a topic triggering to stay away. We list them here for a friendly heads up: a warning that something difficult is coming up, giving the reader time to prepare.

Now, make yourself comfortable and get ready; the first story begins with the flick of a page.

Amelia and Antonica
Manager and head editor
Ink & Locket Press

# Trigger warnings

# These Bodies are Battlefields

Tash McAdam

She's here again, watching. Well, dozens of people are watching, maybe hundreds. I'm quite the draw, after all—youngest person competing on the pit-fight circuits, and a girl, to boot. At least, that's what they see when they look at me. It doesn't matter how I feel about it.

The only time I'm free is when I fight. Here I can be not only what they want, but what I want, too. People love to come and see me, shattering bones and bruising flesh. I'm special. A human weapon, made of rage. And who doesn't love to watch the beauty of violence? It's all there is, in the aching mess of the lower city. We live and breathe the fights.

But this girl, she's different. My age, or thereabouts; both of us too young to be here, in this place, with these people. Most sixteen year olds are busy with their apprenticeships, not tearing themselves bloody against men five years their senior or betting gold on fist fights. I mean, I don't know if she gambles, because I don't know anything about her, but I can't think of any other reason she would be here, every time, haunting me with her liquid-brown, dreamer eyes. I always look for her, anyway, and she's always here when I fight. Ever since the very first time I stepped into the ring, when I barely managed to walk out again.

She doesn't cheer and scream for me like the crowd does, pulsing and sweating like an animal. Just stands, watching, following my every move, her thin face steady and serene. Her cheekbones are as sharp as the well-kept knives I've spotted at her belt. She always stands next to the splintered wooden pole in my corner, always looking at only me. She never takes her eyes off me.

Shifting uncomfortably, I meet her gaze now and try to smile at her, as I always do. She blinks languidly, telling me something in a language I don't speak, and I look down again; the heat of her eyes unsettles me. Still, her calmness sinks into my skin and I stretch my hands out, staring at them so I don't have to look back at her. The fabric wrapped around my fists is tight, secure, bright white against my hickory skin. Soon it will be stained red.

The haze of the packed room settles into my hard bones. The way the air tastes like copper and violence. The smells of sweat and leather are comforting. The stink of unwashed men drinking cheap ale feels like home. The packed canvas matting gives a little as I stretch myself, bouncing on the balls of my feet while I wait for my opponent. I've seen his poster, it's been stuck to tavern walls for weeks. It seems he's some kind of celebrity where he hails from. I've never heard of him, but I eye him with interest as he emerges, running my hand over my close-cropped curls. I'm damp with sweat already.

He's big, like they often are. I'm lean and wiry, at five foot five, and I'd never be able to keep up in strength alone, but just because they could fell me like a tree with one hit doesn't mean they'll get that chance.

They're just not used to fighters like me. I know bodies. I watched my father heal them. Learned where and how to hurt them most. It used to be that I'd get a good few blows in for free before they took me seriously, but these days my reputation precedes me and I don't get that luxury. No more numbing their arms before they've even tried to hit me. No more shattering blows to the cough point between their collarbones, ending the fight in one swift, stiff-fingered strike. Now I fight long and smart. Well. Smarter than them, anyway.

This one looks like so many others. He lumbers up the stairs, bald head marked with the blue tattoos that tell his story. A Clansman. Usually better at casual brawling than the average city dweller, but not often clever in the ring. This weather-beaten man is seamed with marks of battle; a scar twisting the shape of his cheek: he almost lost an eye once. If I'm lucky, he'll be wary of blows that burst the eyebrows, his flinch response heightened by past fear. He's pushing six and a half feet, though, so I doubt I'll get many clear shots at his face. But I see the close-to-invisible hitch in his stride when he climbs the stairs, foot turning inwards just a little. The muscle on that calf is just the slightest bit smaller than the muscle on the other. I'd guess a break in the foot that's still a little weaker than he's used to. That foot, I can reach.

The crowd roars and shimmers with anticipation. My breathing comes a little faster, veins starting to tingle, and it's excitement in my blood, not fear. I'm not afraid of pain. I suppose that's just one more thing that makes me different. In place of fear, I feel a thrill, and anger. It's part of me as much as my fists and feet, an animal inside me ever since I was small, bred on curses and the disgust I saw in the faces around me.

I learned to use it, tame it. To chain it and force it to obey me. I welcome it now, my oldest friend, who has kept me alive and moving for so long.

The familiar ball of rage in my stomach bursts outwards and

I grin at my enemy. It's not a kind grin; my face is too easily "wolfish" or "cruel" for that. Not even my mother told me I was pretty as a child. But she told me how to hit the nerve clusters that would drop a man in his tracks, taught me how to crush a windpipe with a knife formed by the side of my hand, so I never minded that she didn't tell me I was beautiful. Perhaps I wasn't like other children, but she wasn't like other parents, either, and neither of us had time for soft affection and kind words. We had better things to do, my mother and I.

The man facing me is not my mother. If I lose my focus, lose my wits, he will break my bones into splinters. I'll never fight as effectively again, if he hurts me very well. So I cannot, and will not, let him hurt me.

My mother was killed in a ring just like this one, when her feet moved too slowly to dodge the last blows. They called her the Dancing Flame, and I follow in her nimble footsteps. The prize money for this fight is good; it will keep me in my lodgings for several moons. And maybe this time, the girl will wait for me after the fight. Maybe I will look at her and she will look at me and it will be true that she's not afraid of me. I have never seen fear in her eyes.

The announcer climbs to the platform next to the ring, bell clutched in her meaty hand. Her studded leather gloves ting against the metal softly, and the crowd quiets, stills. It feels as though everyone in the place is holding their breath except me. But I breathe long and deep, the taste of sweat coating my throat. The girl, the one who's always there, meets my eyes, blinks at me, and I don't even hear the speech. I get lost in her instead. Her delicate nose and stubborn mouth, her wide-set eyes that sparkle at me like sunlight through a jar of honey.

I don't need to hear the announcer's words, not really. I've fought in this pit, for these people, on more than a dozen occasions. My hand-wraps are tight, my feet are firm, my head is clear and my girl… *the* girl is watching. Like a good luck charm. Even if I don't know her name.

My attention is called back to Daneel, my trainer, when he hooks his arm over the rope and cuffs me around the ear. It is a gentle blow, and I growl at him in mock anger. He gives me a delighted grin, broken teeth like tombstones.

'Smash 'em, Ice.'

I nod, and he jumps down from the side of the ring with a whoop.

The bell rings and the mountain man explodes toward me, all raw strength and power. I sway around his outstretched arm, redirect it past my ear with a brush of my hand and then I'm inside his guard, thrusting my hand, fingers outstretched, into the ball of his shoulder. I hit his brachial plexus nerves, exposed from his first swing. The best part about nerves is that you can overload them with repeated hits. I know that shooting numbness, the tingling in your fingers. It's not fun.

He doesn't react as much as I'd hoped, his meaty frame offering some protection from my fingers, and I almost lose my head to his other fist thrumming through the air. But I'm balletic to his violence, dancing away from his strikes, taking shots where I can find them and hitting pressure points again and again. He gets angrier and angrier, keeps trying to hit me, his face reddening and his iron eyes flat and dark with fury. It's clear to both of us, and probably the crowd as well, that if he can corner me, get one good blow in, he'll flatten me.

His arms whip through the air like the limbs of a tree. He's a good fighter, better than I expected, but he's too emotional, too pumped with adrenaline. He hasn't trained enough, only used to overpowering people. His body doesn't know the dance like mine does.

My double-fist strike to his kidney leaves him staggering into his next turn. I see fear in his eyes when I stamp on his bad foot and feel the bone bow under my strike. He backs away, limping a little, hurting now, wariness painting his expression. The fighter who gives in to fear will always lose. You can't commit if you're scared of being hurt—I have seen it in my fights and in many, many others.

I stand in the middle of the ring, shoulders heaving. I'm getting tired, but don't dare to look at how much time is left for the round. He closes on me again, knowing his strength and size are his advantage, and I can't avoid every hit this time, too slow, too tired. His fist bursts into my side, catapulting me onto the mats. For a moment, everything is pain. I can't tell if it's the bell ringing or my head, but since nothing else hits me I assume I must have made it to the end of the round. I scrape myself off the ground and freeze, leaning on my elbow, face to face with the girl. She looks at me with a serious expression, and then, to my surprise, a teasing smile streaks across her face.

'C'mon, gorgeous. You gonna let him get away with that?'

I don't know what I expected from my watcher, but a semi-flirtatious pep talk was not it.

I scowl. I can't help it, it's an instinct—but I'm taken aback by the playful light in her eyes. I can hear Daneel hissing at me to get up. The next round is about to start. The girl winks at me, and the pain in my side retreats a little. This close to her, I can see the scars. White lines wrapping round her throat, an X on one cheek and a slice through her full lower lip. Knife scars, for certain. I don't have time to wonder how she got them—I have to get up.

The rope under my hand is heavy and worn as I haul myself upright, protecting my floating rib. It's cracked, I think, and if he gets one more hit on me, I'm finished. Hell, I'd have been finished already if not for some great timing on the round's end. I grab the water Daneel is proffering and swill a mouthful before spitting it into my brass catcher, and the girl wrinkles her nose.

'If you lose, you owe me twenty guilders,' she calls.

Without deigning to reply, I turn back to face the ring. The only chance I have to win is to end it quickly. My side feels as though it is on fire, and the logical part of me knows I should bow out. A cracked rib can easily turn into a punctured lung, and any child of a healer knows just how likely that is, how fragile us sacks of meat are. But there's no one here to stop me; Daneel never would. He loves me like a child, no doubt, but his pride in my fighting spirit and skill is part of that love. And there's no one else who cares if I walk out of this ring or am carried out, as long as there's blood streaking the floor. Except for maybe the girl. After all, she has twenty guilders on the match.

The bell rings, and the decision is snatched away from me because the sand is already trickling through the glass, counting out the minutes.

My warrior friend limps as we circle each other, as wary of me as I am of him. I have to angle myself to keep my injured side away, but my guard is weaker on this foot, and I know I'm too slow to hurt him like I did before. I have to ruin him if I'm going to walk out of here—preferably without him laying a hand on me. I hawk spittle up in my throat, and he flinches back like I'm going to spit it at him. That second is enough. I shut the pain of my rib down into a tiny box in my head where I can deal with it later, and I swing for him. My feint goes out straight for the nerve cluster in his upper arm, which is already bruising from my earlier blows. He falls for it, twisting to avoid my hand, but as he turns he drives an uppercut toward my nose. There's no way I can get out of the way—I'm already committed to my real move.

My free hand chops him in the carotid artery right as his fist destroys my face. Through the pain, I feel the rubbery give of his neck. A perfect strike in the perfect place, but is he too strong to fall?

My nose has burst like a ripe peach and stars stab me in the eyes as I stagger backwards, bouncing off ropes that drive into my back. Blurry, black smears cloud my vision, but I hold my guard up, hoping I'll be able to protect myself at least a little if he's managed to stay on his feet. A warm hand wraps around my ankle and I gasp. I think someone is trying to hobble me, but then I know, somehow, that it is her.

Nothing hits me, and my sight clears. A foggy, distant roaring becomes sharper in my ears, and I realise the crowd is screaming. In front of me lies the Clansman, moaning, his eyelids fluttering. His skin is paler than milk under all his ink and the bushy ginger beard.

I swallow the blood that fills my throat and raise a single hand for the cheers. My ribs hurt too much to try to move the other arm. But I've won. The attendant checks the guy on the floor and nods for a healer, who races in with fluttering hands. All I can do is grin, even though it stretches the sore flesh of my nose. I revel in the pain. My victory tastes sweet.

‡

After I change out of my fighting gear, I tuck the bulging purse of coin into my breeches. I stuff the sweaty clothing into my bag and finger the bloodied bridge of my nose with an aggrieved sigh, wishing I had a mirror so I could set it. The bone is off kilter, and I'm ugly enough without the twist.

My face is puffy and tender, my ribs aching, so I ignore my fans and well-wishers as I push out of the small room I use to change. The other fighters usually strip off in front of the crowd, but I have no wish for anyone to see my body. With my breasts bound tightly under my loose-fitting shirt, I can pass for male if people don't look closely, but I know from experience that once people have *seen* you, they can never unsee you. Their eyes change.

The small hope I had that the girl would be among the people waiting for me is quashed as soon as I leave the building. As usual, she's gone before I have a chance to speak to her, although I don't know what I would say even if she was waiting. I'm no good with words—they catch in my throat and I stumble on them. Fighting is the only language I speak fluently.

The throbbing in my body matches my footsteps as I hurry

down the alley toward my lodging. It's not much, just a small room in a tavern on a side street, but it is more a home to me than any I've had since I was a child. I can't wait to lie on my bed, rub balm on my bruises and relax. If the pain stops me from sleeping, there are many small jobs that need to be done. Hand-wraps to squeeze the blood from and knives to sharpen—an activity that always helps soothe my mind towards slumber.

The night air is cool and welcome against my overheated skin, even though I know I'd be holding my breath if I could smell it. Squishy piles of manure and garbage slip and squirm under my leather-clad feet, and I am almost glad for my broken nose, and doubly glad for the prize money that once allowed me to buy these good boots—my only pair, but waterproof and comfortable. My head throbs and pounds as the adrenaline of the fight drains out of me. By the time I'm halfway home, I'm so busy trying to control the pain sinking into my skull that I'm taken completely by surprise when someone steps out into the street in front of me. The moonlight casts definition on the tattoos on his head and frames his beard in shadow. My friend regained consciousness fast.

At the sight of him, my hands stiffen into blades of their own accord. I doubt he's here to congratulate me on a good fight. Then another man steps out to stand with him. A shuffle behind me makes me jump and I glance back, cursing under my breath as another cuts off my escape route. Three of them, and me with a broken rib and pounding head.

My voice is calm, though thick and nasal, as I hold my ground. 'You don't want to do this, lads.'

'Tha's our money you're saunterin' off with.'

I can tell by his hard voice that I won't be able to reason my way out of this, and I gulp down panic as I push my back against the wall to make it harder for them to rush me. There are worse things that happen in dark alleys than having your money stolen, but if I hand it over there'll be nothing to give my landlord on Sixday, and I'll be out on the street. And more to the point, I doubt they'll simply let me go if I hand it over. I bruised his pride as well as his body.

Adrenaline rises in me and I snarl, 'I won this, fair an' square. Walk away.'

'No,' he grunts, and charges.

I duck under the first blow, my ribs screaming in protest, and smash my fist into his groin. The leather of his pants protects him a little, but not enough, and he doubles over. I want to hit him in the back of the neck while he's exposed, but the other two are already on me. We trade blows in a flurry. The men are messy and undisciplined, getting in each other's way, but I'm hurt and small and it doesn't take long before I'm pressed against the wall with a forearm braced across my trachea and lights dancing in my eyes.

The man leans in, pressing his body against me. I try to squirm away, work my knee between us to hurt him, but pain and lack of air conspire to stop me. The last thing I remember before I black out is a shadow swinging toward his head.

‡

I wake up in a bed. It takes me a long time to realise it is not my own, the blankets silky and unfamiliar under my palm, but as soon as I do, the memories of the previous night assail me and I sit up. Bile immediately rises in my throat, and I have to squint my eyes shut and breathe deeply to keep from vomiting. Something cold lands on the back of my neck, and I flinch.

'It's okay. You're safe.'

The voice is familiar, but I can't place it and have to force myself to open my eyes. It's her. The girl from the fights. She sits on her haunches, crouched beside the bed, dressed in breeches and an old beige shirt that hangs open to her belly button. Scars litter her pale skin, drawing my eyes down. I flush as my gaze freezes on her chest, and she rolls her eyes at me, sitting back to close the gap in her top.

'Where am I?' The words stick in my mouth like week-old bread.

'My place. Fifth Street. I didn't exactly know where you lived.' She looks uncomfortable for a moment, her brown hair falling into her face as she ducks her chin.

I'm still confused, but half willing to accept that as a partial explanation. I cough, and wince as the pain rips through my side. 'What happened?' I force the words out past my closing throat, demanding control over my body. It gives it up unwillingly, but I feel better for the victory.

'You were attacked. I... helped.' She says it with a slight grin and I quirk a bruised eyebrow at her in question. She rolls her eyes again; she strikes me as someone who does that a lot. 'They'll live. Probably.'

She lifts her hand and her sleeve falls back to show the distinctive hilt of a throwing knife. Expensive. And the room I'm in, with a proper bed, a chest of drawers; light streaming in through a glassed window. Also expensive. It's not quite palatial, but it's the kind of home I could never dream of affording. Who is this girl? I want to ask questions, but gratitude outweighs my curiosity for now.

'Water?' I ask instead.

Her nose crinkles up when she smiles fully, and I am fascinated by the emotions that flicker across her face, like sunlight on the surface of a stream. Her fingers are long and delicate as they close around a clay mug and pass it to me.

I take a large sip, wincing as the cool liquid soothes my throat. I can still taste blood on my lips, and wonder what I look like. The damp cloth she dropped on my neck has fallen, making a wet spot by my thigh, and as I pick it up to clean my face off I realise my shirt is missing. She's left my tight breastband on, but I freeze, feeling naked and exposed, then I haul the blanket up over my chest with a wince at the too-quick movement. Her face falls and there's a question in her eyes as they scan over me, but I won't answer it. I glance around the room like I might be able to escape, then bury my face in the cloth under the pretext of cleaning the blood off. It feels like most of it has already been dabbed away.

Her back is to me when I look up, and she hands me a shirt without looking. Gratitude roars through me like a fire, and she busies herself at the desk as I awkwardly struggle into it, hiding the body I hate.

'I wanted to check your ribs, and your shirt was ruined, anyway. It ripped, and then you fell in the mud.' There's a defensive note colouring her voice. I button the new shirt with one hand, wondering what this is all about.

'Thank you,' I mumble. 'For… saving me.' The words are thick and awkward, just like they always are.

'You saved me, once.' Her voice sounds dreamy and distant, like she's not in the room at all, anymore. I can see one hand lifting, and she presses it to her face, rubbing gently at her cheek.

I lean forward, confused. 'What?'

I fight for money, that's all. I fight because I am made for it, because I am made for nothing else.

When she turns, the light is back in her eyes, and a playful note in her voice. 'Nothing. You need a bath. Do you think you can make it to the tub?'

For the first time, I notice a small, copper washtub tucked under the window, and the thought of sitting in cold water makes me grimace. But I am sticky with sweat and who knows what else. I must have fallen in the alley when I passed out, so I'm probably covered in shit. I'm surprised she let me in her bed. Her bed. The thought makes my cheeks flush again and I'm grateful for my dark complexion, which must help hide it. I've never been a blusher, although it seems I am making a habit of it around her.

I nod, but my eyes flick from her to the door. She gifts me with a short, sharp grin of understanding, already making her way across the room. 'I'm going to get some food. I'll be back in half a bell.' The door closes behind her with a snick, not even giving me a chance to respond.

The bath is unpleasant, as expected, but it does feel good to get clean. There's blood in my short hair from a cut behind my ear I don't remember getting, the skin swollen and tender. I must have hit the ground hard. I clean my face again with the rag, gentle but making sure all the blood is gone. My nose feels enormous—I can see it without crossing my eyes—but when I tentatively stroke it with my fingers it feels straight, albeit swollen. She must have fixed it for me while I was passed out. I'm grateful, again. My side is a heated, swollen mess. I can feel the bruising thick and hard under my fingertips, the purpling visible when I peer down at it.

The cool water is soothing, although I can't help thinking a *hot* bath would make me feel more human. Still, I can't expect her to have water heated and hauled up for a stranger. She's done enough. I wonder what she meant, saying I saved her, and manoeuvre myself, with some difficulty, out of the bathtub. By the time she's back, I am dressed with my boots on, standing awkwardly in the middle of the room. Her hands flick through the air and I flinch, surprised when a bread roll hits me in the sternum.

She gestures toward the bed, and I sit down awkwardly on the edge of it. I feel like I owe her, and if she wants me to stay, I shouldn't leave. But I don't want to intrude on her space any more than I already have. I wonder where she slept while I was unconscious in her bed, and pick at the crust of the warm roll with uncomfortable fingers.

'How did you get me here?' The words sound more accusatory than I intended, ugly and violent, like the rest of me. I duck my chin in shame.

'I carried you.'

I can tell I'm looking at her sceptically. She's taller than me by a good few inches, but looks like a harsh wind would knock her over.

The smirk on her face makes something in my stomach twist, and I look away again. 'You're really short. And I'm stronger than I look.'

'You set my nose for me?' I mean to say thank you, but somehow the words don't make it out with the question.

Her deft hands roll her hair into a bun and secure it in place, and I can't take my eyes off them. 'Yes. It made you look rugged, but I thought you'd prefer to be able to breathe properly. The scar—well. Not much I could do about that. But it draws attention to your eyes, and I think it will make you even more handsome when it's healed.'

My breath catches like a ball has just thumped into my chest at impossible speed. She looks concerned as I gulp for the air that's been sucked out of the room.

*Handsome?*

The vicious sting of a lifetime of insults is soothed by the simple acceptance I hear in her compliment. And it *is* a compliment, for once: not mockery for my strapped-down chest, my graceless face, my unfeminine posture. The word sets something warm and deep in my belly, and I relax fully for the first time, maybe ever.

'I don't even know your name.' For once, I don't sound cruel.

'I'm Tia. And you're Ice. Although I doubt that's your real name.'

'Real enough.'

My voice is rough again at the perceived challenge, and I hate myself for it. There's no way for her to know how I hate my "real" name, my girl's name. Ice suits me fine. I have frozen blood in my veins, and like a glacier, I can destroy much larger things than myself, given time. I chose it when I was twelve, and it feels far realer to me than my old one.

'Just 'cause someone gives you something, doesn't mean you want it,' I tell her. 'I could give you a black eye but I doubt you'd want that.' I wince as soon as the words are out—I didn't mean to threaten her. I was just trying to explain that my birth name isn't mine, isn't me. That it was thrust on me by my father when I was too young to argue. *Isabelle*. Ice is better. Ice is me. Cold and hard and unforgiving.

Silence stretches out and when I look up, I'm convinced I'll see fear on her face, but she's beaming at me. A wide grin, lighting her up like a paper lantern. I'm startled into smiling myself. Somehow she's seen through my clumsy words to what I meant, or, at the very least, to something that doesn't upset her.

'What did you mean when you said I saved you?' The question tugs at me, and in the moment I can't help blurting it out. Her eyes darken and her face stills into a mask. I don't like it, and open my mouth to retract the question, to leave it be, but she cuts me off.

'Your first fight. He was my uncle.' Her hand is on her face again, rubbing at that X-shaped mark on her cheek.

My mouth drops open and something in my chest cracks open as I remember that fight. That *murder*.

I remember his body pressed down upon me, my face pushed so hard into the floor that I thought my eyeballs would pop. I remember the matting sliding under my limbs; scrabbling to get purchase against fabric slicked with my own fear-sweat as I struggled against him. Trapped and trapped and trapped, my mind not letting me think through the hold he had on me, too panicked to solve the puzzle of limbs I was captured in. I remember Daneel's frantic face as he screamed at me from the sidelines, his words drowned by the roaring in my head. I remember the weight crushing me and the wet whispers and foul things hissed in my ear, until the bell rang and he climbed off me and I could breathe again.

For a heartbeat, I feel again the fear that he awoke in me—that true fear of total helplessness, the kind that numbs and cripples. The fear that still tugs at me, always, trapped in chains of anger and hate, kept small in the darkest places inside of me. Sometimes I feel that without the anger to hold it in place, I'd never move again. I'd just drop to my knees and never get up.

I remember trying to patch it up with fury then, and failing. I drowned in it, letting him toy with me, slow and unsteady on my feet, unable to think as his punches shredded my face and bruised my flesh. Broke my arm. He pinned me again, and I could feel his excitement, his pleasure. Anger had come back for me then, burned through me, and I shoved his nasal bones into his brain just to get his dead shark eyes to stop looking at me.

It was ruled an accident—we all sign waivers before we fight, sometimes people die—but it wasn't an accident. He was a hollow man, as men sometimes are, and I killed him for it, for my fear.

*You saved me, once.*

The things he had said to me when I was trapped underneath him...

Her words take on new meaning and I grab for the wastebasket as my stomach roils, but I don't vomit. She sits next to me on the bed, leans against my side, her hand hot against my back. 'I always wondered how I could thank you.'

Her words send a wash of anger through me that drives out the nausea, flooding me with familiar, comforting rage. There's fury throbbing in my veins, burning static rods in my skeleton, and I want to *hurt*, to throw myself into the adrenaline-fuelled giving-pain-taking-pain dance that will push out these other *things* inside me, this twisting in my guts I don't understand. But her hand is burning the skin over my spine, keeping me glued to the bed. There's something in the air that feels like it will shatter if I move, and so I just breathe in, breathe out, try to imagine what it feels like not to need the rush of violence to understand myself.

She sits quietly, doesn't say anything else, but I can still hear her words echoing through the silence that's filling the room like poisonous gas. I don't know what to say. I'm frozen, with an empty head and knuckles creaking under their own tension. I don't want to be thanked for killing someone.

She said the men that attacked me had lived. *Probably*. With new understanding I look at her and realise that she doesn't care, and she arches an eyebrow at me, seeming to look right through me and see that thought exactly.

'Empathy is a nebulous concept at best. And you fight men twice your size for money, so I really don't think you're in any position to talk.' The lightness in her tone cuts through the swirling turmoil inside of me, my muscles loosen and I feel my face soften out of its habitual half-snarl.

And then she kisses me. Her lips are hot against mine, and all I can think of is the warmth and softness of her; and in my body, the anger rolls slowly into something else, something that might be peace. But I don't stop, I don't end, like I always thought I might. I just let the hard tension fall out of my bones and melt away, until it is as though I've never felt anything but the calm chaos of her body against mine.

‡

Daneel claps me on the shoulder and I lean into him, giving him a sweaty hug before pulling back and looking for her. She's right where she should be, a huge smile on her face. The smile I love to see.

I squat down, grab her by the hair, and she rises eagerly for my kiss. The crowd hoots and hollers, some with joy, some with disgust, but it doesn't mean a thing. She pinches my cheek when our lips part, and it stings and focuses me.

'Later,' she says, with a promise in her eyes. I straighten up, happiness burning through me like a wildfire, igniting my bones, my tendons and muscles. The sound of my audience is like music and my feet itch to dance. The fabric wrapped around my fists is tight, secure, bright white against my hickory skin. Soon, it will be stained red.

# Sole Survivor

Lewis Bright Rees

'I'm—'

'No names. Not real ones, anyway. People die out here all the time, for all sorts of reasons, and you don't want to get attached.' Temple lights a cigarette and sits at the window, pulling back the curtain to peek at the street below. 'You know, you're the first person I've met in two years who didn't shoot on sight? You're new to all this, I can tell. You're too soft. If you want to survive, you're going to need to learn the rules—and one of the most important ones is: don't use your real name. Don't let people get that close.'

'Why not?'

'The closer you get to the fire, the hotter it burns,' he says with a shy smile. He takes a drag of his cigarette. 'Names these days are as valuable as diamonds: you only want to give them to the people you'd go to the ends of the Earth for.'

Only two people, he says, have known his real name since the lights went out. 'Both dead now, as far as I know. Melody died in the night. Cancer. Not a pretty way to go, but a damn shot better than most people get these days. Last I saw Wander, we'd been ambushed by some Smilers, going on four years ago now—I reckon. Time don't mean a thing when you're living one day at a time.'

'I'm sorry,' I say.

I barely remember the old world. Everyone's lives have been defined by the infected: a stark red line drawn between what came before and what came after, and I don't know whether I envy those old enough to remember more, or not. Would I rather live in this ignorance, or have tangible memories of how life used to be?

I'd just turned four when my parents took me to Camp Greenbow—the old summer camp where they'd first met, as counsellors. They always used to tell me they'd take me when I was older, so I just figured that four was old enough. And I was one of the lucky ones: we'd never had a run in with the infected, so at the start, it just felt like a long vacation. It wasn't until we'd been there for a couple of months that I started to put the pieces together; until I realised I was never going home. Until I learned that the Smilers are the monster in every closet.

'Yeah, well. There's no use crying over spilt milk,' says Temple at length. 'I've done my grieving, and I've learned my lesson. The only name anyone needs these days is the one they choose for themselves.'

Those last frantic minutes in the woods haunt me. Our home and everything we'd ever known, burning behind us. There were seven of us then. I'd met up with Carlos and Marla since, lost them both. As far as I know for sure, I'm the only one left.

I think back to that last kiss. He didn't want to split up, none of us did, but the alternative would have been travelling together and the Smilers were already on our trail. Better to split up, force them to separate into smaller groups if they wanted to follow us. We were all unarmed, hungry, exhausted;

we were all terrified. There's no way we could have fought a pack of them off.

He had run his hand through my hair and given me that smile, that heartbreaking smile he always shot me when he wished more than anything that he could take away the pain.

'It's going to be okay,' he had lied. And those beautiful hazel eyes filled with kindness, always the opposite of the sobriety in mine.

'So what should I call you?' Temple asks. There's something about him that I trust. I know he could shoot me at any second, but I don't believe that he will. He makes no effort to reach for his gun or mine. His movements are slow and deliberate, like he's trying to avoid spooking a deer. His eyes are as grey as a rainy day, but I find them comforting all the same.

What should I call myself?

'Romeo,' I say.

‡

He walks with a limp; not bad enough that he needs to rely on a cane or a walking stick, but bad enough that he sticks mostly to the roads. I've been doing my best up until now to avoid the roads. The thing about line of sight, I think, is that it works both ways. In the forest you can hide; get the jump on your enemies if you need to, or at least plot your escape. On the road, exposed and out in the open, they see you coming from a mile away.

And the thing about the real world—the great, wild expanse that exists outside the walls we build—is that we all have our scars. Some of us just wear them on the inside.

'How long have you been alone?' he asks. Poor guy. I guess when you spend your life out here, you'd do anything for some company.

'A couple of weeks. Not long.'

'Fair enough. I won't ask you to elaborate.' He lights another cigarette. I'll bet his backpack is full of them. 'It's bad form to ask where someone's come from,' he informs me. 'They've never been anywhere good.'

'It wasn't too bad,' I reply. 'Pretty good, actually. It was home, at least.'

'The only difference between hell and home is the people you're with.'

'My boyfriend was there.' I step over a fallen tree, then turn back to help him over it.

'I'm sorry for your loss.'

'He's not dead.' I help him down to the ground. It's hard to pin his age. Early fifties? Maybe. More agile than you'd think for a guy around that age. 'I'm trying to stay optimistic.'

'Yeah, well. Hope for the best, prepare for the worst.' He lets out a grunt as he hits the uneven ground. 'That who you were waiting for?'

'Yeah. Him, my brother, his family. I can't be the only one who got away, right?'

'Prepare for the worst,' he repeats. He takes a shaky step forward. 'You got a destination in mind?'

'Sanctuary. That was the plan; we'd all meet up there.'

'Quite the journey.'

'You been there?'

'No, but I hear good things.'

'Why not?'

'I guess I just don't put too much stock into their ability to protect themselves,' he says plainly. 'QZs were a dime a dozen when everything first went to hell, and now Sanctuary's the only one for a thousand miles. In the early days, there were millions of people trying to get into them; all of them fighting, plenty of them dying. All a crowd that big ever achieves anymore is to attract more infected.'

'But there's less people now, right?' I ask. 'They must have space for another handful.'

'You could have filled the *Titanic* a handful at a time; it still would have sunk in the end.'

'So what's the other option? This?'

'It's as good an option as any,' he says. 'By all means, head for Sanctuary. You might get lucky—I mean, it's been over a decade since I stopped trying—and if that's where you're all headed then that's where you'll find them. All I'm saying is, you might not get as lucky as you're hoping.'

'What happens then?'

'Same thing that happens to everyone. You live or you die. Only thing it depends on is how fast you learn that this world doesn't owe you anything. If anyone else is still alive, call it a blessing, but don't expect that your luck won't run out.'

'Yeah, well. I'll cross that bridge when I come to it.'

‡

Darcy always wanted to see the best in everyone, even when they couldn't see it in themselves. Even me. When we grew old enough for the grim reality of our lives to sink in, but before we were old enough to realise how much we meant to each other, I envied his positivity. How could you not envy someone who looks over the ruins of civilisation and says we could build it up again, as easily as picking the world off the ground and putting it back on its bike? I want nothing more than to believe it would be that easy, or even possible, but how can I? When the monsters in the closet have ventured out of the darkness to show the world their twisted, mutilated, *joyful* faces, how can anyone maintain that optimism?

I think the moment he first told me about that dream was the moment I fell in love with him. It wasn't until we came together, though—fitting together as perfectly as two pieces in a puzzle we didn't even know we were assembling—that I started to realise it was just a mask.

We'd gone out to a town fifty miles away to search for supplies—medicine, mostly, but canned food is always useful, even if you're farming. Six of us went, all together; for Darcy and me, it was our first time out scavenging. Our first time being more than twenty miles away from home. We'd sent scouts out first to check the town; to check for the sounds of screams or sobs or bestial roars or, god forbid, the cold, sadistic laughter of a Smiler. To check for smoke or voices: the telltale signs of raiders. They told us it was clean, but in the time it took for them to come back and for us to prepare to leave, the raiders had moved in.

At first, we just thought it was a Screamer or two: unpleasant, but nothing too dangerous—they always seemed to be too consumed by their own fear to pose much of a threat unless they were cornered. We worked through the town, making our way past the abandoned homes and through overgrown gardens to the centre, where all the stores were. Darcy and I pointing out our favourites of the houses; imagining a world where we'd live in one of them together. We stayed clear of the screams, more or less. We didn't think to wonder what was setting them off until we'd wandered in too close.

His hair was long and unkempt, falling down over his shoulders. So emaciated that the skin seemed to hang off his bones. He opened his mouth and let out a shriek—a bloodcurdling scream so loud I felt my eardrums vibrate. He turned and started to scurry away, and it wasn't until then that we saw the chain around his neck.

We turned in the opposite direction and ran; forgot all about the raid, all about our fears that the winter would be a long one—we'd had rough winters before, when there were more of us. If we were careful with rations, we could make do. We ran until the town was far behind us, receding into the distance.

'The raiders…' Darcy said, panting still. 'Were they doing what I think they were doing?'

'Using him as a guard dog, looked like,' said Marla. She was so cool about it; so calm, as if it were just a case of going to the next town. But then, she'd already been scavenging a dozen or so times.

'That poor guy…'

'He's infected,' I shrugged. 'He doesn't know any better.'

'You don't think he's still in there somewhere? The real him, I mean.'

For some reason, his fretting had unnerved me. It wasn't our first time seeing a Screamer—they used to wander by the camp from time to time—and we'd had run-ins with raiders before, so we all knew that we'd been lucky to get away without a fight. I suppose I expected him to be more relieved. 'Well, they're keeping him safe,' I said tentatively, wrapping my arm around his waist. 'That's something, right?'

'I guess,' he sighed, and leaned into me. 'I don't know. I've just been thinking a lot, lately. Maybe they are still there—the infected. Like, their brain is screaming out for help, but their body just moves on its own. He could be… he could be alive.'

'Hmm,' I replied. I'd seen him sad before, but not like this. Even after everything we'd heard, he was the one we all turned to—the one who'd cheer us up. I knew him better than anyone, but it wasn't until then that I saw the *real* him.

That mask was for all of our sakes, I suppose, but I can't help thinking, sometimes, that he wore it just for me.

'Is it always so hard?' he'd asked Marla.

'Hard? Hell, that was easy,' she said. 'We didn't have to fight, we didn't come across any Fighters or Smilers, we didn't even catch the raiders. We got off as light as we could have.'

I watched Darcy's Adam's apple bob as he gulped.

Marla was his best friend, apart from me and his dog. He looked up to her—I mean, we all did, but he grew his hair long because he wanted to be as cool as she was. He wanted the fire to dance in his eyes like it danced in hers, when he told us a story around the campfire.

I don't know how I'm going to tell him what happened to her and Carlos.

There was always so much fight in her, so much bluster. We

used to joke that she was so stubborn, a hurricane couldn't knock her down when she had her mind set on something. When the fire in her faded, that's when we'd all started to face the grim reality that we'd die in a place we once called home.

‡

We leave tracks behind us in the snow; I'd be more worried about it, but it's snowing all the time so they'll probably disappear fast. I used to love the snow, but now that I'm travelling, all I can think about is that I can always see my footprints. Another step away from camp. Another step away from Darcy. Another step closer to Sanctuary. Another step that can be tracked.

It seems so much more real when you have proof of the journey.

'So how far are you going?'

'I haven't decided yet.' He takes a drag of his cigarette. 'There comes a point where the destination doesn't mean squat.'

'You could come with me,' I say. 'It's got to be worth the shot, right?'

He doesn't reply. He stops in his tracks and puts his finger in the air.

'Temple?'

'Ssh!' he snaps. I narrow my eyes at him, and he slowly raises his hand to his ear. I can see fear in his eyes, for the first time.

And then I hear it. A laugh in the woods; a shrill, high-pitched peal of laughter.

'How many of them?!' My voice comes out in a panicked whisper, as loudly as I dare.

'One. One too many.'

'You know they can gag themselves, right?'

'They only do that when they need to sneak up on someone,' he murmurs. He keeps his eyes fixed dead ahead, in the general direction of the Smiler. I see him slowly reach for his crossbow. 'But Smilers don't like to travel alone. There's more;

and close, too.'

'Think we can outrun them?'

The laughter continues.

'Not with my leg the way it is.' He unholsters his crossbow. I take the hint and slowly reach for my pistol, but he raises his hand to stop me.

'You shoot that thing and every Smiler around is gonna make a beeline straight for us,' he says softly. 'And I don't intend to die today.'

'So what do I do?!'

'Just stay close to me. We're going to duck into the woods, quiet as you like,' he whispers, and starts to slowly shuffle through the snow. I follow behind him, not daring to move so much as six feet away. I keep glancing back over my shoulder, so sure that the laughter's getting closer; certain that I'll see it standing in the middle of the road.

'Do you think it knows we're here?'

'If I did, you'd be seeing a me-shaped hole in the brush,' he mutters quietly.

The laughter stops. I stand stock still, a couple of feet away from the safety of the forest, and I can't move, like the blood in my veins is frozen. I'm too afraid to even breathe, even though I know there's no way for the Smiler to hear it from so far away.

A moment passes, and then the laughter again. I let out a sigh of relief and shuffle forward.

'There should be a stream not far from here,' Temple says quietly, scanning the trees all around us, crossbow raised. 'Nothing too deep, if we're lucky. It's only a matter of time before the Smilers find our footprints. If we get in and walk downstream a couple of hundred feet, it should buy us some time.'

'Why don't we just take it? There's two of us.'

'Next lesson, Romeo: flight, not fight.'

What sort of rule is that?

'Never forget what they are, Romeo, or what they'll do to you,' he elaborates. In the distance, I can hear the stream. 'And never let yourself get confident. Let yourself think you can take one and before you know it, you think you can take half a dozen. There's more here, too close for comfort. In the grand scheme of things, what does killing one really achieve? It's better to take the path of least resistance, as it were. If you don't leave early, sooner or later you won't have a chance to leave at all. How many did you kill when you left camp?'

'Well… I had no weapons then.'

'That's a good mindset to keep. No matter if you have a knife or an assault rifle, it's never going to be enough; and unlike the Fighters, the last thing a Smiler wants to do is kill you. I hardly need to tell you that; nobody walks away from them without seeing some stuff. Hell, seeing their faces is more than enough for most.'

I shudder at the memory of chewed-off lips and cut-up faces; splinters of glass in their gums; gaping cavities where they've cut off their noses or ears. 'Why do they do that to themselves?'

'Same reason they do anything else.' We're approaching the stream now; barely more than a trickle of water weaving through the trees. He unsteadily makes his way down the bank, gasping audibly when the frigid water, only a liquid by virtue of constant motion, seeps into his shoes. 'It makes them happy.'

I step into the stream, and curse under my breath when the water soaks my skin. I open my mouth to ask him how he knows this will work, but he silences me with a finger to his lips and starts moving.

We walk for a mile in the water; long enough for the sensation in my feet to disappear. I stumble more than a few times because I can barely feel the stones beneath my feet. We don't talk; there's no sound but the gushing water. Snow falls lazily from the sky, but the clouds aren't so much grey as they are black, hanging pendulously in the sky. It won't be long and we'll be facing another blizzard, I think.

'All right, this seems a good a place as any,' he says. He hardly stumbled all the way down the river, despite his limp; he must be used to this. He climbs out of the water on the opposite side to where we got in. Everything below my waist is soaked through. I almost want to stay where I am just to avoid the wind chill.

'We're about a mile away from the next town. Should be able to hole up there for the night.'

'There won't be Smilers?'

'If there are, we just mosey on to the next one.'

I can't help but sigh at that. Another town farther away from Darcy.

'You left a note, right? If he finds it, if nothing else, he know you made it this far.'

'If he even finds it.'

'Sanctuary's to the east; if anyone else who escaped is half as smart as you, they'll be following the river. It's the snowman that really gets me, though.'

'It just… it used to be our thing. If he sees that snowman then he'll know.'

We're silent for a few moments. Whenever I think of Darcy, the reality of my life creeps up on me. Losing someone, over time, becomes a certainty. After all, death is one of two things that everyone on the planet has in common. Still, losing him seems wrong. Unnatural. He should be with me. Sanctuary was always a dream we shared; a journey we used to talk about making together. Making it without him just feels… wrong.

'You think he's cold?' I ask.

'Probably, but it's better than being dead, right?' Temple replies.

'He always… He doesn't like to be alone,' I say. 'I hope he found someone.'

'You mean one of the other survivors?'

'Yeah… I know our dog was with him, but it's different. I like to think he found someone.'

'If he found someone, he might not have made it this far.'

'It can't all be bad, right?' I ask. 'The world can't just be raiders and the infected. We're proof enough of that.'

'Sure, but good people can do bad things when their backs are to the wall. Remember that, Romeo. When the chips are down, the only person you can truly rely on is yourself.'

Maybe I just don't want to be the only person alive who knows my name.

'I don't want to think like that.'

'Neither do I. More than anything, I wish I could still look at people and assume the best. You're out here too long and you learn that most people are only in it for themselves. You either step in line or you die.'

'If I thought like that, you wouldn't be alive right now.'

He laughs. 'You wouldn't stand a chance, kid.'

I smirk. 'I don't know, old man. You're pretty slow.'

'Yeah, and pretty experienced. All it takes is a moment.'

I turn to him with a retort on my lips, but I blanch.

'Temple!'

The thing about line of sight is that it works both ways.

He looks back just as the Smiler raises the golf club. It swings at the empty air where his leg used to be.

It's a man; or it used to be, at least. Tall and imposing, yet skinny and malnourished. Still, I don't doubt its animal strength. Its eyes are wide and manic, the sort of blue I once would have called beautiful. Dirty blonde hair, matted with filth, in places hanging down past its shoulders and in others shorn close to the scalp; I can see bald patches where it's cut huge patches of skin away, leaving nothing but scars to grow back. Its whole face is drenched in blood. The gag it wears is pulling its face back into a grim parody of a smile.

We've fallen right into a trap.

The Smiler raises its golf club, eyes shifting between the two of us, trying to decide which one of us is the greatest threat. Or maybe it's trying to decide which one of us would be the most fun.

I don't give it time to find an answer; I raise my pistol and shoot it right between the eyes. The shot rings out through the woods as the Smiler falls to the ground. In the distance, I hear the flutter of a flock of birds taking flight.

Temple grabs my arm and pulls me forward. We run as fast as we can through the woods, all too aware of the sounds of our pursuers; at first just twigs breaking and the underbrush being trampled, but then the laughter, the cacophony of laughter, from high, child-like titters to booming cackles so deep I feel them in my bones.

It's too late for stealth; Temple unholsters his own pistol.

'What do we do?!' I yell.

'Calm down, I've been in worse scrapes!'

'You call this a scrape?!'

Despite his age and limp, he has split-second reflexes—before I can even register that one of the Smilers is breaking through the treeline, he's already shot it mid-stride and it tumbles to the ground less than a foot away from me. I can see more coming.

'How many are there?' I yell.

'Does it matter?!'

I get one in the leg and it tumbles to the ground, laughing the whole time.

We surge forward through the brush. I don't know how many there are, and I don't dare look back; there could be five or there could be fifteen. All I know is that whenever one gets too close to blocking our path, I shoot. They used to be men and women. As young as me, as old as Temple. My heart isn't in my chest anymore. I feel it beating in the hollows behind my eyelids.

Temple and I work as if we've known each other for years, instead of days. Two limbs in the same greater body; two functions of the same machine.

Survival is a choice.

I choose not to be captured here, and I choose not to die.

We break through the treeline onto the road and we both run south, following the unpaved road around the bend. We're so deep in the forest that I can't see any hints of a town nearby—I can only believe Temple when he says that it exists. He keeps his eyes forward with grim determination. Even with the limp, he's fast. My lungs are about to break through my ribcage but his breathing is even, almost calm, like this is just another day. The tragedy, I suppose, is that that's exactly what it is.

Somewhere nearby, the gentle babbling of the stream becomes the great roaring of a river. How long have we been running? I don't know. I can still hear them laughing, but I don't see them when I risk a glance behind us. I don't see their silhouettes in the trees or hear their footsteps in the woods. Just the laughter.

We fly around another bend and I can see the town through the trees ahead of us; nothing too big by real-world standards, I know, but it looks huge to me. I can see myself getting lost in the twisting streets and narrow alleys. Between us and the town is a bridge over the crashing white peaks of the winding river: concrete, just wide enough for a single car to cross. The trees are thicker here—so thick that I'd think it was the middle of the night if I didn't know any better—but I can see the snow falling in sheets on the town; enough snow that it will break up our silhouettes and hide our footprints.

'We hide?' I hiss. My chest is burning and my heart pumps battery acid. It takes all of my strength just to keep standing.

Temple doesn't break his stride, much less take the time to answer. He grabs my arm and runs towards the bridge but, instead of leading me across, he leads me to the left of it and down the bank. Before I can even ask what he's doing, he ducks down as low as he can and squeezes into the narrow space under the bridge.

Every instinct is screaming at me to make a break for it. My legs itch to run toward the town and find an apartment or basement I can hole up in until they creatures pass—but at the same time, they feel like they've been pumped full of molten lead. I don't know if my lungs will be able to survive the journey, but my brain begs me to find the strength I need. Just another hundred metres to safety, it screams, and I can think of the next step once I'm inside. But my heart screams louder.

I've encountered enough Smilers to know that they don't give up. That town is an amusement park for them—a place where they can play hide and seek for as long as it takes.

Temple didn't survive this long without learning a trick or two.

I think of Darcy's face; I think of how hard he fought to save everyone. I think of our last kiss, and how that can't be our *last* kiss.

I duck down, shut my eyes tight and crawl into the darkness next to Temple, withholding a gasp as the frigid torrent seeps into my shirt, holding my breath again even though there's no *way* the Smilers could hear our breathing over the rush of the water. I shift myself around until I'm sitting back to back with Temple. I reload my gun as quietly as I can and hold it firmly in my hands, waiting for the first mutilated smile or bloodied hand to cross my field of vision.

The laughter is barely audible over the torrent, but it's getting louder. I hear their footsteps overhead and I'm far too aware that they're only a matter of feet away; closer than I ever feared, just weeks ago, that they'd get to me. It hurts to breathe; less a gas escaping my lungs than a mass forcing its way up my throat. I feel Temple tense behind me and I know that he's itching to tell me to keep it down. I think of Darcy, but not as he was. Not as we were. I think of what he must be doing right now, and how hard he's fighting to get back to me. If I believe in anything in this great big cruel world—if there's one hope worth clinging to—it's that I'll find him again. I can't die at the hands of the Smilers.

I can't die so far from home.

The footsteps fade into the distance and I finally let myself breathe.

‡

They came in the night, as the stories always go. The end of the world never comes in the bright light of day; it comes in those dark hours when a romantic might fear, despite all evidence to the contrary, that the sun will never rise. They corralled us into the camp cabins; everyone crammed into two houses that some of us once called home, and that we would all soon call prisons.

I'm just thankful that it wasn't our little cabin; I don't know how I could ever look back at my home fondly if, in those last few days, we had been trapped there instead. It might have destroyed me, if my bedroom, our escape from reality—where Darcy and I could forget that there was more to life than each other—had been tainted by that fear and desperation, in which the only hope that kept you going was that the Smilers would take somebody else, anybody but you.

I wish I could say that I had felt sad or angry when my father was chosen, but all I felt was relief. Anger, maybe, but I was always angry with him. Angry that he threw me out, much as I hated sharing a cabin with him after mom died; angry that he never accepted Darcy and me—even after the Smilers descended on us and his prejudices seemed pettier than ever. The rest of us stuck together—we can say that much, at least. My father was never the sort of person to care about others; he was the sort of person who'd do nothing for anyone else but still feel entitled to help when he needed it. Even if all he needed was someone to cover his guard duty while he nursed a hangover.

He was one of the first ones they took, but he understood something from the start that it took the rest of us a while to accept: the best we could do was be the last person standing. We never spoke about it, but I know I'm not the only one who was relieved when they took someone else. But then came the guilt, because when the Smilers come, you pray that someone you've known all your life—someone you've *loved*—will die screaming so you can have another day. Even when it was Darcy—my boyfriend, my soulmate, the love of my probably tragically short life—being dragged away by a monster in a human mask, its skin scarified and cut and peeled away, bloodied lips pulled back by fishhooks and wire in the rough facsimile of a smile, I was relieved. Fear, sadness, loss like icy daggers in my chest, but more than anything, I was relieved.

In the end, nobody escapes the Smilers: that's what we were always told. The Fighters are so blinded by their own rage that you can escape if you're smart, and Screamers and Weepers are mostly harmless, but with Smilers, you're as good as dead. They fed us, at least. Gave us water. Not enough to thrive, but enough to keep us alive. After all, it's more fun to torture the living than to mutilate the dead.

None of us dared to dream that there was a way out of it.

They might all be dead by now. I saw Carlos and Marla die, and the best thing I can say is that it was, at least, fast. Carlos had taken a bullet to the head before he even understood we were under attack. Marla lasted a little longer, but as strong as she was, killing people—actually pointing a gun and pulling the trigger… it's a lot harder than I think any of us expected. She fought hard, took a couple of the raiders down, but we were up against people who'd spent years out here, probably, honing their skills. I barely got out of there alive. And just like that, the death count grew by two.

Say what you will about me, but I'm not weak.

That's my main worry about Darcy; not that he's weak, per se, but that his strength lies in a different realm. He's too idealistic. I don't know if he could ever bring himself to kill anyone, and I'm quickly learning that, far too often, kindness isn't an option. Survival is hardwired into our brains, and I have no doubt that when it comes to it, he'll fight, but could he live with the knowledge that he ended a life? Or would he shut down like Marla did? He blew up the camp, that much I know, but only once he'd been chosen by the Smilers; only to survive. Even then, he waited until we were all out of danger. He just wanted to get as many of the Smilers out of the way as possible, and I don't think anyone could argue that Smilers are people. Could he have done it if they were raiders? Could he have ended their lives, or would he just have rescued us and run?

We're like two halves of the same whole—paradoxically equal to, and yet opposite, each other. He got all the empathy, the people skills, and I got the calculating intelligence. He's better with a knife or a bow, I'm the better sniper. I can sneak around, track animals; he's more of an act first, think later kind of person. Together, we're almost a whole, functioning person. But what do you do when you lose half of yourself? How much can you lose before you have nothing left?

So many people are out here, wandering the wastelands—the dead zones between Sanctuary and whatever settlements people have managed to cobble together. They never know safety, they just know… they know this. They know survival. They don't know life. I just hope that they've learned to enjoy the little things.

‡

We wait until we're sure. We follow the river east, watching the buildings recede into the distance until, just like that, they're gone.

'That was some quick thinking,' I say; the first words to pass between us in what feels like hours, but can't be more than one.

'Like I said, I've been in worse scrapes.' He replies. He keeps his crossbow in his hands, watching the treeline, daring a Smiler to make itself known.

'So what happens now?'

'We've bought ourselves some time. Not a lot, mind you; we're gonna need to keep walking, and if we're lucky we'll make it to the next town some time before midnight. The Smilers'll search this place for days, I'm hoping, but I'd sooner have it as a dot on the horizon than risk being too close when they leave. Hopefully your friends manage to avoid them. Maybe the Smilers'll find someone else here to keep them occupied.'

I stop in my tracks. 'How can you say something like that?'

'It's easy enough; you just stop caring.' He lights a cigarette as casually as he does everything else; as casually as breathing. 'Better them than me. For what it's worth, though, I really do hope your boyfriend and the others are okay. It's an easy life, being alone, but I can't say it's much to write home about.'

I open my mouth to say something, but my head and my heart are fighting it out. Do I call him out? Do I ask him how long it took for him to stop caring about anyone but himself? There are so many tragedies in this dying world, and maybe the biggest one is how so many stories end; how the burden of memory falls on the shoulders of so few. There used to be so many places like the camp, or so Temple says: little sanctuaries where the Smilers were nothing but the boogeymen, and the world after the infection was a million miles away.

I could punch him, but one look into his eyes and that thought disappears. Everything he's told me, he's learned the hard way. He's survived, but at what cost? How many people has he lost? How many times has he walked away from tragedy alone, the only one left to tell not just his story, but those of the dead, too? There's only enough space in a man's head for so many stories.

'Me too,' I say in the end.

Darcy. Jerry. Heather. Sawyer. I hope I'll see you again. Please don't let the burden of our memories fall on my shoulders. When I get to Sanctuary, please be waiting for me there.

I expect him to say something—to try and reassure me, keep me going, anything—but he's already walking ahead of me in silence. I can't be sure, but I'd swear his limp is a little more pronounced, and I can only hope that it's just from exertion.

I take a deep breath, grip my pistol tight, and follow. And we walk in silence, the promise of Sanctuary in the distant tomorrow.

# The Seeing Hands of Captain Zerach

Kayla Bashe

Zerach realised it was morning not because of the dim light from her boarded-up window, but from the shrieking and squabbling of grackles and vultures outside the fortress. 'Get away!' she imagined them yelling at each other, 'This soldier's stinking corpse is mine!'

She took careful steps from the left side of her bed to the chamber pot; a measured shift forward and she encountered her robes, folded on the chair in front of the desk. She rubbed her thumb over the delicate embroidery, chives and chrysanthemums in goldwork. The metallic straight stitch had a rougher feel than the linen leaves below. She ran her scarred hands through the worst of the tangles in her dark hair, and dressed with economical movements. Out of habit, she took up the old workbag hanging on a hook by the door. Her fingers had closed on its strap before she laughed and let it fall. *Won't be needing that anymore. It's not as if I'll be permitted on the front lines.* She took up the oaken staff instead, carved with a rearing gryphon—her coat of arms—and steadied herself to face the day.

It was quieter than it usually was in this part of the castle. Cooler than she'd expected, too, even after the rain had stopped. It was morning, so where was the scullery maid who always rushed, laughing, along the corridor, who'd bumped into her yesterday and stammered an apology while unable to stifle her giggles? (And then she'd seen Zerach's scars, and a gasp had broken from her. She'd gathered up her things with a clatter and rushed along. *Poor child.* She'd encounter a lot worse as the war drove on.)

Zerach traced a hand over the uneven brickwork in front of her. If she concentrated, she could feel the edges of an old carving, the eldritch sigil with its twelve spined arms. How long ago had they captured Fort Khalfa? Maybe she'd ask someone to look it up for her—but when there was time, when they'd won. *If* they won.

After the carving came the staircase. She tripped at the bottom, only barely regaining her balance by slamming her staff on the flagstones. *Dust and spring frost,* there were always more steps than she remembered! Two weeks in Khafa and she was still making foolish mistakes. But there was no immediate sign of panicked underlings, no one running to her side as if she'd break from a simple stumble. No one had seen, then. Bless small mercies.

'Good morning, Zerach.' Her first lieutenant, Abasai, came to meet her by the entrance to the great hall. She nodded in response and slipped her arm through his. 'We're at the long table near the window again.'

'We?'

'All us mages. There's reinforcements over from the lowlands—'

'I don't suppose there's anyone I know?'

No answer. Abesai blew out a breath. 'Hold tight.'

They moved through a knot of people and drew into a quieter area. One male voice rose in proud explanation over the rest. 'From what I hear, the main opinion? Luck. At the very last, carelessness. For months and months it was rumoured, though only by those in the know, that Zerach was infinitely more fallible than the legend she became. That… oh, perhaps… No, I shouldn't say. Surely some censor will deem me incorrect. There are always those who bristle at honesty.'

'Strike true with words, as if a sword!' a younger voice urged.

He went on: 'I've heard words—said under the influence of pomegranate wine—that speak of, well, her *prowess* in bed. Not that I'm jealous, of course. It's enough to know that I gained my position on my own merit. But truth is often found in the words of the people, after all, and—'

'And do you believe these rumours, Tiberias al Kordova?' Zerach's disdain elicited small, startled gasps among the group.

'I'm just reporting what I hear,' Tiberias replied, voice laden with courtesy. Wood scraped on stone as he pulled a chair back for her. 'You look lovely, by the way.'

He took her elbow to help her sit, and instinctively she pulled away.

'Well! Forgive me.' He put more affront than necessary into his tone, making his young subordinates chuckle amongst themselves. 'Far be it from me to startle an old comrade injured in battle.' Zerach gave pause. *Sarcasm, or genuine apology?*

*You think everyone's an enemy,* Ta'ir had always said, tracing calming caresses down Zerach's tense arms. She had always scoffed and called Ta'ir naïve, said she was just too trusting, but so often, her optimism had paid off. Besides, Zerach told herself now, the army needed both her *and* Tiberias, working together. Troop reserves were running low and mages rare; discord could spell disaster in battle.

'Or it could be completely rational not to enjoy strangers steering you like a child,' Zerach muttered, finding her fork, but still, she kept her voice low.

A plate slid in front of her. 'Stuffed pepper at sundial twelve, lamb at six, spiced carrots at nine,' Abasai informed her.

'My thanks.' She chewed with deliberate bites. 'Tell me, are the curtains still up? Have there been any more infiltration attempts?'

'It's like a parody of a wedding, all white sandstone and black linen. At noon sometimes, we still hear them creeping outside, their claws on the stone.'

'Right.' *It could be worse.* 'How are we managing in terms of supplies?'

'Attempts to harvest food and water… most haven't succeeded. Everything's from root cellars, winter stores and the underground well.'

A scream from across the hall stopped Zerach before she could reply.

'It's still there,' someone was shrieking. 'Those scales—its scarlet eyes, like branding irons—its blood-dripping teeth in that twisted mouth. Fuck, I can still sense it!' Terracotta smashing against stonework. Drawn swords and shouts, 'Hold him, don't let him harm himself!' At last a scuffle, and the knight was subdued. For moments, hushed silence permeated the hall. Then tentative voices entered quiet conversation, and the noise uneasily resumed.

'They're carrying him to the infirmary,' Abasai answered before she could ask.

*Another warrior fallen, then,* thought Zerach. She tried to count how many they'd lost in the past few days; she didn't know. The uncertainty worried her.

'Will we lose our thoughts the way he has?' It was one of the new mages, a quaver in her lowlands-prim voice.

Abasai gave an audible shudder. 'The longer you're fighting them, the worse it gets. Their rows of slanted teeth and burning crimson eyes—they're horrible to look at. All your senses turn against you. Rot and blood swarm in your lungs, a thousand locusts sting your skin—the inside of your mouth is all hornets and piss. And you smell death, all the time. Not as an old grave, but fresh sticky blood. You hear the cries of children, of young milk-goats… And the whispering. The voices that say it'd all stop if you'd only do as they ask.

'There aren't words for what it's really like. I can poke around the edges, but—there aren't words. I wish there were.' He leaned against Zerach with a heavy breath, like a dog seeking comfort, and she let him rest there for a minute before nudging him off with her fork.

'Don't tell tales, you fool. You'll be fine as long as you keep your wits about you and don't lose your head or do anything stupid. I spent months fighting them; I should know well enough.'

'Really?' the young mage asked.

'Of course. Face-to-face, they're hardly fearsome.'

It was a good lie. They seemed to believe it.

‡

Zerach returned to her chambers to find that the young soldier who'd been assigned the task of reading battle correspondence to her had been sent to the infirmary during the night. Khafa's harsh, dry air took its toll on lowlanders, and a single gust of sharp sand could blind someone for days, causing absences Zerach had learned to deal with. But it meant that Abasai had to take up the responsibility, and reading aloud was not among his many skills. Crawling through a report on supply lines as she patiently listened, he stumbled over words she knew, turned pages and pages back when asked to repeat a paragraph, or interrupted his reading with conversation. She was almost grateful when he was called away to some more vital task.

Zerach sat on the low stone sofa after he'd swept from the room, pressed to its coolness as she unconsciously stroked the closed book.

Footsteps. She raised her head. Only mages wore those heavy boots.

'It's only me.'

Tiberias, unwilling even to make the effort of naming himself—but she knew his voice.

*Anger will serve nothing,* she reminded herself. *The grievances of one are nothing. Without unity, all tribes will fall.* The curve of her smile was a saltwater lake.

Fabric caved as he chose a nearby chair. 'Tell me, Zerach. What is it you do here at Fort Khafa?'

She tapped the book. 'I am consulting. Most don't serve as long as I have and survive.' She spoke with confidence and pride. Since her arrival, she'd forged reams of new strategies and advances—the troops of the last desert battle had returned with reports of the lowest casualties yet.

'I suppose they must read you their reports? Make maps from clay, so you can see the land? Were you given an escort your first fortnight here?'

'Ye-es.' Like a wildcat prodding at a snare, she knew his words must hold some trap. But what? For once, his tone seemed genuinely inquisitive and kind.

He circled her, his footsteps soft as sand-shift. At last he said, mildly, 'Take no offence, Mage-Captain. I respect you greatly; your past victories were a great inspiration to us all, and I learned much from hearing of your deeds. But… I have heard the warriors speak of you. They—though I cringe to hear it—say you are a great burden to His Majesty's army. A helpless, old invalid, her training outmoded, her magic faltering. That you accomplish nothing that could not be done by a sighted warrior in a third of the time—that, well, you accomplish nothing.'

Her hands tensed. Folded. 'And what do you think of these rumours?'

'I merely repeat what I hear, and this is what I know: as much as it distresses me, your presence unnerves the troops. They worry that our leaders' continued employment of you is a sign of corruption. Ridiculous, of course. But, were you to leave your post and return to your cottage in the hillside… there would be no accusations of cowardice against you, Mage-Captain. I think it's admirable that you still attempt to contribute what little you can.'

The noise of his gait receded. At last a door closed. Zerach rested her head in her hands and took deep, slow, empty breaths.

‡

'Zerach, come with me—please?'

'What is it you want?'

Abasai paused. 'It's not what I want, it's what the War Council wants.'

Zerach laughed. 'Splendid. Perhaps they plan to use my scarred face as a weapon of psychological warfare now. Perhaps I will be sent to terrorise the human tribes who've allied themselves with our enemies—come to think of it, that would be quite effective. I'll suggest the idea myself.'

'Don't be like that—look, I can hardly see the scarring if we're standing in a shadow, and everyone's glad you're back on your feet. You know, you give a lot of the injured soldiers great strength. They say that if you could get through the burn treatments and rehabilitation, so can they.'

Was that really the case? She wasn't sure how to feel anymore, who to believe.

As they neared the fortress's war-room, the stone corridors grew louder and busier. More than once she had to nudge a rushing page out of the way with her staff. In the room itself, mint tea and silence permeated the air; a quiet crafted by spells so that important conversations couldn't be overheard. She raised her head. 'Well?'

'We've intercepted a letter leaving the fortress—there may be someone within our forces feeding information to the enemy.'

Zerach nodded, jaw tightening. A traitor would go a long way towards explaining their recent defeats in the south. 'That's a significant discovery. I'm not sure how it concerns me, though.'

'We need you, Zerach. There's a spell on this—something complex—preventing us from decoding the letter's contents.'

'And you think I can help you?' Disbelief and sarcasm dripped from her words like blood from a shield.

'You're one of the best we have left—certainly the best we have here. Please, at least try.'

'I doubt I'll be of much use.'

Still, she took the sheet of parchment and pressed it to her forehead. Since the acid, her senses reached for other forms of understanding magic than sight, and she felt it now flooding all of her body: an out-of-tune stringed instrument playing a strange scale. The distant shimmer of a goat-skin tambourine. Burnt cumin and moss-rose leaves.

Zerach coaxed herself deeper into the pattern, as subtly as she knew how, like feeling her way along a labyrinthine stone tomb. Her body remained in the war room, but she could feel herself travelling, felt the sensation permeate her body. Under her left hand, the slimy taste-texture of enemy workings spread over the spell's walls, while her right hand twitched with rough flashes of familiar strength. Dust swirled in her head, forcing her to backtrack. She pulled the music into rhythm, tendons in her wrist straining as harmony formed.

'I'm making progress.' Her own voice sounded incredibly distant, and she knew she approached the centre of the maze, the heart of the spell. From there, she would be able to analyse its making. 'I—'

Light flared into her vision, an explosion of fire where there had been fog. Zerach knew she was falling. Her legs crumpled under her; she could do nothing to stop it. Her head knocked on the marble floor.

*Oh,* she wanted to say. *It's a curse. It's a trap.*

Then she was falling farther. Falling inside herself.

‡

In the dream, Zerach saw her reflection: her faded old robe, her uneven dark braids and the splashmarks of white acid across a face once renowned for its arrogant elegance. Her wavering image was the only thing that existed in the endless dark.

A clawed hand gripped the thought of her bare shoulder, monstrous snakeskin on flesh.

'Look at you, Mage-Captain,' came a voice. 'Everyone exchanging pitying glances whenever you open your mouth. Still behind on your correspondence. Still stumbling down stairs.' The fragments of truths sank into her secret heart and burned. Her body stung all over. Before she could cry out, a soothing mountain spring washed the sensation away.

'I can give you everything back, Mage-Captain. Your sight and your armies.'

A landscape stretched out in front of her: the green mountains of her childhood, with its secret tombs hidden in limestone, its marigolds, myrtle, cedar, figs. Abruptly, the scene changed: Fort Toqeph, the day before they'd taken back the ruined city of Kewara. Soldiers cleaning their weapons and playing bone-dice, yet all supremely alert, looking up and saluting as she walked past. A glow of pride reinvigorated her tired body.

'Old victories to relive, new ones to challenge. All the comrades in arms that you've cherished and lost.' Something began to materialise in her palm: the portrait from her locket, its image as fuzzy as her memories. How many smiles had crinkled the corners of those honey-sweet eyes? A yearning to remember tugged at her soul.

The scene shifted again: the view from her own mudbrick cottage in the hillsides, a perfect spring day. Below, beside the onion beds, a brown horse reared gracefully, its powerful legs thrusting at imaginary foes. A tall, dark-haired woman, her hands on her hips, nodded in satisfaction. *Look up,* Zerach prayed inwardly. *Turn your smile on me just one more time. Honey eyes sweetening pomegranate lips.* She remembered, but—*Show me your wild and perfect soul.*

'And I can return your heart-wife Ta'ir, dead and gone these past two months. You could stay here forever, living in a perfect dream of your own design.'

The words slammed into her. Only two months. Somewhere low in her guts, a laugh broke its shell, the same laugh that bandits still feared in their echoing caves. As strong and bitter as wormwood. 'That means I haven't even been blind for a month!'

Magic rushed back into her on a red tide of rage. The beast loomed before her. She pulled her body into the dream, like walking through a web of wire; with each tug of effort, she shredded and remade her skin. She manifested her own solid form, her clouded-glass dagger, and seized the monster by its tattered neck. In a single movement she wrestled him back into the featureless space of before. They fought, snake against battle-mage. Its body wrapped around her torso, but she jabbed her knife into the thinner skin beneath its throat. The dream slowed down her movements; still, she held her own.

'I've only been blind for a month,' she panted. 'One damn month. At one month of magic, I couldn't even light a candle. King Sulieman, blessed be his name, was still shitting himself at one month old! A year from now, I'll have clouded-glass goggles and a gyroscope in my eating knife. I'll walk with more dignity in my bruised-up toenails than all your soldiers will have in their deaths!'

Movement came faster, easier. She didn't even need to breathe. *It'll get easier and easier every day without her, every day without sight.* 'I am Mage-Captain Zerach Salaan from the tribe of the goats. My roots are sunk so deep in stone that no lightning can touch me. And as for my heart-wife—if you think she would be happy to know that I stayed in a beautiful dream with her ghost instead of going where I was needed, you don't know the first thing about her. Time wears all things but one down. It takes the edge off grief like a sandstorm on ruins, but it cannot alter love.

'You think I want to retreat into my memories?' She pulled it closer with a twist of her fingers and a gust of cold wind, and pressed the knob of her staff into the vulnerable place at its throat. 'Listen well, beast. Those memories are why I fight.'

The dust of the explosion choked her breath, propelling her up a mountain and back into her skin.

‡

Zerach woke to cold marble under her head, worried voices exchanging suggestions far above. Instinctively, she grabbed her staff and sat up.

'Thank the King of Kings,' a voice breathed.

Memory snapped back into place: she'd been so close. 'Give me back the letter. I think I know what I'm doing.'

'Are you sure she should—'

'Contrary to *rumour*, I'm still one of the best. Bring it here.' Snapping her fingers and having people rush to fulfil her ideas—being not just Zerach but Mage-Captain, a creature with infinite deviousness and a thousand strong arms—oh, King of Kings, she'd missed this.

The parchment was thrust back into her hands. Now familiar with the tapestry of texture and sound, she applied pressure to the puzzle, forcing it to solve itself. A nexus revealed: coriander and sharp leaves. It was a tangle of cactus spines, but she recognised it now.

'I know this spell,' she said. 'In the mountain war between the tribes, a few kings back, Sulieman Dovid used a passcode based on his seven husbands. Sometimes we still use it for ceremonial documents, but only mages above a certain rank are permitted to learn it. And the only other mage-captain here—' Paper crumbled under her fingers. 'Tiberias al Kordova sent the letter. He's been sending information to the enemy. Stop him, now.'

A quick rush of departing feet responded. She would have joined them but her head was still spinning; the floor unsteady beneath her feet.

*I'll forget what my wife looked like in the years to come. Her silent sigh of joy when we made love, her morning grin. But I know she'd be proud.*

'What does it say?' She held out the parchment. It was taken gently from her.

'We will have it decoded as soon as resources allow,' said her lieutenant.

'Why would he support them?' a lieutenant asked, his confusion practically audible.

'Cutting his losses,' she ventured. 'Better chance of survival.'

'Survival?! But they hate humans!'

'Only on religious principle. They're pragmatists; they'd likely be willing to work with one member of a lesser race if it meant exterminating us all—especially if he was willing to swear himself to their gods.'

'Perhaps.' Abasai sounded uncertain. Zerach almost envied him; she could not afford herself the luxury of doubt.

'Abasai!' came a shout. 'Cover the left corridor!'

He left with running footsteps. Reflexively, she moved to follow them, but the stones tilted under her and she had to sit back down.

*What must it be like,* mused Zerach, in the quiet, *to pledge one's soul to those beasts?* For surely Tiberias had done so, to be trusted by the creatures. He was living in a dream of his own importance; she was glad she'd had the strength to resist a similar trap.

According to the enemy's scrolls, Zerach remembered, anything that walked on two legs was an abomination, to be hunted and killed unless it swore allegiance to their unholy gods. There'd been apes in this land, once. Little pale-fuzzed creatures that lived in sharing clans of a few dozen, chattering their gentle myths about the Great Mother Tree. The first human settlers had found only their hand-tools, cave paintings and bones.

'Then we send a peace mission on donkeys,' Ta'ir had said once, the evening wind catching her dark curls. Campfire light dancing in her eyes. 'Or we put the parley flag in our mouths, and approach on all fours.'

Zerach, roasting meat on a stick, had swallowed the last bite and twirled the skewer in her hands. 'Or we fight and survive long enough, and they realise that we're abominations worth buying armor from. You never know.' She'd rested her head on her wife's shoulder, glad that the night hid her exhaustion, more thankful still for the familiar fingers tangling in her hair.

Screams smashed her memories, jolting her back into the present.

'Tiberias is gone! We've lost our chance to capture him!'

'How did it get through—'

'She'll be defenseless—'

Bodies hit stone. Unconscious, not dead, she hoped.

The wooden door ripped like paper. Where was her staff? Zerach felt around, but only touched cold roughness. Cursed be, it must've rolled farther, perhaps all the way to the wall. The creature's slithery legs—undeniably six of them—slid against each other as it sniffed the air.

Hide or fight? She had no chance, either way. These things died slow. Damn everything. Stall, then. Muffle her senses against its poisonous madness and hope for reinforcements. You don't try to take one on alone unless you're already infected. In one quick movement, Zerach dashed to the window and wrapped herself in cotton drape.

Footsteps slicked closer. She felt like a fraud, hiding from the very thing she daily ordered soldiers toward. Her boot nudged something—her staff.

In their last moment together, Ta'ir had pressed it into her hand. 'Take the refugees and go, my heart. I'll hold them off—'

They hadn't said they loved each other. They hadn't needed to. Love flowed through her voice, like water through desert canyons at the flood season's heart.

*Ta'ir died helping others to safety. Protecting them with her warhorse, with her very flesh. She didn't die cowering.*

*And neither shall I. Because I'm still loved—and I can still be brave—*

With a single stamp, she flipped her staff up into her grasp and began spinning the call of a spell.

Suckers ripped back the curtain—

No blood rushing to suffocate her. No untellable horrors or endless void. Just hot, fetid breath on her face, like a thousand dead cats. The madness these creatures carried had decimated her soldiers and haunted her nightmares, yet now, the pain emanating from its form didn't even brush her skin. She knew it was searching her face, asking: threat or prey?

*Threat,* she thought. *Always and forever a threat to your war.* Zerach completed the spell's sequence of movements. Sharp heat flared against her face, the desert-thunder shockwave of magic striking home; the explosion knocked her back. Her body burned, her hands spasmed around the polished wood. The wall took her weight as she slid towards the floor.

A door creaked open. 'Oh, gods,' came a voice, awed and fearful. She imagined what they saw: her empty eye sockets, blood spattering her limbs and spiking her hair, the wildflower robe now forever ruined. Down at the laundry vats, they'd weep over the embroidery, and she'd rip it from their grasp to wrap herself in it again, to wear it until it reeked.

'How did you survive?'

'Their cloaking…' A cough snaked up her throat, and she clutched her staff until she could speak again, her free hand gesturing furiously. '…The way they play havoc with people's minds… it doesn't infect through all the senses, only sight. I don't feel the fear anymore. It was trying to push at me. Nothing. It skittered right off.'

She accepted the offered arm to help her to her feet; her legs were unfeeling, her chest made of light. 'We fight blind and we'll win.' Though her voice barely worked, Zerach laughed.

‡

Zerach taught the troops how to follow her movements by command and instinct, how to sense magic in fingertips and scent. Captain once more, she slept curled around her staff. As long as she made schedule, no one cared if she stumbled; once again she breathed in strength and roared out fire.

When the next battle came, the mages fought blindfolded on the ramparts, working spells that would keep the front-line soldiers safe from the beasts' madness. Over the course of the first few hours, hope grew in Zerach's chest. Though outnumbered, they had the higher ground, and their shield-lines seemed to be holding.

A scream split the air, mere feet from her head; a body landed with a dull thud against the already blood-spattered stone.

'What is it?' she shouted.

The response came from a panicked mage nearby. 'Tiberias is leading them! He knows what we're doing—he's working against us, breaking through our shields!'

Zerach pushed through the throngs, determined to get down to the battlefield. Instead of running down the narrow staircase, she hoisted her staff and slid down the spiral railing from her post, trusting her body's instinct and memory. Talons slashed at her face as she landed on solid ground. Flinging out nomad's fire like a shockwave around herself, she battered the creatures back.

From the depths of her muscle-thick belly, she summoned the Voice of the Gryphon—a name given by soldiers and enemies alike. It had lain silenced for fortnights, but she called now and the power answered, a contralto profundo bellowing like a storm over the battlefield, startling all who heard. 'Come down and face me, goat-chewed Tiberias! Or are you a coward as well as a panderer's get?'

Silence for a breath, then speech, nearer and sharper than the clang of swords. 'Face you? Luck-captain, you can't even *see* me.'

A dangerous underestimation. She traced the pathway of his snort and struck before he'd finished dodging. It was only a wounding blow but still laden with power, the wicked curved blade scything out from her staff. Tiberias, the coward, called up a fizzing nimbus of cloaking strength and flashed away. If she could, she'd have tracked him to the ends of the Earth. But it was almost enough to know she'd got him fleeing scared.

Without the help of the traitor mage, the enemy beasts turned uncertain. No longer able to rely on magic to communicate between squadrons, they fell back to banging their hypnotic skin-forged drums.

Returned to the wall, Abesai aimed Zerach with short bursts of instruction, and a new energy crackled through the defenders. Their enemies weren't invincible—they could be beaten. Still, waves of soldiers faltered in the frenzy and were grasped by madness, as did a few mages who couldn't resist the compulsion to peek. But it was a much slower leak than ever before—there was no soldier unprotected against the infection, no mage turning on an ally with brutal savagery.

Invincible to the raging dust-storm, Mage-Captain Zerach raised her arms atop the battlements. The wind of blood and lemons tangled her cropped braids.

Her legs gave out before her strength did, and the battle-commander ordered her below to drink something besides kafe.

'We're still fighting—'

'And you'll be no good to anyone without some rest. You've done enough. You've done more than enough.'

There was a note of genuine respect in the woman's voice, and it took Zerach a moment to realise it had always been there.

She just hadn't trusted herself enough to believe it was real.

Steadying her shaking hands, Zerach snapped out a salute. 'And I'm glad to have done my part.'

She meant to reach her room before her willpower could fade, but halfway there, she was forced to pause in an alcove to catch her breath. All at once, getting up seemed like the most unnecessary scrap of foolishness. She pulled her staff closer and tucked her arms under her head.

Zerach dozed lightly as a jackal, the sounds of battle raging outside the walls, the drumbeat burning in her chest. She rested on a hard wooden bench, a cup of mint tea cooling by her slack fingers.

Footsteps woke her.

'Abesai?'

'It's me.'

At once she yanked herself into full awareness. 'Well?'

Exultant joy rang through his voice. 'We're slaughtering them like gazelles in a valley. When their drummers faltered, their lines broke; then one of our women got hold of a drum and lured their cavalry straight into our grasp. It's incredible: a whole throng of our people can already fight with opened eyes without screaming and clawing their own skin. We've driven them back, for now. And it was all because of you.'

'Any word on Tiberias?'

'None—we think he may have retreated to their headquarters. From the contents of his letter, we can assume he's in a position of high command.'

Zerach felt around for her tea, catching the mug before her sleeve could knock it over. A smile scythed across her lips. 'Good.'

'You wanted to kill him mere clock-turns ago.'

'And now I have an enemy I know how to kill. Anyone who is not exactly like Tiberias—a woman, an invert, someone with wounds or from the nomad tribes—he thinks less of. Even though I'm all four of those things and I've bested him at every turn. That'll be his undoing. Because we're going to recruit more of me. Anyone who's left the mage service because of sand damaging their sight, any blind youth with magical talent. We'll take away the creatures' advantage and crush them in a fair damn fight.' Approving noises from Abesai as excitement carried her to her feet. 'We have to start writing letters. You transcribe, I'll dictate—and don't get ahead of me again. I'll fetch my writing things. Oh, and—' She broke off.

'Yes?'

Asking for help felt like pronouncing the words of a difficult spell. Each syllable stung the space behind her teeth. But just like she trusted her magic, she now trusted herself to speak up. 'The next time I do my braids, can you sit with me? The blue glass beads are the same size as the green, and the gold ones have the same markings as the silver, and I know I've been getting the colour patterns wrong.'

'It would be an honour.'

Before, she might have taken the stairs slowly, worried about falling. This time, she glided up, her steps as smooth as sand, just letting her body follow the familiar curve. She reached solid rock again without a single stumble and let herself grin. That one small victory, she knew, would be the harbinger of many more.

# Seida the Fairy-Troll

Claudie Arseneault

Fairies are meant to fly—to zip around, looping and twisting, *buzz-buzz*, look at my pretty shimmering wings, or something. All slim and graceful, with pretty round mouths. Oh, and let's not forget polite and demure, too. You've got to be *shy* and *obliging*. I guess, maybe, I was never meant to be a fairy. Not with the swears rolling off my tongue all day, not with the burnt, twisted frame I sometimes dared to call wings on my back. The joke around the tree was that my mother got knocked up by a troll, and out I came. Didn't care much for it. Just another way for folk to say I was big, buff and ugly… and sorry, but I was big, buff and *majestic*.

Most days, I avoided the canopy hall at rush hour. I preferred my cozy home down by the roots, where no one could come and ruin my day. No doubt it contributed to the myth of Seida the Fairy-Troll, but maybe I wouldn't *be* such a grumpy recluse if these coneheads weren't assholes all the time. At least there was Jasmine. She would float down to my hole every now and then for lunch, and she was nice. Didn't laugh at me, just gave me the latest news from up top, helped me treat my tattered wings and listened. More refreshing than a cool breeze on a hot summer night. My kind of girl, too—all sharp angles, beautiful nasal laugh and big brown eyes. I made a move, once, but she said she was asexual, and maybe aromantic, and she wasn't interested. Good on her; at least she kept coming back to my place. I was afraid I'd scared her off.

Maybe it had been her calling me up to the Great Tree earlier, when the little alarm buzzed and lit up blood red. It was a lazy system, but built on mutual laziness, I suppose: they couldn't be bothered to float down to tell me I was needed for a job, and I sure as hell wasn't going to climb up every day to check. Besides, fairy work involves lots of flying around and doing magic dances—not exactly my strong suit. They had an image to maintain, anyway, and I didn't fit, so I wasn't often called upon. I liked working, though—even dull jobs changed the routine—and that light had never flashed *red* before.

I grabbed the Great Tree's bark and started climbing, my thick muscles easily lifting my weight. It was a long way up, but not a hard one. Just had to take it one handhold at a time and let your mind fall into the zone. Exercise had its own rhythm, breath and heartbeat syncing, thoughts evaporating. It made everything not suck for a while. They could laugh all they wanted at my 'worm crawl', but the climb was the best part of visiting the canopy hall.

A film of sweat soon covered my dark arms. Every now and then, my wings flicked behind me, itching to start beating and flying. As if they'd forgotten they were little more than a broken frame and a bit of charred tissue. I kept going, forcing them to fold awkwardly behind my back. By the time I reached the canopy, my breath was short, my back and arms just about ready to explode. I rolled my shoulders in an attempt to release some of the tension and walked towards the Great Tree's trunk.

I entered the large hollowed-out section of the tree, the cavern expanding dozens of feet above and below the sapwood. Tunnels and structures branched out of the walls, their mouths often surrounded by golden and glowing fungi. Suspended in the middle of the chamber was the canopy hall, its inside obscured by twisted branches and moss. My way of entry tapered into a platform from which other fairies could just leap off and attend their business.

I came to an awkward halt, glaring around and hoping that whoever had called me wouldn't waste too much time showing up.

This hub was always a mess of fairies, heading out to grant wishes, rushing in from missions or just meeting for a gossip before heading inside to eat. But today? Full on chaos. A maelstrom of wings and shouts, fairies zipping by so close to me I almost stumbled and fell. I couldn't make out a clear conversation, but the hall thrummed with anxious voices.

The fear permeating everything disturbed me. Danger rarely came to the Great Tree; fairies aren't warriors, we're diplomats. Our role is threefold: to act as messengers between planes of existence, to resolve conflicts within these planes or between them, and to maintain the Great Tree and its portals. The tree stands at the heart of everything, and its massive branches stretch out to every portal, every facet of the universe.

'Seida!'

Chief Julian's voice pierced through the chaos, deep and loud. I spun as he rushed out of the canopy hall, wings fluttering so fast they were practically a blur. His didn't have the iridescence so many fairies sported, just thin all-white wings that contrasted with his smooth brown skin.

'Thank the Great Tree you're here!' He landed next to me, his wings slowing down to a lazy flap. 'Thank the Great Tree you *exist*, even.'

'Oh, I do thank it. Every day. You know me, very religious.'

He scowled, and I grinned. I hadn't participated in our religious festivals in years, and didn't mean to start any time soon. I mean, we *lived* in the Great Tree, cared for its holy branches and seeds. Why get all fancy about it? It was enough for me to lay my hands on the cool bark of my house every morning. More private.

'You're never this happy to see me,' I said. 'What's going on?'

'We've got a portal sundering.'

'Send a team?' I could feel the frown on my face. Portals split and broke all the time. Well, not *all* the time, but often enough for us to be ready and keep specialised fairies on call to fix them. A quick paste, a bit of tree-shaping magic, some friendly jokes between coworkers—pretty routine stuff. Why was everyone freaking out? And why call *me* in for a portal break?

'You're the team.'

He crossed his arms. This obviously didn't please him any more than it did me. I waited for more, expecting Julian to give me a full debriefing, but he just stared over my shoulder. What was up with him? Our interactions were never pleasant, but this awkward silence was new and disturbing. We didn't get along precisely *because* we threw the truth at each other, and he was holding it back this time.

'Okay, spit it out.'

'It's Hell's portal.'

I stiffened. He wanted *me* around Hell's portal?

'Send someone else. I learned my lesson.'

I spun on my heels to climb straight back home, trying to quash the memories creeping in the back of my mind. Julian flew right by me and into my path the moment I stepped into the sunlight. He almost earned himself a solid punch.

'We can't. Seida, you're the only one who can do this.'

My gaze shifted down to the lowest of branches, where our only connection to demons rested. Why anyone would ever send a fairy diplomat to those fiery abominations was beyond me, but *apparently* it was our sacred duty to keep it open, just in case. And they wondered why I didn't dig a lot of our religious spiel.

I couldn't see most of the portal from here, but the air around the lower branches wavered from heat. And were those flames licking out? *Shit.* Not a good thing to have around our highly ignitable Great Tree. Whoever thought this was the brightest place to build a smouldering hot portal needed to rethink their life choices. In fact, whoever decided the portal should be accessible to adventure-hungry fairies with no respect for rules should've lost their job. Or wings. That'd be fitting.

'Why me?'

A joke about being the expandable one crossed my mind, but stuck in my throat. I wanted nothing to do with Hell's portal. The last time it'd cracked, it had stolen my wings.

Julian snapped his wings, jolting my attention back to him. 'We need someone without these babies. Jasmine is on her way with protective sheets to avoid burns, but it doesn't stick to wings. Of those of us who can actually access the portals, you're the strongest climber by far. And sure, messengers and diplomats can fly in and out of the hottest hell without a problem, but they know jack shit about reparative magic. You *can* fix a portal, can't you?'

The question stirred bitter anger in my stomach. 'Of course I can. I'm a goddamn portal fairy too, not some pet monster you keep around for a laugh.' A full-blown rant was forming in my mind, built of frustration and a growing, niggling fear. Jasmine came flying out of the canopy hall before I could start, a large bag cradled in her flimsy hands. 'So, basically, either I go down there, or we all burn.'

He nodded. I swore.

'Fine. I'll fix it.' I needed every ounce of willpower to keep my voice firm. Despite the years, any mention of the cursed portal turned my legs into wool. I hated it, hated the way I quailed as if I was still that scared child. I'd grown strong and steady, and I wasn't going to let even a gate to Hell scare me.

'I'll fix it,' I repeated, more forcefully this time.

Jasmine landed next to us and threw a displeased look at Julian. Her lips rarely held anything but a smile, and the fairy captain cleared his throat and stared at his feet. Satisfied, Jasmine put a cool hand on my forearm. I sighed, relaxing at her touch.

'I had to prepare it really fast,' she said, 'so don't stay any longer than you have to.'

I snorted. 'As if I would.'

Jasmine retrieved a large jar from the bag, uncorked it and reached in. When her hand reappeared, she was holding a strange fabric that looked like an inch-thick sheet of sludge. The translucent yellow glittered in the sunlight. Without waiting for my approval, she slapped the sheet on my chest and started wrapping it around my body. I grimaced at the oily texture and coolness. Better that than to burn, though. I let her plaster me with the gooey stuff, cringing as she floated up to spread it around my face and on my hair, weighing down my massive curls. She flew once more around me to make sure she'd covered every little spot of skin and cloth, then applied some of it on my broken wings. I was glad it was Jasmine doing it. I hated when strangers tried to touch the frames.

'Okay, you're ready.'

'I'm always ready. Usually it's to fuck shit up, though, not repair it.'

Jasmine's nasal laugh covered up the disapproving grunt from Julian. I ruffled her hair, rubbing in a thin layer of slime, and approached the edge of the branch.

'We'll fly you to the ground, and you can climb to the portal,' Julian said as I peered down the tree. He barked out names and two fairies flew over, probably wishing they hadn't been around. 'Everyone get a hold of Seida. And stay around. She might need quick help back up.'

I sure hoped I wouldn't. The last bad encounter had been quite enough for me. I gritted my teeth as thin hands wrapped around my arms and lifted me. Julian picked up my legs, and they flew down in unison, with me dangling between. Very dignified. Would *totally* do again.

It didn't last long, but those minutes hanging between two fairies revealed a whole new perspective of the Great Tree to me. With my nose inches away from its bark while I climbed, I'd never paid attention to how large and bountiful my home was. It stretched its branches hundreds of feet into the sky, green leaves catching the sun, speckling everything beneath in small shadows. Portals decorated the branches, sometimes standing proud atop them, sometimes hanging down from vines. Fairies zoomed in and out of them as I descended, buzzing around like insects, breathing even more life into the place.

My feet touched the ground before my shock had passed, and I tripped in surprise. I swatted my carriers away in an attempt to cover my stumble and cleared my throat. Julian muttered something about my rudeness as they flew back up, but I didn't care. I needed some of my self-respect back, and that helped.

My stomach twisted, but I didn't give myself time to think about it. Not until I was well on my way. I started forward, forcing my mind to focus on the climb and the strain in my muscles. This wouldn't be like my first visit. I wasn't a wilful child anymore, disobeying the rules to prove myself, to show I didn't fit any of their lies. When adults told the seven-year-old me I was meant to be slim and graceful, to keep my mouth shut and listen and heal, I'd known they were wrong. And I'd figured the same would be true of their warnings about Hell's portal.

That flight to the portal had been my last flight full-stop. This time, I had to heave myself on to its level, hands slick from Jasmine's protective slime.

The portal loomed at the other end of the large, flat branch, foreboding and familiar. Craggy dark stones the length of my forearm arched around the gate, creeping under the wood like bony black fingers. The stone on the top of the portal was fissured, bright red and fuming. Blinding white energy spurted irregularly from it in crackling jolts. The portal curved up to about seven feet—tall enough even for me to get through, unlike most fairy doors. Yet smaller than I remembered. But I had been so young, and the belching smoke it'd been spitting must have made it seem bigger.

I shouldn't have gone closer, shouldn't have approached the armoured centipede crawling out of it—but it had looked just like a bigger version of the bugs I'd played with all the time. That is, until it'd snapped at my legs and dragged me into the searing heat.

I swallowed hard, sparing a glance to the thick scars on my calf, and headed towards the gate.

A warm wind picked up around me as I approached, blowing me back and forth. I kept walking, struggling against the push and pull, grateful for my heavy build. Most other fairies would have been blown away; even at double their weight, holding my own required serious effort. The storm pulled at the frame of my wings, and for a moment I feared it'd rip what was left of them out.

I took each stride one at a time, my eyes fixed on the prize. The bursts of energy seemed to grow worse but perhaps it was just in my head, where memories of a burning inferno were superimposed on the current flames. Perhaps it was just the quickening of my heart. Sweat rolled down my neck, drenching my shirt. I could feel the heat through Jasmine's slime.

I extended my hand as I neared the portal, but hesitated. What if another creature crawled out? What if I couldn't do this? A lump blocked my throat. I hadn't created any kind of major reparative magic for years and fixing a portal was hardly the same as fixing a tear in my clothes. But what were our other options? No one but me could stand in this burning cyclone.

I took a deep breath, stretched my arms. Focused. Ignored the imagined cries of the centipede, the tingling in my scarred leg. Fairies draw their power from their grace. I could be graceful if I wanted. In my own way. It'd help if I didn't have the entire fairy population looking down on me, though, flying around the branches above, just out of reach of the heat.

I brought my arms up, palms outward, and closed my eyes. The winds pushed at me, but I stayed put. I had to take it slow. Focus on the body, on the strength in my muscles, on the energy within me waiting to be unleashed.

Heat filtered through the protective ooze. Just a speck, at the base of my wings. In my mind it flared, catching the thin fabric that had once hung there, fire coursing all the way up to their tips. Phantom pain pierced my shoulder blades, then lit up my calf where the centipedes' teeth had dug in as I'd kicked at it, panicked tears rolling down my cheeks. Its shell had cracked under the assault of my bare feet, freeing me inches away from the portal.

I groaned, struggling to keep the memory away and calm down. *Inhale, count to seven, exhale.*

I wrestled control over the screaming child in my head, flailing and rolling to extinguish the flames in her wings, her leg bloodied and hurting. Nothing would have the time to come out today. I would see to it. I channelled the fear into my arms and hands, building up strength in my muscles. This was my grace, my power. I did not dance, gathering power through fluid spins. I amassed it through immobility, focus and sheer strength.

I only needed to move once, to release my magic in a single blast. I itched to do it *now*, to just let go, but I let the tension in my bones escalate until it felt like I would tear apart from holding it back.

Then I spun.

A whole three-sixty, hair flying, a cry bursting from my lungs. I brought my arms down and slammed my palms into the portal's frame. Out went years of fear and guilt and shame over my recklessness and the price paid, over the terrible loneliness that had followed. The shock rippled through my body, leaving me out of breath, and white light erupted from my fingers, spilling over the broken stone and rushing for the cracks above.

The fiery wind closed on me, circling ever faster into a disorienting spiral. It crushed my lungs, but I couldn't let go. The pull of my magic glued me to the portal as it repaired the damage, but the buffeting gusts tore away my coat of slime. The heat cut at me, my skin blistering. *Should have asked for two layers of goo.*

I let out a ragged cry, my rough adult voice echoing the child inside, across time. My knees felt limp. *No, no. Don't slip, not now.* I forced myself to focus on the state of the portal, my eyes watering against the thick, burning wind. The uneven, cracked stones had become almost as smooth as a newborn's ass. I could do this. I wouldn't burn, not this time. Just a little longer, and I would beat the portal.

As the last fissures in the portal sealed themselves, the gusts died and the heat was stifled. Everything stopped at once—no more sounds, no movement but my singed hair falling down and my shoulders easing in release—and then the air around was sucked toward the gate. I swore as it pulled me in, dragging me towards Hell. I grabbed at the stone door, squeezing the frame under my armpits as my feet went flying inside the fiery underworld. The intense heat ate away the protective slime, and my heart stammered as I realised how little time I had before my feet would catch on fire. Flames licked the stone and a tightness wrapped around my chest. The portal was shutting down, a film of black, opaque energy closing on me. *Shit.* That ungrateful dolt of a door! I fixed it up, and now it was trying to crush me to death?

'Oh no you *don't*.'

I drew what strength my strained muscles had left. My wing-frame expanded, pushing the closing portal back half an inch—enough for me to pull myself out and collapse on the ground as it snapped shut. My stubby wings beat lazily behind me as I heaved, arms shaking, my gaze lost in the singed wood underneath me. My head buzzed, my clothes were smoking, and I hurt in so many different places it was hard to choose which was worst. My leg, probably. My scars blazed with angry pain, as if condemning me for returning here, where I'd lost so much long ago. No bitterness roiled through my stomach in response. I had let it all out with my spell, leaving me empty and exhausted, but serene.

Jasmine's tiny feet landed right before me, and I lifted my head. She smiled and offered her hand without a word. I took it and pulled myself up, even though there was no way her tiny frame could lift me; even though my soles flared when I stood up. Julian and his two carrier-fairies had floated back down, too. Slouched over, my head still ringing, I met the Chief's gaze.

'Don't you dare break it again.'

Indignation flashed through his features, and he seemed about to retort—probably some excuse about the natural delicacy of the portals—but thought better of it. Instead, he nodded.

'No, Miss, we won't. Let's bring you home. Jasmine says she has an ointment for your burns.'

Now *that* was something I wouldn't refuse, even if it meant being carried again. I'd just had my fill of adventures and people for the next month, at least. To be left alone in my little troll cave by the roots, with Jasmine and some pain relief? It sounded like a paradise well earned.

'Perfect,' I said. 'Nothing else I'd ask for.'

'Not even a feast?' Julian dropped the question in a casual, almost playful tone. A feast? Why the heck would they invite me to a feast? My confusion must have shown, because he went on. 'We close portals every day, but this one had cracked hard. It would have killed us all, Seida. Impressive work deserves recognition.'

Hundreds of protests rushed through my mind—this was my job, someone had to do it, my single spin-release of reparative magic couldn't compare to other fairies' elaborate dances. My brain just couldn't fathom his offer. *Recognition?* I was the fairy-troll, the recluse who couldn't behave, who disobeyed rules because she could. But I swallowed down my refusals and squared my shoulders.

I *did* deserve this. They had needed someone big and buff, and I had been majestic.

'Sure, I'll take your feast too, once I'm rested. You better cook me something good, Chief. Good and *cold*, if possible.'

'You have my word.' Julian flapped his wings and gestured for the two fairies to carry me off.

As they lifted me off the ground, I cast one last look at the smouldering portal. I could almost see my seven-year-old self, tall even then, lying smoking on the branch. I'd watched fairies fly high above, unaware the disaster far below—or unwilling to notice. I'd been a stain on the branch, all too aware that the searing pain in my back and legs was punishment for defying their rules. For being different.

And yet, here I was again, being carried to safety mere moments after my face-off. They had hurried to my side, promised to tend to my burns, even prepared a feast. I stared at Hell's portal, a stunned smile creeping on my face. It didn't twist my stomach the way it used to, and it never would again.

# COLOSSUS OF EPHESUS

TYLER GATES

Twenty thousand people screamed for blood.

Helios charged the manticore, his gladius shining gold in the sun as the blade bit into the beast's sinewy hide. The creature roared as its purple blood gurgled onto the white sand of the arena. Helios's eyes watered from the stench. A scorpion tail lashed down at him. He planted his feet firm to the ground and raised his shield, but the hooked tip crashed through, splintering the wood, swelling with milky venom.

Helios struck, removing tip from gland with a flash of his sword, the barb lost in the sand beneath his feet. The manticore reared back with a shriek as sharp as a scream. Helios leapt forward for the finishing strike, dragging the weight of his shield beside him.

The manticore swiped, its claw tearing through leather guard and lacerating his flesh. Helios gritted his teeth against the pain. Sweat trickled into his eyes behind his bronze visor. He tightened his grip on his shield, ignoring the ache in his muscles, and waited for the next strike.

It came fast.

Helios slashed at the manticore's paw and it reeled back in pain. He charged with his shield, bashing a mouthful of wood into the beast's human face. It groaned. He struck again and heard a sickening crunch, and the manticore staggered and froze, Helios's blade resting deep in its lungs. It opened its mouth to roar but choked as more purple blood, dark as blackberries, spewed free. With one last guttural groan it collapsed in the sand, dead.

The crowd's applause was thunderous, their cries a song that pumped life back into Helios's tired limbs, burning glory into his heart. It was a storm, it was chaos… and he bathed in it. He knelt down and pulled his gladius free from the manticore's corpse, its blood coating the blade. He raised it to the sun and the people of Ephesus shouted, '*Invictus, invictus, invictus!*'

*Undefeated.* Helios stood a titan, soaking in the warmth of the sky and the love of the crowd. In that bright moment, he touched heaven.

In the dark tunnels beneath the arena, slaves flocked to him. He dropped his shield with a sigh and removed his bronze helm; black hair clung to the sweat on his face. Nimble fingers removed armour and scrubbed dirt from his wounds with a damp cloth, and the gladiator was stripped away to expose Helios beneath, just a bruised and bleeding man.

A shadow emerged from the darkness, and Helios recognised the sweet, perfumed stench and pretentious grin of Sabinus.

'Did you have to be so quick to kill it?' he said. 'There are only three manticores left in the world, you know. It cost me a fortune, getting it out of Parthia.'

'Terrible investment,' said Helios.

Sabinus laughed. 'Twenty thousand people out there disagree with you.' He patted Helios on the back as the two made their way through the bowels of the arena. 'Still,' he frowned, 'a longer spectacle would've pleased me.'

*A longer spectacle would've killed me*, he thought. But that wasn't what Sabinus wanted to hear, he knew. 'Manticores are a nightmare for any man, even me.'

Sabinus chuckled. 'Yet here you stand, alive to tell me what a poor businessman I am. I hear the people talk. They say you are Mars himself! I'm inclined to agree with them.' He stopped and pointed a finger to his own smiling face. 'But remember, god or no, your life is mine.'

*How could I forget?* 'I live to please you, dominus,' he said with a stony gaze.

'That's all I ask,' said Sabinus, his voice an echo in the dark.

‡

The barracks smelled of shit and blood, the natural perfume of any gladiator school. Helios sat on a rough hay bed beside the medicus, a leathered-skinned Greek named Tryphon, and gritted his teeth as the man applied an oregano salve to his arm.

Pericles entered from the training yard, grave-faced, bruised and trickling with sweat. He frowned at the sight of Helios's deep cuts. 'How's he doing?'

'Remarkably well,' said Tryphon, 'for a man who just fought off a manticore.' He layered cloth over the green paste and smoothed it down.

Pericles sighed with relief. 'So you weren't stung.'

'If I were,' said Helios, 'they'd be wheeling my corpse to the cemetery.'

Tryphon rose to his feet. 'I'll be back in the morning to apply more vinegar to the cuts.'

'I look forward to it.'

The medicus shuffled to the doorway, and then turned and snapped his fingers at Helios.

'Oh,' he said, 'the dominus wanted to see you as soon as your wounds were tended.'

'He'll just be a moment,' Pericles answered for him. 'I have my own tending to give him.'

Tryphon grunted and waved dismissively as he exited.

'Those bruises look painful,' said Helios. 'More lessons from the magister?'

Pericles sat down on the bed opposite him. 'I'll have worse in the arena.'

'You haven't spoken the oath yet; you can still leave.'

'And go where?' He leaned forward and took Helios's hand. 'Everything's here.'

They met lips; heat filled Helios and soothed his inflamed wounds. Some muscles relaxed, others tensed. Pericles pulled back. 'We shouldn't,' he said. 'Your wounds…'

Helios touched his cheek reassuringly. 'There are worse ways to feel pain.'

Afterward, the two lay tangled together in the bed covers, beaded with sweat. They stared up at the ceiling and Helios let the quiet build around them. If he were with anyone else, the silence would suffocate him; he needed the noise, or thoughts would flood his mind to fill the void.

'My day will come,' said Pericles, his voice barely above a whisper. 'Once I'm a gladiator, I'll be a champion.' He looked to Helios then, brown eyes mottled with gold and burning with determination. 'Perhaps even your rival.'

'Perhaps,' he allowed, 'in time.' *When you're ready. If one could be ready.*

Helios had known his fate the first day he'd entered the arena. *If I do not die today*, he had thought, *I'll die tomorrow.* The roar of the crowd had frightened him; men, women, and children looked down at him with hungry eyes. They were his judges, he realised. It was they who he fought for—they who were his masters—not Sabinus.

*Fight for them, and die a gladiator.*

Only he never died; time and time again he was victorious. His love for the crowd had grown, and glory came to matter more than anything else. In time, he'd forgotten the name his mother gave him. *Helios* was all he knew.

Pericles snored softly beside him. He thought back to the manticore, its tail dripping venom that could fell a hundred men. How long could he have held against it? For the first time in ages, he feared the answer. *This man makes me weak.*

Crickets chirped outside. He had kept Sabinus waiting too long. He climbed out of the bed and dressed, careful not to wake Pericles. He stirred, rolled to one side and murmured something in his sleep. Helios watched him and for half a heartbeat considered staying. But he knew he couldn't. His hands balled into fists and, before he could change his mind, he walked out the door, cursing.

Under the cloak of night, Helios made his way up to Sabinus's villa. It rested on a hillside, overlooking the ludus. Helios followed the dirt path from the gladiator school to the house's pillared entrance, eyeing the guards at the doors.

'I'm here to—'

'We know why you're here, dog,' spat one of the guards. He knocked on the door and waited.

Iron hinges groaned as the doors swung open. Helios was welcomed by a hundred candles surrounding the tiled pool, casting a thousand dancing shadows on the marble walls. Clouds of steam rose off the water. Sabinus was resting against the back wall of the pool, bare-chested and red as a pomegranate. A girl with a swollen cheek attended him, holding a plate of berries, nuts and chicken.

*He's drunk*, he realised. Behind him, the doors slammed shut.

'Dominus.' He bowed stiffly.

'Helios!' Sabinus gestured with his hand. 'Come. Join me.'

He tensed. 'I haven't washed since my fight,' he protested. 'I'd soil the water.'

'Who doesn't love some filth?' Sabinus grinned.

Trained to obey, Helios dropped his loincloth on the mosaic floor and stepped into the hot pool. The dirt and blood of the arena melted off his aching body. For a moment, he almost forgot to keep his wounded arm above water.

'Wine?' said Sabinus.

'Best not,' said Helios, too curtly. 'The magister would have me whipped if he smelled drink on me.' *And I don't know what else you've laced it with.*

'You make me more money than the magister.' Sabinus snapped his fingers and two slaves hurried away. 'He should be lucky I don't whip *him*.'

A slave boy rushed to Helios with a cup of wine. He sniffed it and took a reluctant gulp, almost choking on the bitterness.

'How's the taste?' said Sabinus, taking a sip from his cup.

He wanted to spit it in the pool. 'I'm not much of a wine drinker.'

'Perhaps some food.' Sabinus gestured with his finger to the girl behind him and she knelt down with the plate. He plucked two grapes from the pile, threw them in his mouth and crunched.

'Apologies,' said Helios, 'but I should return to the barracks before I'm missed.'

Sabinus gulped. 'I won't keep you.' Helios rose to leave the pool. 'However, I'd like to show you something before you go.' *Fool. Like he'd let you leave that easily.*

The master clapped his hands.

Squeaks and rumbles echoed in the corridor that led to the garden. At the back of the atrium, two broad-shouldered slaves wheeled in a statue atop a block of polished marble. Its stony eyes stared into the abyss, its face familiar to Helios, like his own reflection in the water.

'I give you the Colossus of Ephesus.'

Helios stared at his immortality etched in marble, and wanted to ask how Sabinus would make him pay for it. 'I'm honoured, dominus,' he said instead.

Sabinus glided towards him. 'You've brought Fortuna to my house, Helios. Wealth, prosperity and influence are all mine because of you.' He touched Helios's face with a clammy hand, soft fingers against rough skin. 'You've given me everything… well, almost. A master should have *all* his slave has to offer.'

His hand lowered, passing over neck and chest and lower still, until it disappeared beneath the water's surface.

Helios closed his eyes, remembering the heat of the sun and the feel of arena sand under his feet. His heart beating in his ears as the crowd shouted, his sword wet with manticore blood as he held it to the sky for the gods to see. He remembered the warmth of Pericles, his brown eyes speckled with gold, bright as the sun.

*Everything's here*, he heard Pericles say.

Someone snatched Sabinus's hand and lifted it out of the water. When Helios looked down, he saw his own hand grasping his master's.

Sabinus gritted his teeth in anger. 'Let me go.'

Helios released him and turned his back, startled by himself. He climbed out of the pool, steam rising from his body. He'd only had a mouthful of wine, yet he felt half drunk.

'Where are you going?' snapped Sabinus.

*To him.* He picked up his loincloth and headed to the doors, glaring at the two slaves to move aside. They did.

'Jupiter help you if you step out of that door!'

He pulled the doors open, stopped and looked back to the red-faced Sabinus. 'Jupiter help us all, dominus.'

‡

Helios joined his brothers in the training yard the next morning, his eyes sore and heavy from a sleepless night. Despite how he felt, the green tirones looked worse. They stood bloody and bruised before the stern-faced magister, filthy and brimming with pride, for they were all to be sworn men of the arena. *I don't know what I feel more—pride or pity.* Many of them had marvelled at the arena from the outside, but nothing had prepared them for what awaited within. Half would be dead by year's end; the rest would become seasoned warriors, hardened to stone. None showed more promise than the agile and determined Pericles, his face now bright with joy. How youthful he seemed to Helios now.

Sabinus shoved into the circle of gladiators and senior trainers who surrounded the recruits, clutching a red-hot branding iron. Helios stood back, hoping he'd pay him no mind. The master's eyes studied each greenhorn in turn, his face twisted into something between a grin and a snarl.

'You came here as slaves and criminals, broke men and conquered peoples,' Sabinus cried. 'Today, you are gladiators.' The yard erupted with cheers. 'Today I welcome you to House Sabinus, where fortune and glory rain on those who earn it. Step forward and swear the oath for gods and men to hear.'

Sabinus turned to Pericles first. 'Kneel.'

Pericles dropped to his knees and stared at Sabinus, unflinching, as if to show no fear or weakness. 'I will endure to be burned, to be bound, to be beaten and to be killed by the sword, in honour and in name of my dominus, Sabinus.'

In answer to his vow, Sabinus pressed the iron into Pericles' chest, burning it deep into the flesh. Pericles groaned through the pain, gritting his teeth so hard he threatened to shatter them. In the next moment it was over. The greenhorn stood straight as an arrow, showing his discipline. His flesh sweltered where the iron licked it, the sight compelling Helios to touch the spot where his own scar had burned. *The mark of a slave condemned to his fate.*

By noon, most of the gladiators were paired up to train and the rest had departed for the arena, some never to return.

Helios approached Pericles at the centre of the yard. The man still looked dazed by the fresh mark on his chest. 'What will my gladiator name be?' he asked.

'That depends on what type of fighter you are,' said Helios. He struck the air with a wooden sword, enduring the ache of his healing wounds.

'I want to be a murmillo, like you,' he smirked. 'You'd hate that.'

'Why would I hate that?'

'Because then you'd have competition.'

Helios grappled him with his free hand, tripping him to the ground. Pericles stared up at him with his brown and yellow eyes. *He has courage.* The greenhorn swept Helios's feet from underneath him, knocking him down, and there the two sat, laughing and soiled with dirt. Helios didn't see Sabinus watching until he stood back up and glanced across the yard. The man's gaze was more petrifying than any Medusa legend.

A voice rang out. 'Helios!'

He turned to see Tryphon shuffling towards him and sighed. 'Greetings, medicus.'

Tryphon grunted. 'My arse. You've been avoiding me all day. Come, I need to wash your wounds.'

The medicus's quarters were barely larger than a gladiator's cell. Surgical tools lined the walls, and bowls of different herbs and elixirs scented the air with mint and liquorice—smells that cut pleasantly through the ripe stench of the ludus. Helios took a stool and sat unmoving as Tryphon tended to his arm.

The man peeled away the itchy cloth and dried paste. 'You're healing nicely. Good, you'll be fit enough for the lion.'

Helios frowned. 'What lion?'

The medicus dabbed a fresh cloth in a bowl of vinegar and pressed it to his arm. 'I overheard Sabinus talking with the magister; he's scheduled a lion for your fight tomorrow. What did you do to earn that bit of bad luck?' He was being coy. Every gladiator knew the servants whispered to each other. No doubt Tryphon had known what had happened with Sabinus as soon as sun met sky.

*Let them cluck like hens. What does it matter to me?* 'I reminded him he's just a man, powerless like the rest of us.'

Tryphon looked up with a faint smile. 'Well, like most of us.'

The day moved quickly back in the yard. Vermillion clouds streaked a bruised sky when Pericles finally collapsed, exhausted, in the dirt.

Helios helped him to his feet. 'Mars himself would be proud.'

'I'll see what his temperament is when I set foot in the arena.' Pericles looked to the falling sun. 'Whatever my fate is, I have no regrets.' There was something sad in his tone.

Helios gave a reassuring smile. 'No regrets, only glory.'

*That's all a gladiator has.*

‡

The crowd's cheers reverberated throughout the bowels of the arena.

Helios stood at the tunnel gate, peering through iron bars as gladiator fought gladiator. Slaves huddled around him, securing greave and arm guard straps. He equipped his murmillo helm, its distinguished fish-fin crest polished to a shine. He grasped his heavy shield, emblazoned with a gold sun, and awaited his gladius.

A boy appeared at his side, presenting him a wooden sword.

'I'm to fight a lion with a training weapon?'

The boy nodded.

Helios's jaw tensed, anger creeping through him like fiery snakes. 'Sabinus had better hope I don't live to shove it up his arse.'

Outside, the people screamed no mercy as the triumphant gladiator hacked at the throat of his enemy. He thrust the bloody head in the air for the crowd to savour. Helios snatched the wooden sword from the boy.

Attendants raked the bloody sand as the magistrate announced the next bout. The gate rumbled open and sunlight flooded the tunnel entrance. The people beckoned Helios forward, their deafening applause almost a prayer to his ears as he stepped into the arena. *You are Mars himself*, Sabinus had said. *But remember, god or no, your life is mine.*

He thrust his wooden sword above his head and met the crowd with his own loud cheers, as if he wielded the sharpest steel. *Pluto take your pride, Sabinus. This is* my *arena!*

The magistrate's bellows cut through the crowd's cheers. 'But who will challenge the undefeated champion of Ephesus? Citizens of Rome, I give you Leo!'

Across the sand, a second gate opened. From the darkness emerged Pericles, wielding a spear and bearing matching armour with a small, round shield.

*No. This isn't right.*

His helm was like nothing Helios had ever seen, the visor twisted out into a snarling mouth of fangs. On his chest was the mark of Sabinus, still raw and blistered.

High in the crowd, he saw Sabinus grin.

The magistrate signalled for the battle to begin.

For the first time since his youth, Helios was scared. His arms trembled and the wooden sword felt heavy as lead. *I knew this day would come—but not today, not like this.*

Pericles had not moved. His hand gripped his spear so tight, his knuckles had whitened like pearls. For eternity they stood there, frozen, eyes locked.

The crowd sensed their fear. He heard men curse and call him craven. One woman questioned his manhood.

'*Fight!*' he heard the magistrate shout. Suddenly the people's love turned to venom, their groans of displeasure rumbling through the stands like a swarm of angry wasps.

'Come,' pleaded Pericles, his voice hollow in his monstrous helm. 'The crowd needs its champion.' *He needs me to attack first*, Helios realised. *My strength gives him courage.* The thought made him smile, despite everything.

The sword was heavy, so he dropped it. 'No regrets,' he said to himself.

He charged. Pericles found his courage in time to sweep

out of the way and lunge with his spear. Helios spun, blocking with his shield.

The two circled each other. Helios's breaths drowned out the crowd; the people dissolved around him, no more than spectres with mouths opening and closing to the pulse of his heart. The arena was the whole world, and only he and Pericles inhabited it. In this phantom realm, he was a spectator. His arms and feet moved on battle instinct, his thoughts nothing but wisps without weight or form. In the lion helm, he saw the snarling grin of Sabinus, taunting him with an unspoken threat. Hate boiled in his stomach, leaked to every muscle, drove every move. *If I don't hate, I will falter.* He pressed toward the lion's face with his shield.

Pericles—*no, Leo*—struck past his defence, spear grazing Helios's chest as he caught the weapon's shaft in his free hand. The lion pulled the spear back hard, its iron head lacerating flesh as it tore free. Helios cursed and rushed forward, twisting behind his shield as Leo lunged. The spear deflected off the wood, and shield bashed into gladiator.

Leo groaned.

Helios lunged again, knocking the spear from his opponent's hands. The third hit sent him to the ground. Dazed, Leo rolled over to recover the spear. Helios snatched it first and stopped the tip an inch from his opponent's throat. The anger left him then, gone like smoke after a fire.

A cacophony of noise rose around them, but Helios hardly heard it. 'Do you yield?' His voice was hoarse.

'Only to you.' Pericles sat up and tugged his helm free, revealing brown eyes speckled with gold and a radiant smile that softened his heart. His dark hair stuck to his forehead in clumps, his face wet with sweat.

Helios smiled. He dropped the spear and helped Pericles to his feet, raising his shaking, sweaty hand in presentation to the people of Ephesus. Among the joyous masses, he saw Sabinus redden and clench his teeth in smouldering hatred. *Go on, rage.*

*I'll defy you again and again, you bastard.*

When Pericles's hand suddenly slipped away, Helios was too slow to stop his fall. He crashed against the sand, vomit splattering from his mouth as his limbs squirmed. Only then did Helios see the manitcore barb stuck in the back of his left leg, blood and venom congealed at the wound and caked with sand.

'No!' he shouted, dropping his shield and falling beside him. *This is my fault.* 'You can't die. Not in my arena, I *forbid* it.' No matter how hard he blinked, tears returned to burn his eyes. 'I'm the Colossus of Ephesus, champion of the arena, and you will live!'

He pulled the sting free, but the venom had already spread. The muscles in Pericles' neck hardened, and after a few short breaths he stopped still. His soul escaped with a sigh, the sunlight gone from his eyes.

With a dead heart, Helios looked to the sky and watched the sun fade behind clouds, shadows creeping over the arena. Never had the sand beneath him felt so cold. Never had he felt such darkness in glory.

Around him the crowd rose, chanting, '*Invictus, invictus, invtictus!*'

Helios looked to Sabinus and saw the dominus raise his arms in celebration with the crowd. Helios cried out with an anger so great his body shook.

The people fell silent. He shot to his feet and retrieved Pericles's spear with his off hand, keeping the manticore sting clutched tight. *If I don't hate, I will falter.* With all his strength and rage, he threw the weapon into the crowd. People scattered in panic. Sabinus ducked, and the spear clattered against the stone seat behind him. Guards stormed the arena, armed and armoured.

'Take him alive,' ordered Sabinus.

Through Helios's blurred vision, the faces in the crowd twisted into snarling lions, their eyes wide and shiny, mouths dripping with blood. They shrieked like the manticore, hungry for death.

*Everything's here*, said a voice in his ear. But it wasn't, he realised. Not anymore.

Helios raised the manticore sting to his neck and felt its stab like a hot knife.

'Stop him,' Sabinus shouted to the guards, 'If he dies, I'm ruined!'

Helios could only laugh as the sound of his slowing, pounding heartbeat drowned out his master's panicked cries.

He collapsed, his vision fading to black as he gazed over to Pericles one last time. The strength in his arms and legs evaporated, the venom seeping into his blood and burning him away. In the heat, he felt a hand touch his face, and as a light breeze blew over him, a shape embraced him. A sweet voice whispered in his ear and lifted him, up and up into the warmth of the sun.

The whispered words echoed in the wind.

'No regrets.'

# The Metal Mermaid

## Kelly Matsuura

Ontario, 2064

'Squad Seven, forward!' Sergeant Kent pointed left, then right, indicating the team to fan out either side of him across the road. 'Nothing and no one gets past us, got it?'

'Yes, Sarge!' the squad responded.

Reiko took her place on Kent's left and aimed her gun at the bus speeding along the old freeway towards them. A second bus and a tanker truck followed, but she didn't let them distract her—there were three other squads out there ready to stop them.

The loyalists' first bus skidded to a rocky halt, narrowly avoiding tipping onto its side.

'Fire!' bellowed the Sergeant.

The air exploded with sizzling flashes of orange, blurred with the occasional blast of blue from Squad Four's mounted zanka gun. Streams of yellow and green fired back from every window of the smoking bus.

Reiko kept low, her shield firm in front of her.

'Toby! Shield up!' she called to a teen on her right. He was a good soldier, but Reiko knew he was still getting used to his robotic arm. Poor kid—he was only a year younger than her, but he had almost as many metal implants as she did. Toby glanced her way and smiled, then inched forward and released a new torrent of fire at the now-burning bus.

Reiko caught sight of a Unity fighter jumping out of the back window, and swung to the side to take him out. She wished the bus was loaded with Bone Heads, not humans—but that was just the war these days. The aliens recruited men and women to do the grunt work while they stayed safe in their airships.

The laser fire gradually slowed and stopped as her team members realised there was no one firing back. Reiko looked to the second bus, where the two rear squads had taken out the driver and were checking inside for survivors and any salvage-able goods. Most importantly, the fuel truck had been secured.

'Incoming! Get down!' someone called. Reiko looked to the sky and swore. The loyalists did have an alien escort, after all.

'Take cover!' She grabbed Toby by his good arm and pulled him towards an abandoned car—one of dozens left littering the roadside since Landing Day.

They waited for enemy fire that never came. The octagonal spacecraft zipped overhead and carried straight on.

'Looks like it's headed to Toronto,' said Reiko, relieved. 'Probably just a transport ship that saw the bus burning.'

'The Bone Heads are gonna figure out pretty damn quick what happened—and that we got their fuel truck too,' bit out Toby. 'There's gonna be a fighter ship here in no time.'

'The boys are on it.' Reiko pointed to the truck, where Squad Five was now inspecting the cabin.

Reiko yanked Toby to his feet and looked with trepidation towards the crumbling, dying city in the distance. Hovering over the skyscrapers were the enormous steel stations of the Bone Heads, thousands of workers and soldiers on board. Reiko often wondered if the tales were true: if every city on Earth looked just the same.

'Do you think there are any civilians still there?' Toby asked.

'No,' said Reiko. She looked Toby over. 'My parents volunteered with the evacuation teams that went looking for survivors. None of them came back. But not all of them died over there.'

Toby's eyes widened. 'You think your parents are Unity fighters now?'

Reiko pinched her lips together before answering. 'No, Toby. I don't.' She knew her parents would have died before pledging loyalty to their invaders. For three years, she had fought in their honour, vowing to protect whatever free cities remained.

'I'm sorry, Reiko. I didn't know.'

'It's all right. My sister's safe in Port Huron, at least.' Reiko forced a smile. She had long prayed that the war would magically be over by the time Jessa turned fifteen. Serving at the enlistment age wasn't mandatory, but she knew Jessa. She was every bit as stubborn as Reiko was.

'Soldiers, back to transport,' a sharp voice cut in from the other side of the smouldering bus. 'Oh, hi Reiko!' Makeisha's perfect, angelic face came into view. 'You guys okay?'

'We're fine,' Reiko replied tersely. 'Come on, Toby. Kent is signalling us.'

'Huh? He—'

Reiko kicked him in the shin. She had no intention of conversing with her ex-girlfriend today, ranking officer or not.

‡

Reiko was last to meet her squad at the old tractor shed the following morning. The base, set up only a few months ago, had once been a dairy farm: although there was little fresh food growing on the land, the farm buildings were all in good condition, and there were enough working solar panels to power the small military hospital, charge their weapons and run tech equipment for ground operations. And having lights and heating made life a little more comfortable for the soldiers. Reiko wasn't the only one who struggled to get out of bed sometimes.

'Sorry I kept you up so late, sweetheart,' Dylan ribbed, joining her at the rainwater tank as she filled her canteen. He was good looking, she mused, if you like muscled, tattooed, douchebags. Reiko did not.

'Yeah, well, *someone* has to teach you how to pass as a human being,' she shot back, and her squad guys snorted with scattered laughter. It looked like Dylan's team had left him behind—but that wasn't her problem. She grabbed a daypack, checked her gun and dropped a spare solar-charger in her vest pocket.

'Hey. Your squad's on recon today, right?' Dylan asked.

'Yep. We're hiking to the old showgrounds to check out the buildings there.' She rolled her eyes—he knew as well as she did that there'd be nothing to find there but ruins and worn-out loyalists left to die. It was some council member's show of power, nothing more. She lifted her foot on to a tree stump and tightened her bootlaces, glancing out over the green fields and wishing there were cows to graze there. What she'd give to eat a fat steak again. 'Where are you supposed to be?'

'Huh?' Dylan tugged the side straps of her protective vest and slapped her shoulder. 'There you go.'

Like she didn't know how to wear her vest right. Douchebag! 'Where's your squad?' she tried again, but he wasn't listening. He peered over her shoulder at the screen on her wristwatch. Reiko yanked her arm out of sight.

'How many credits have you earned this month?' he asked with a smile.

'None of your damn business.'

'Whoa, I was just curious.' His hands went up in defence, but the grin stayed put. 'So, you wouldn't be interested in earning triple credits today then, I guess.' He turned back towards the barracks and shrugged, hitching his canteen to his pack.

Reiko knew this game. Here he was, playing it cool, but he'd probably been sent to reassign her. Pathetic.

'Triple credits, was that?' she asked in her most feminine voice. 'What's the gig?'

'Ah, well. It's not the usual thing.'

Was he nervous? Now she *really* wanted the job. 'Spit it.' She crossed her arms.

'Okay. It's not Kent asking, it's Mack.'

'Your sis—Hell no! She has a nerve asking me for anything after humiliating me like that.' Makeisha was the last person Reiko would stick her neck out for.

'This is war, Rei. Do you think she wants to beg anyone? You're the only one who can cross the river.'

Reiko huffed. The Tungi River was over two hundred metres wide and partially frozen all year round—and the Bone Heads had dropped a few of their venomous fish species in there, too.

'Come on, you know that until we can get the cybernetics facility going again, you're the only soldier equipped for the swim. I'd go if I could, but my only robotic part is my left foot.' Dylan glanced down at his boots.

'Don't look so sour about it. My lungs are a prototype, remember? The robotics guys don't know how they'll hold up long term. And I'm sure you think having half your body replaced with metal is cool, but my dead nerves are all human.'

'I get it,' Dylan promised. 'Look, are you in? A Unity plane dropped a supply load across the river yesterday and no one's picked it up. Reckon the loyalist buses were a distraction. If we wait any longer, we could miss our chance.'

Reiko cursed. They no longer had any boats, and the nearest bridge was blown up months ago. There was no other way.

'Reiko, we're heading out,' Pyke interrupted. 'You ready?' The rest of her squad stood together, packs on and waiting for her answer.

With a sigh, she waved them off. 'Nope. Got another assignment.' She turned back to Dylan and dropped her heavy pack on the ground. 'Okay, what's the plan?'

Dylan dragged his boot through a patch of dirt and squatted down to draw a map.

'The package is small, so it's likely medical supplies or guns.'

'Where do I go in?'

'At the shallow rocks, here.' He jabbed at the ground. 'The current isn't strong this month, so if you swim pretty straight, you'll find it right on the bank. We'll get you two floatable barrels to fill with as much as you can manage, then you swim right back. It'll be your call whether you go back for a second run or not.'

Reiko nodded. 'Okay. I'll see what they have and decide.'

'Good. I'll be your spotter. I know you won't have your radio with you, but if I see any Bone Heads or rebels over there while you're in the water, I'll turn on the soundwave transmitter.'

'Can I have Avaline spotting too?'

Dylan smirked. 'You're doing her now, are you?'

'Maybe.' She wasn't, but perhaps if Avaline saw her crossing the entire river underwater, she'd be impressed and finally put out. That girl liked to tease. 'She has the only functioning zanka gun,' Reiko added.

'I heard she likes dick,' Dylan whispered.

Reiko slapped his arm. 'No way. Makeisha sure does though. Tonny, Elias, Beck... I caught her doing Patrick, remember?' That was a tough image to erase from her mind. 'Urgh.'

Dylan groaned. 'Never tell me crap like that about my sister again, and I'll put in a good word for you with Avaline.'

Reiko stuck out her hand. 'Deal.'

He shook it, smirking. 'Let's go. You need a scuba suit, and I need to find our hot blonde gunner.' He turned towards the supply house.

'Oh Dylan, one more thing.' She put her sweetest voice on again.

'Yeah, mate?'

'Tell Makeisha she's paying me two hundred credits right off, *and* triple credits for any kills,'

Dylan laughed. 'You got me, damn! Okay, one hundred for swimming across. One hundred for swimming back with the bounty. And triple credits for kills—done. Let's hope you don't get much chance to earn them.'

'*And* I get the two hundred even if the package is worthless.' Reiko stood firm, one hand on her hip.

'That, my friend, is a solid deal.' He punched the details into his wristwatch and winked. 'You'll have the first hundred before you dive in.'

'Thanks.' For once, the douchebag had helped her out.

Reiko went back to the supply house for a wetsuit and boots. She was fine with the cold water, but if any of the fish attacked, she wanted more than her knife at hand to keep them off her skin.

Her comm beeped just as she was closing her locker. She took it out again and read the screen: Makeisha had deposited the hundred credits, as promised. Reiko tapped a button to check her total credits. Fourteen thousand, four hundred and ninety-eight.

She grinned; she was so close to what she needed to become a squad leader. She would get her own little house too. She could invite Avaline over, break out the massage oil, and… Reiko grinned, shaking herself back to the task at hand.

‡

As they approached the departure point, Reiko was pleased to see Avaline already there, setting up the zanka.

'Hey, hot stuff,' chirped Dylan.

'Dylan,' Avaline said dryly. 'Just so we're clear, if anything bad happens to Rei, I'm frying your balls for breakfast tomorrow.'

Reiko chuckled. So Avaline wasn't a fan either—that made

Reiko like her even more. 'Great to see you, Avaline.'

'You too.' Avaline beamed, flipping a chestnut-brown ponytail over her shoulder as she turned to Reiko. 'And don't worry, I've got your back today.'

'Thanks. I'm ready when you two are.' She pulled on her diving hood and smoothed it down. Avaline ran her hands once over Reiko's suit, adjusting the fit and checking for holes.

'Careful, you'll turn her on,' Dylan teased, looking up from his tablet.

'Shut up, Dylan.' Avaline scolded, a soft blush marking her cheeks.

'Yeah, we're working here,' added Reiko, hiding a smile. 'Okay, let's do this.' She pulled her gloves on and waded into the rocky shallows.

Dylan held up the soundwave transmitter. 'Remember. You hear this, you turn around, no matter how far across you are. Clear?'

'Clear!'

'Good luck!' Avaline waved.

Reiko reached for the rope that connected the two plastic bins she would have to swim with. Dylan must have added some weight already because they half-sunk below the water's surface, making them easier to tow and harder to see from the sky. 'Thanks, Dylan,' she called over her shoulder.

'No worries. Godspeed, soldier.' Dylan gave an odd little salute. Was he actually worried about her?

'Bombs away!' Reiko called back, and dived under the surface.

The swim was almost pleasant—the water was less murky than she remembered, and she managed to swim a fair distance before spotting any of the alien fish. Her cybernetic lungs fed her body smoothly through the water; her legs were her own, but she revelled in the boost given by her mechanical knees.

She popped up only once, to confirm she was swimming straight and check the distance to the bank. As the water became shallower, she spotted a huge red dragonfish—that's what she called it, at least. It was the only fish she thought pretty. It was venomous, though, she was sure: the spikes on its back were enough of a warning. She swerved left to avoid the sharp thorns it puffed out in attack, then blew out a stream of bubbles in relief, grateful for the agility her various body modifications provided.

Reiko crouched low as she stepped onto the bank, trailing her eyes over the clearing and tree line. Clear. She tugged the scuba hood off her head and smoothed down her wet hair, then threw a wave back in the direction of Dylan and Avaline, where she knew they'd be watching her through scopes, fingers on their triggers.

She pulled the containers onto the bank and skipped over to the dropped cargo, which was wrapped in a shiny grey tarp and stamped with Unity's logo: a solid, black alien eye, encircled by five human eyes of varying colours.

'Let's see what we've got.' Reiko withdrew a short blade from her diving belt and started cutting the ropes securing the cargo. Once the ropes were free, she ripped through the tarp, revealing the weapons stash inside. 'Oh, yeah!' She grinned.

This was pay dirt—the laser guns were alien-made but sized for human hands. The army had been gathering similar guns from the battlefield, but without a compatible system to recharge the unique battery, they were useless.

Reiko dug deeper into the load and finally found what she had been praying for: three bulky charge stations, fitted to hold six batteries each. All the engineers back at camp would need to do is hook up the chargers to the solar generator.

'Seriously, what idiot sends the weapons and chargers together?' she murmured.

She removed the chargers from the crate with some difficulty. They were bulky things; she would only be able to take one back in each floating container—assuming she could even fit them through the opening. She could probably squeeze a few hand guns in as well.

Was it worth a return trip for the last charger? The extra guns would be useful, but there would always be more to recover from the loyalists and Bone Heads on the battlefield, and they had at least fifty back at camp already. But then, the more guns they accumulated, the more they needed the third charger.

She toed the soft ground with her diving boot. She could bury the charger and a few more guns. Then, if the rebels got to the site before she returned, they wouldn't have the chargers, which they surely needed as much as Reiko's camp did. She chose her spot and started digging, using one of the long-nosed alien guns as a shovel.

Her ears pricked up at a rustling in the trees to her right, and Reiko froze. There was a second rustling, softer than the first, but definitely something there. There were hardly any animals on this side of the river.

'Damn!' she cursed softly. She snatched up one of the other guns and hoped it was charged. That would just be her luck, to be sitting on a pile of weapons that had never been powered up. She flicked the switch and breathed a sigh of relief when two bars lit up on its barrel.

She tucked the gun into her belt and grabbed two chargers. She had to at least try to get back into the water with them before anyone caught her.

Too late. Three men emerged from the forest—a dozen more behind them.

Reiko dropped the chargers, grabbed the gun and pointed it straight at the closest man. She blinked, not believing her eyes. He had the signature exposed skull-cap of the Bone Heads—a smooth dome of porcelain that began just above the alien's sunken eye sockets and ended high on the back of his hairless head. He was also a good foot taller than the men behind him. But he was dressed in civilian clothes.

The Bone Head raised his weapon at Reiko, and she pulled the trigger on hers. A burst of orange light shot out, and her arm jerked from the kickback. She flinched as a streak of yellow came flying towards her chest. She hadn't even see him pull his trigger.

She hit the ground, her chest burning so hot she felt like she would explode. The sky bloomed with colour above her and she struggled to get up, to keep fighting.

Blue laser rays flew past her eyes, just a metre away. Avaline!

'Get up,' she told herself, her voice sticking in her throat. 'Get up, Rei.' But she couldn't move. Her sight blurred, and she gave in to darkness.

‡

Reiko woke up in the dim nighttime glow of the infirmary. She felt around for the controls and raised the head of the bed so she could sit up.

She was hooked up to a monitor by an array of tubes—no surprise there—but putting a hand to her chest, she felt only a thin gauze patch over her wound. Okay, so what absurd, cutting-edge surgery had they done on her this time?

She pressed the buzzer and checked her wristwatch while she waited for someone to respond. Her credits balance hadn't changed. Her heartbeat thudded in her still-sore throat. What did that mean? And what had happened to the rebels? She had a million questions; she was tempted to call Sergeant Kent right away.

'Reiko,' came a familiar voice. 'My favourite patient.'

'That's just because I'm your most regular patient,' she quipped. 'Just give it to me straight, Doc. What did you do to me?'

Dr Goderich sat on the edge of the bed. 'Sure. As you know, the new lab is still being built, but we've been able to resume some projects right here in the hospital. Your lungs were hit when you were shot, so we repaired that, but your chest was still a mad mess of burns. I took the liberty of making you my first live test subject for regenerated tissue development.'

'You... you regrew me?' She gingerly touched the gauze again.

Goderich chuckled. 'Yes. I injected the damaged area of your chest with a serum that kills off damaged cells and replicates healthy ones. You'll have a faint scar where the new tissue meets the old, but you should find the contour of the muscle is smooth.'

'Wow. So, no new metal parts?'

'Not necessary. *This* time, at least. And I have more good news for you.'

'Oh?' Reiko said faintly, still fingering the bandage.

'Your friend's had a rough twenty-four hours, but he's doing well today. Dr Gravenhurst gave him a set of metal lungs, identical to yours. It's been exciting to see your success with the procedure, and to finally have the ability to build the system again.'

'Wait, what?' She leaned forward and grabbed the doctor's arm. 'Who are you talking about?'

'Your partner, Dylan Keswick. He brought you back across the river.'

'He did?' Reiko couldn't believe it. They had all known full well that she was expendable. Dylan must have broken protocol. 'That idiot! He can barely swim, and the water...'

'Right,' Dr Goderich nodded. 'Even after replacing his lungs, there was no guarantee the rest of his body would recover from the hypothermia—but he proved to be every bit as tough as you, dear.'

'Can I see him?' Reiko had to know everything that had happened. Why had he risked his own life?

'I'm afraid the nurse gave him a sedative to sleep through the night. He's going to be staying with us for a few weeks, but you can see him tomorrow before you check out.'

'I can go?'

'You'll be on medical leave until I clear you for duty, perhaps two weeks. But yes, you can go back to your barracks and take care of yourself. We're pretty tired of seeing your face around here, anyway.'

'Doc!' She punched his arm lightly. 'Thanks for patching me up again.'

'Any time.'

‡

Reiko meant to thank Dylan when she stepped into his room. She really did.

'You stupid idiot!' she blurted out instead. 'What were you thinking?' Tears stung the corners of her eyes.

'Hello, Rei. I'm glad to see you're alive too.' Dylan smiled, and grimaced as he tried to sit up.

'Here.' Reiko picked up the bed controls and raised the head for him. 'Water?'

'No, I'm fine.' Dylan looked her up and down. 'You doin' okay?'

Reiko sighed. 'Yeah, thanks to you and Avaline. I don't know what happened after I passed out, but I guess she shot down all the rebels and you swam across?'

Dylan frowned. 'That's not what happened. No one's filled you in?'

'No. The doc's discharging me this morning, and I have to report to Sergeant Kent later. I know Avaline tried to see both of us last night, but they wouldn't let her in.'

'Wow, okay. So, did you notice that the guy you shot was a Bone Head?'

'Yeah—but he was dressed in human clothes. I remember that. I think… the others were all human, but I didn't get a good look. He died though, right?' Reiko asked, worried.

'You blew his face off. He's dead, all right. But I saw the group moving through the woods on my satellite screen—I was already in the river before you could have seen them. I tried the soundwave transmitter, but you were swimming so fast! I didn't know what else to do—I just dove in. I expected to get out of the water and face instant attack, but they were all dead.'

'Avaline shot them all?'

'No. She shot a few, but they all dropped the second their leader did. It looks like the rebel teams are now being led telepathically by Bone Heads.'

'What, like they're linked up?' Reiko felt her eyebrows shoot up in surprise. 'Like… a hive mind?'

'Exactly. I mean, we always suspected the Bone Heads are telepathic, but now we have proof. They're using it to control Unity fighters. With one shot, you took out *forty-three* rebels, Rei.'

'Are you kidding?' And here, she thought she had completely screwed up the mission. 'What about you? Will you be punished for breaking protocol?'

Dylan grinned. 'Technically, I didn't. Makeisha ordered me to bring you back safe. I doubt she really expected me to swim across the Tungi, though.'

'Bring me back safe, eh? Well, that *is* the biggest surprise of the day,' said Reiko, only half joking. 'But thanks, Dylan. I owe you one.' She held her hand out.

He took it and pulled it to his lips. 'Actually, I do have a favour to ask you.'

'Do I dare ask?'

'So, when I get back to duty… can you teach me to swim underwater? I have lungs like you now, so I have a feeling we'll be working together a lot more.'

Reiko laughed. 'Right, of course. But, seriously, the water temperature is still a huge issue. I know you made it across and back—dragging me, too—but it's a miracle you survived.'

'Well, I may have a solution for that. Since I'll be laid up for a while, I've got time to develop it a bit more, and Makeisha thinks she can get me some tech support.'

'For what?'

'A temp-controlled diving suit. I've seen you do that swim a few times, and I've been playing around with the idea for a while. You know, the fabric the Bone Heads wear regulates their body temperature, so it might be suitable for freezing temperatures as well. If not, we can try to develop our own.'

'Awesome. We need every advantage we can get in this war.'

Reiko began to take her leave, then stopped. 'My balance didn't update,' she told Dylan, and left the sentence hanging in the air: he deserved a chance to explain. But he only frowned.

'That's weird.' He paused, and his expression tightened. 'Well, you know what? We'll find another camp, another hive-mind leader. Take out a dozen loyalists with one shot at a Bone Head. Even without triple credits, you'll get your promotion in no time.'

Reiko gave a short, uneasy nod. She promised to visit every day while she was off duty on medical leave. She knew how boring it could get, lying in a hospital bed for weeks on end—and anyway, she would need to help him with his project.

She picked up her bag and said goodbye to the nurses, wincing at the pain in her chest as she spoke. At least she could walk, she thought grudgingly, and wouldn't have to spend her recovery time confined to her barracks.

Dylan's words replayed in her mind as she passed through the dim halls. The idea of killing hundreds, if not thousands of humans just to take out the Bone Heads didn't sit right with her. How many of the aliens were even linked in to this hive mind? And if the loyalists were being *controlled* by the aliens, they were victims, weren't they? Sure, she thought, it was an easy way to score credits—and other soldiers would probably jump at the opportunity to wipe out more loyalists—but that wasn't going to be her path, she decided.

She'd get back out on the battlefield and lay waste to the Bone Heads with their own damn guns. She'd go back across the Tungi for the chargers too, and as many guns as she could transport back. And the hive-mind leaders… that was a question for another day.

Nearing the hospital exit, her heart flip-flopped at the sight of Makeisha and Avaline, side by side, waiting by the guarded iron doors. It was odd seeing them together, but she knew she owed them both a thank you.

'Reiko!' Avaline skipped forward, her face lighting up. 'I want to hug you, but that'll hurt, right?'

'I don't care—I'm so happy to see you.' Reiko accepted a kiss on the cheek, then pulled back with a frown. 'What… what are you wearing?'

Avaline's smiled faded as she tugged on her jacket. Her new sergeant's uniform. 'Well, I earned enough to get promoted. I got my own little cabin too, it's so cute. I want you to come over for dinner tonight—if you feel up to it?' She took Reiko's hand and squeezed.

Reiko pulled away, feeling her expression sour. 'Dylan said you only shot a couple of rebels, and that they would have died anyway when *I* killed the leader. And you got, what, fifty credits to be on guard?' If Avaline had really been that close to her fifteen thousand, why hadn't she said anything?

'Sorry, Rei, but… you didn't kill the leader. I did. Kent gave me three hundred for taking out the rebel team.'

Reiko balked and turned on Makeisha. 'Did you do this?' she demanded. 'It's not enough to break my heart, you have to make a fool of me and cheat me out of credits too?'

Makeisha stepped forward, her expression calm. 'There was a vote. We reviewed the satellite footage of the fight and the majority of the council agreed that Avaline's shot killed the leader, not yours. I'm sorry for this whole ordeal, Reiko. I don't like seeing you hurt.' She reached out, but Reiko took a step back.

'Just get away from me. Both of you,' she snapped. 'I shot that Bone Head in the face with an alien gun. Get forensics to check the body, that'll prove it.'

'They can't—' Avaline began.

'Sergeant London, why don't you go in and say hello to

my brother?' interrupted Makeisha. 'I'll walk Reiko back to the barracks.'

'Fine. I'm sorry, Reiko.'

'You're disgraceful,' Reiko spat at Makeisha, without a glance at Avaline as she made her away down the corridor. 'This is super, *super* petty of you.'

'Reiko, do you really think that because of a few silly rumours you spread about me, I'd go out of my way to convince the council to vote against you? Heck, I voted *for* you. The footage was hardly crystal clear, but I could have sworn you shot the Bone Head first. He fired just a second after you, but the laser from his gun struck yours and curved the shot. That's why your wound wasn't fatal.'

'I hit him in the face, didn't I?'

'Yes. Avaline's fire hit a couple of rebels on his left, but I don't think she hit the leader at all.'

'Then why did she get my credits while I got medical leave?'

'You know how these things go sometimes. The council had to make a call, and it was seven to four in Avaline's favour. Look, I know this doesn't make you feel better, but I reviewed your stats and you're next in line to reach fifteen thousand. I have every confidence that you'll be back in the field and have your own squad in a matter of months.'

'You're right, that doesn't make me feel better,' Reiko grumbled. 'But... Dylan said you ordered him to protect me. So, I guess I should trust you when you say you're on my side.'

Makeisha smiled and brushed an angry tear from Reiko's cheek. 'I owed you.' She hesitated. 'Look, Rei, when we were together—I was just living in the moment. It was careless of me not to consider you may have had deeper feelings. And when it comes to the war, you're one of the best soldiers we have.'

Reiko let her head fall, overwhelmed by both Dylan and Makeisha's support. 'Thank you.'

'Any time. And, can I give you some advice?' Makeisha added. 'Don't blame Avaline for this. She does think she killed the leader—and besides, she played a huge role in your rescue. She had the medics down by the river before Dylan even got back with you. She really deserves her own gunner squad.'

Reiko nodded. 'You're right, she does. I guess I just… felt betrayed. I really like her, you know?' She felt her chest flutter just voicing it.

Makeisha gave a small smile. 'Don't let yourself distrust other women just because I messed up, yeah? Avaline likes you a lot. I think you'd be great together.'

'Really?' Reiko asked, incredulously.

'Really,' she grinned in return. 'I gotta check on Dylan.' She brushed past towards the hospital.

'Mack,' Reiko called, and Makeisha spun back around. 'Hey, can you give Avaline a message?'

'Sure.'

'Tell her I'm sorry. And… that I'd love to have dinner tonight.'

Makeisha grinned. 'Take care, Rei.'

Reiko checked her credit balance once more.

*So close.*

She'd get that promotion—and maybe one day she'd get a seat on the council too. Hell knows she'd do a better job than the idiots running things now. The war was far from over, but they were slowly pushing the Bone Heads off the planet, one shipload at a time. The aliens really only had two options: die on the ground, or go the hell back where they came from.

Switching her comm back to the menu screen, she gazed up to the sky. High among the fluffy clouds and the bright blue she loved, she scowled at the alien ships hovering over the vacant, crumbling city of Toronto. Her metal lungs filled, suddenly, with a lightness like helium, forcing its way up her throat.

'Watch out, Bone Heads,' she shouted to the sky. 'We're coming for you.'

# HOWL

NATALIE CANNON

It begins with falling.

Well, actually it begins with running, running after Rafe, running in the midnight of Regent's Park because laughter spills out easier when you're teetering along the banks of muddy ponds, running under splotches of amber street light between the cold dark, running too slow and losing sight of the tall shadow in the lead, running into shrubbery and under a clump of trees, and then it's feet skidding, mulch springing and falling face first in the mud as something large and furred collides with my back.

My hands reach out to bounce me into a roll, and my eyes glance around to land on the glistening jaws biting into my ankle. Son of a—

I scream for Rafe, the teeth sinking into me, the sharp sting of pierced flesh, and I kick the dog in the face with my other foot. It yelps and lets go and spins away. I forget the dog with its yellow eyes because my leg is kind of on fire, and by "kind of" I mean that I'm lying on the ground with my back arching upwards, death-gripping my ankle with clenched fists and where is Rafe, God, where is he? I need a hospital, something, anything and then finally: Rafe's voice beside my ear, 'Heather, what happened? Heather!' The warmth of his face next to mine, his week-old beard scratching my cheek, his solid hands, his elbows hauling me upwards. I trip a little, then there's the ground (Skate straight, Heather, skate straight).

'Rafe, we need to go A&E,' I breathe, inhaling a mouthful of his jasmine perfume. 'It's probably infected.'

One arm is around Rafe's shoulders as we hobble, the other is fisted into his shirtfront (he went for boyish tonight, but still so many goddamn buttons), and I try to close my eyes against the pain, concentrate on moving forward. My foot feels like it's been burnt to charcoal because, no really, there's fire and it's climbing. I spread my free hand against Rafe's chest as far as it will go and find his heartbeat hammering away. God, I have to say something because Rafe's going mental and, wait, has he been talking this entire time? 'Rafe, shut up and flag a taxi. I need a rabies shot. I'm fine. Well, not fine.' I make my lips stop moving.

Rafe stops, and I open my eyes. The world can't decide if it is to blur or crystallise, and I'm slumping and drowsy. Just let me sleep through this, that'll be better, won't it? I'm lurching towards the cab, the pain radiating upwards, farther, farther in little finger sparks. The shoulder slips from underneath me, and I'm free in the air and falling (I always wanted to skydive but I never have), a soft landing against the cab seat and maybe now everything will be quiet.

But no, Rafe's hitting my face and speaking, loud. Oh God, what if he's bored, what can I think of to entertain him this time? I don't have any more make-up tips to trade—

'Heather! Heather, don't fall asleep!' I'm boneless and floating and nothing is real, not even Rafe, not even the fire.

‡

'Just come home safe.'

My eyes snap open. Was I dreaming? There's a wetness on the corner of my lips from drooling. I swipe it away quickly, before Rafe sees. He probably saw already and doesn't care, but it's a bit embarrassing anyway, drooling on the spotless pillows of the… hospital bed?

'There you are, love.' A nurse smiles over me, lips broad and coral (Mom would like that shade, would smack her lips in pleasure trying it on). I blink back to full awareness, like fighting out of the anesthesia fog that's somehow necessary for uprooting a couple of wisdom teeth. I try to sit up, but the nurse gently pushes me back down. Her nametag is affixed to a shirt covered in cartoon cats, and it declares her name to be Glenn. (Was there a singer named Glenn? Or an actor?) 'Had a scare, did you?'

I nod, numb. What else can I say? I'm supposed to be the doctor, not the patient—at least in Rafe's eyes. Where is he?

'Looks like you're in a bit of shock. Can you speak, dear?'

'Yeah.'

'Oh, you're American too. Where you from, then?'

'California. Los Angeles.' An eighteen-hour plane ride, body willed into stasis, and it only takes eighteen hours to leave everything behind.

'And your birthdate?'

'October 30th, 1987.' My ex-girlfriend Allysa used to say everyone either loved or hated Scorpios; Rafe used to reply that he was a Gemini and in his expert opinion, that was bullcrap.

'Looks like you know yourself, then. Your friend gave us your NHS card, so that's all squared away.' I remember: the stacks of visa and National Health Service paperwork had towered over the desk in my parents' house for months.

I stretch out my fingers, but they're too stiff to work properly. I mentally confirm the diagnosis: shock, dehydration, animal bite.

'Very good,' Glenn says, nodding at my hands. 'Now, I'm

going to let you sit up. Your ankle is all bandaged, but do we have your permission to give you a rabies shot? It's just a precaution. The doctor also prescribed you to drink plenty of fluids before you go.'

'Rabies would be good. Did Rafe—my friend—tell you what happened? This enormous dog just attacked me.'

Glenn shudders in sympathy. 'Frightening story, the whole lot. I don't go near that park, myself, you know, if I can help it. We've got dog bites out of there for years, but nobody's ever caught a thing. I think someone's letting it out, or else it's getting out on its own. Happens sometimes. Irresponsible.'

Glenn's head of wispy orange hair bobs up and down in agreement with herself.

‡

I wake up on the couch, spine popping against the leather as I turn to see my foot swollen and straining against its bandages, propped up on the armrest of the couch in our little London apartment. (The third-story stairs were mountains to lug everything up, mountains.) It's still night—there's a silvery 3am darkness outside our windows but it's almost as clear as noon out there. I hear feet padding to my side and turn my head to see Rafe approaching. His loose patchwork dressing gown fans out, enlarging his thin frame. 'A dressing gown'll connect me to the culture,' he had whined on our first shopping trip, and we'd bought it despite going over budget.

Rafe's eyes scan over me, the short black sticks of his hair in complete disarray, his left hand twitching. The writer (I'd never met a writer before Rafe; I'd spluttered into my Starbucks when I found out, which did nothing to snag me a date at the LGBTQ+ Student Mixer) practically glides forward and sits on the coffee table to face me. A thermometer is produced from somewhere (table? Pocket? He knows where the first aid kit is?) and easily slipped between my lips. I let it slide under my tongue, taking a deep breath through my nose to stop any gagging reflex (a trick I learnt from my mother). Rafe silently reaches for my hands and untangles them—I'd woven them together in sleep, a habit from my childhood, ever since sleeping had meant escaping the yelling and throwing. His long fingers find my pulse point and press down into the flesh. I can see the ticking in his eyes. He must have researched something like this for a story.

I close myself to the sight. Knots in my shoulders undo themselves. Everything feels heavy. I can hear Rafe's gentle and steady breathing beside me. 'I'm fine, Rafe. Go back to sleep,' I murmur around the thermometer.

Rafe takes the thermometer out, raising it against the window to see the tiny lettering on the display. 'No, you're not,' he says and the deep rumble of his voice startles me, as always, ever since we met. It was disconcerting at first to hear such a masculine voice out of lips smeared with Sephora Red Velvet, but that's Rafe. 'You've got a temperature, and your pulse is going haywire.'

My eyes snap open. I feel relaxed. I'm exhausted, okay, sure, but I feel fine. 'What?' I say, and the thin snap of my voice shatters the stillness. 'That's impossible. Is the thermometer cracked?'

Rafe's head turns sharp towards me, gold eyes glinting. 'No, it isn't. Something's wrong with you. Why did they send you home? What is it?' Rafe's in a frenzy now, putting a hand to my forehead and the other against his own (perhaps his mother taught him this). 'You feel hot, too. Do you feel lucid? Sit up and tell me if you're dizzy. What were you nagging me about this morning?'

Anger boils up to my face as I look at him. (This morning I'd begged him to eat something besides toast.) I'm the doctor-in-training; I would know if I had a damn fever. 'I know what a fever feels like, Rafe, and I don't have one.'

'But Heather—'

'Piss off. Go to bed!' I shout, sitting up, and Rafe startles backwards, almost falling over the coffee table.

'Heather—'

'Go!'

Rafe's standing on the other side of the room now, and I have a book in my hand, an old paperback that my sister, in one of her fits of spending, FedExed me ages ago but I still haven't read. God, he is so annoying and fretful and stubborn. I wish he would sleep. He doesn't sleep right these days; he had a new idea for a story weeks ago and that always means his body gets forgotten. I try to get up, and pain explodes from my foot, burning up to my knee before jumping to my middle in one bound.

'Go away, Rafe!' I shout. This is his fault, the damn jerk, wanting to play games at midnight in the park. I stumble about, refusing to sit back down, and he comes to stand still and above me, waiting to see what this outburst is about.

I manage to stand but then I'm toppling over the coffee table and into his arms and, oh God, Rafe must have taken a shower because the warm smell of his skin is delicious. I put my arms around his shoulders for balance and nuzzle my nose into his neck, his heart and lungs going rapid-fire. I want to lick him like kids do in kindergarten, but I dig my nails into his skin instead, fighting the urge. We've covered this ground before, and it wasn't pretty.

Rafe attempts to carry me back to the couch, but screw him: I don't need his help to walk. Anger slams into me hard (something's wrong, something's off, I'm not usually like this) and I push him away with all my might. I land on the floor, exploding with pain all over. My legs break, my biceps shorten into my forearms and I'm screaming, clenching my eyes tight against whatever this is. Rafe yells.

Something comes slamming into the bridge of my nose and slides down and outward. There's no crunch of cartilage but my teeth ache, shrilly, protesting inside my gums, and God, my very eye sockets hurt.

My body stops screeching, and the world assaults my senses: Rafe's lavender, jasmine, man-musk scent, a flush of coddled heat, skidding car tires against the paved road, breathing and beating, crickets, creaking floorboards, the spicy stench of our leftover Indian takeaway, still open in the kitchen. Like something's punched at my face, my head snaps sideways, a hunger roaring to life in my belly and a hurt, an insult stinging my cheek, revenge for ancient wrongs smouldering in, breaking down defences until that's all that's left, really. What came before this agony? The only recourse is to lash out, strike, hit, kick, bite, drag teeth across flesh to taste the beating heart, tear apart limb from limb, destroy them, make them understand exactly what they put me through. I've come to this conclusion before.

I have these thoughts all in a moment, knowing my next move will be for revenge. Someone small yells, really loudly, dancing about, trying to grab me. He would be the first.

But then Heather is back. Please God, this person is innocent, no, no, no, I can't. Run, run away from everything because Heather Leelan refuses to destroy; I want to heal people (because he—my best friend—made the hurting stop, gently took me away from it all, made me laugh, made me smile, reminded me what I was). I am a doctor.

‡

I understand I must be a werewolf but not much else. You wouldn't believe it, but when you have eliminated the impossible, whatever remains, however improbable, must be... yeah. Stomach acid burns my tongue, and I gag on rabbit fur. Scenes, memories flash like cannon-fire in my mind (I'd laughed and war-whooped when I got to the end of *Black Flag*; I'd beat it faster than Rafe could have dreamed), running to the park and finding the nearest food, the closest, easiest-to-get thing with a heartbeat.

I shake my head and wipe the vomit from my lips. My other hand supports me against the rough tree bark. And I'm stark naked. Of course, my lips twitch almost into a smirk; of course I'm stark naked in the middle of a grey-morning Regent's Park. How the hell am I supposed to get home? Rafe will be looking for me: my bones know it. Should I stay put and wait for him, or try to make a run for it and hope no cops are on duty this early? Could I cover myself a little, a la Eve?

Shaky all over, like after a nightmare. Childhood memories of fantasy books wash over me like murky smog (the door creaked as I snuck into my sister's bedroom, the whorled wood under my fingers, the balancing act on the chair, reaching for the fantasy encyclopaedia kept out of reach). Silver bullets, no, silver in general is bad; wolfsbane burns. Full moon transformations, the obvious wish to harm humanity. Hunting in packs. Loyal and brave and good mothers.

I huddle in a small clump of trees and bushes, settling on a patch of pine needles, away from my sick. My tailbone aches (along with the rest of me, really), the ghost of the wolf body hangs over the human, nerves redirect signals and codes and which way to the arm now—or that way to the leg—why can't I hear properly, what's happened to my smell? At least my human vision races ahead of the wolf's, much, much better, and I touch my skin; such thin skin that I can feel the morning chill nibbling my arms. I lean my head back against the tree, closing my eyes to better unboggle my senses. I'm so tired. Breathe, breathe, breathe. A pinecone cracks somewhere.

I open my eyes and fold myself closer together, trying to hide myself and my situation (in college, George streaking across the lawn to impress the girls across the street; the utter, embarrassing whiteness of his skin and me pushing aside the curtains to watch). I breathe a shaky smile when Rafe's hand is the one pulling back the branches, his wool coat protecting his legs from the brambles. His gender has flowed to femme today, peasant top loose and welcoming, box-pleated charcoal skirt full and demure. Rafe's gender does what Rafe wants, but I know this morning's expression is meant to comfort me. He even shaved his beard.

But what do you say to someone after turning into a werewolf and almost killing them?

'Hello.'

'Here.' Rafe's gaze sweeps over me (and my vomit and my tree) as he slips off the long coat, some fancy British brand, and throws it to me. I catch it. Rafe bends and backs out, waiting for me outside my protective pine tree circle. (I'd always been a little too good at hide and seek. I could disappear in a crowd of four.)

I slip the coat on, fumbling with all the buttons, and nobody can tell I'm naked. Small mercy in a shitty situation. I whack my way out from under the tree and put my hand in Rafe's. Gently and quietly, he leads me home.

Awful thoughts bombard me with each long stride: do I turn myself into the police? The American embassy? Both seem like terrible plans because one, getting people to believe me without the wolf eating their faces will be difficult and two, I've seen the *American Werewolf in London* movie and that dude got himself shot in an alley while his girlfriend looked on.

We make it to the apartment, me going in first and Rafe resolutely shutting the door behind us. 'So,' he begins. 'You got "turned".'

I stand in the middle of the living room with just Rafe's coat to drown in, and the only thought that stands out is too obvious to say, so I say it anyway. 'I'm a werewolf.'

Rafe peers at me, like I'm a plot hole to fill. 'What'd ya want to do about it?'

'I don't know. Should we—is tonight a full moon too?' Still stiff, still mechanical, I sit on our couch and cradle my face in my human hands.

Rafe whips out his phone and Googles the bad news: 'Yep. Waxing when you got bit; you got the worst of it last night. Waning tonight.'

'Greeaattt.'

Rafe glances down. 'Your ankle's healed.'

I hadn't even noticed. I lift it and give it a couple of shakes. Rafe says, 'Do you want to look online? If anyone's seen a werewolf in Regent's Park, they're probably talking about it.'

The conversation seems surreal, slippery. Are we actually discussing this? Should we be discussing it? How am I supposed to complete my doctor-in-training residency if I'm a werewolf? How am I going to get out of night shifts multiple nights a month?

I feel Rafe bend down before me and part my fingers. 'My friend, what are you thinking?' Remembrance of the last time he did this squirms like a live knife in the heart.

I shake out, 'Am I supposed to tell someone, an authority? Like the police or the American embassy or my doctor?'

'I don't know they'd believe you, *habibti*,' Rafe brushes back a strand of my hair. (The first time he'd said *habibti* to me, I didn't know what it meant, but I'd wanted to hear him call me that again and again.)

'Why don't you take a shower and eat some breakfast.' Rafe says this. Rafe. Now who's taking care of who? 'I'll Google.'

I stand on unsteady legs. 'Rafe, I actually wanted to kill people—kill you. I couldn't control it, all I could do was force it away.'

'It?'

'The wolf. It wasn't... me in there. When it happens tonight, we need a cage, so I don't hurt you or anyone else.'

'The one that bit you must've escaped from its cage.'

I hate when Rafe is right about the important things, but he always is. The knowledge hangs like a condemned man and I let it swing there, twanging the rope with my exit.

‡

Rafe finds some ideas from the internet. I see the sites, and most of them are fantasy/sci-fi stories and otherkin gender identity tips, but ideas are ideas and they're more than I can think of. Rafe dips into his parents' money to track down a large silver cage. We remove all my possessions from my bedroom, lay thick newspaper down (all those times I told him to stop hoarding and start recycling...). I place two raw steaks in a plastic bowl, and Rafe locks me inside the cage and I strip. I hear him wheeze as he moves his bookcase in front of the door for good measure. I wonder if he knows where his inhaler is, but it's too late to shout to him that it's in his purse, where it's supposed to be.

This time, I feel it coming. It itches like an enormous bug bite all over my skin.

No. Not again.

By the time the sun chases the moon away, the entire flat is trashed in my wreckage: broken wood, shattered glassware, and even a substantial dent in the fridge. I keep running.

‡

I remember flashes of the night, my paws aching, my canine heart pounding in moments of stillness, hiding in bushes, voices nearing and fading as I dash here and there. The swifpfft of tranquiliser darts whizzing past me (I'd almost been run over by a Porsche once, the rocking rush and speed so close that I realised the few extra sentences of studying-on-the-go weren't worth it), a growl in my throat—then human again, bits of leaves in my sable hair and a gash across my left shoulder. I'd seen worse, far worse in med school, on corpses and models and simulations. But still.

It's morning, and the sky is an aching blue, but my limbs aren't obeying me. I'm conscious, I'm human, but the wolf is still in control. Perhaps this will become another flash of memory. I'm on a rooftop, in any case. I don't know how far I've run in the night: it's a small city, brick buildings everywhere, descending to the water. I see the ocean, a pier, shops, and carnival rides. There are also three helicopters trying to surround me. It's almost postcard worthy.

I jump to another rooftop and another and another, all at once. Strange architecture, this. The wolf pushes my muscles, combines our strength to leap. Scrambling around with dexterous hands on a rooftop's edge (I used to thread needles with these eyes and these hands, thread needles and sew people up in small, precise stitches), I swing onto a balcony. The window is cold, imbibing the chill of the air, the glass nearly frosted, my handprint upon that glass. I'm on the streets. The uneven cobblestones hurt my bare feet.

Where am I going? I'll be locked against the ocean that way. No way am I going to swim to Russia (definitely not that athletic, college roller-derby champion or no). The wolf swerves north, back to the fields. I pass an old cathedral, spires sending prayers to heaven (stiff, awkward, horribly pink Sunday school dresses with ridiculous frills). I'm losing them. They're losing me.

Last, I hear the pound of my footsteps against the road: it's in my ears like a heartbeat. (Are they human ears or a wolf's, now? I'll never know. I can't tell.) Behind the drumming of my lunging footsteps is the drumming of another thing. The rut, rut, rut of a spinning thing in the air. I turn to see; I turn to watch. There's someone desperate there, a dark face against the yellow fingers of morning, his eyes gold to match, one hand holding the metal of the doorway and another reaching out towards me. The high collar of his jacket whips back and forth. He seems familiar. He seems lost.

The wolf turns her head and continues running.

‡

Eventually, I'm down to this memory:

We are on the couch together, warm under a blanket, Rafe on his back and me on my stomach on top of Rafe's stomach, both of us too contented to figure out whose legs are whose.

It's soon after we moved in to the small London flat. Rafe

dozes, one set of fingers sifting through my hair and the other wrapped around us, holding us together. I'm almost asleep too. But then I murmur something, a phrase out of one of my dreams, one of those things I never really meant to say but do, establishing this as an unreality. 'I'm always waiting for you to disappear on me.'

Rafe lets out a small breath of laughter. 'Why?'

'You seem too fantastic to be real.'

'Perhaps I am. Perhaps you are.'

'Perhaps,' I mimic.

'Perhaps.'

Sometimes, one memory is enough to build a future on.

# Things We'll Never Know

B R Sanders

The screen door opened with a whisper, letting in the dry summer air and the scent of gardenias. Damien knew Phyllis was home as soon as he smelled them. He turned, and there she was, hauling her suitcase backwards across the threshold. She'd smelled of gardenias since she was fourteen. Damien didn't know how. It was some weird form of magic, that she began to smell of gardenias all at once and still did. Tears sprang up in his eyes. He wiped them away with the back of his hand and reached out to help her, the sharpness of the heat stinging on his skin. The summers had grown hotter, drier, longer as the years passed. They were much worse now than they had been when he was a boy. Now every house in Montbello had an air conditioner; had to have one, or the old folks didn't make it through the Denver summers. He'd been smart to take up AC repair as a trade despite growing up in an apartment with nothing but box fans; it had put his baby through college, and then graduate school. A lot of sweat, back in those days, sure, but no danger. 'Shut the door, Phyll,' he said.

'I am, Daddy!'

'Let me help with your bag.'

'I got it.'

'Let me help you.'

She swatted his hand away. Her fingers were long and dark, like his, like Auntie Cam's. She wore brass bangles. She flashed him a wide smile. She'd done cut all her hair off again; she wore it short and natural now. But she looked good. She looked happy. Smiling and happy; not sunburned. Not skinny. Taking care of herself. Damien smiled back.

'I'm grown, Daddy. It's just one bag.'

'You should've let me you pick you up,' said Damien.

'It's high heat, Dad.'

'So?'

'So, car would've stalled out in this heat. You know it would've. Poor cycle cabbie nearly got heat stroke. What, you think you could've cycled me back here at your age?'

Damien followed as she made her way to her old room. It was just as she left it when she'd graduated high school and struck out for college: the narrow room was wallpapered with music posters. Well-thumbed paperbacks stood in foot-high stacks around the perimeter of the room, posted like sentries. 'No, I suppose not. It used to not get so hot here.'

'Yeah, you said. Growing up, you said.'

'Things sure have changed.'

'They always do, Daddy.' Phyllis sat on her narrow bed. She ran her hands over the old blanket and smiled again. 'You look good, Dad. How's your arthritis?'

Damien scowled at her. 'I don't want to talk about my damn arthritis, Phyll.'

'Well, how is it?'

'It's arthritis. How do you think it is?'

'Not great, if you're biting my head off about it.' She fished around in her bag, and out came a small silver device, long and flat. 'So this project I'm working on—'

'I got your email. I know you want to talk about the aliens. You just got here.'

Phyllis sighed. She dropped the recorder back into her bag. 'You hungry? We should eat. I'm hungry.'

Damien managed to hold her off for a day and a half. Made her tell him about school, about the new friends she was making, about why she'd cut off all her hair. He made her come with him on his twice-weekly visit to Auntie Cam at the nursing home. The visit left Damien sad and happy at the same time, and afterwards, when he'd brought her home and cooked her lunch, Phyllis looked at him sternly across the table. 'Auntie Cam was there when the Hy-Messna came, right?' she asked. That slender silver recorder had slithered onto the table somehow, without him noticing.

'Phyll, can't this wait—'

'Daddy, I'm only here two more days.'

'Then you should schedule another visit.'

'You know travel's hard.'

'Then you should go to a school close by, not all the way out in North Carolina.'

Phyllis shut her mouth tight. Damien ate in silence. She looked at him for a long time before she spoke again, and he became overly aware that all the noises in the room—the whir of the air conditioner, the sound of his chewing, the odd creaks of the old house itself—were being captured by her recorder. 'This is for my thesis, Daddy. The college paid my way out here to talk to you and a few other people. I got other interviews scheduled. I'm glad to see you. I love you, Daddy. But I'm here for research. So either you sit for this interview, or I go down to the Blair Caldwell Library and listen to the other folks I've got lined up. And then I won't hardly see you at all until I leave. Your choice. Now, do you want to do this interview, Daddy, or not?'

Damien sighed. He put down his fork. He looked at his daughter and he knew she was a woman who was approaching thirty, who was grown and brilliant and self-possessed. But he still saw Phyllis, little Phyll, who could only fall asleep if he was beside her and who would only drink juice from a cup that matched the colour of the liquid it contained. He felt himself ill-suited to a battle of wills with his baby girl who was no longer a baby girl. He still loved her like she was. He folded, like a deck of cards.

'Fine,' he spat, frowning, growling, rubbing the bald spot on the back of his skull. 'Fine, Phyll, fine, I'll do your damn interview.' But what he wanted to say was yes, all right, whatever keeps you close, baby girl, whatever keeps you in my line of sight a little bit longer.

Phyllis grinned. She helped him clear lunch off the table. She repositioned the recorder and pulled out a thin tablet from her bag, and explained, her voice suddenly formal, what the interview was for (her thesis) and what she needed (history as he remembered it). Consent was obtained, a form was signed; it felt for all the world like playacting to Damien, like the tea parties they used to have when she was little. She pulled a list of questions up on her tablet.

'What you got questions for?' Damien asked. 'I thought you just wanted history as I remembered it.'

'It's a guided interview, Daddy. They're prompts. So I can get the same kinds of information from everyone I talk to.' She smirked. 'What, I can't ask you questions now? Here's the first one: Tell me about your life as you remember it at the time of First Contact. How old were you? What was your standard of living? Where were you?'

Damien frowned slightly. '"First Contact"—it was an *invasion.* And it was sure as hell only "First Contact" for us—who knows how many others they'd contacted before.'

'You don't know that. The Hy-Messna—'

'The aliens, Phyll. Look, I ain't using their language. They can call it what they want. They were aliens, and they invaded. It was an invasion. Anyway that's four questions. Don't pester me. I don't need you to pester me.' He glanced down at the recorder. 'I'll tell you everything, but let me tell it at my own pace, in my own way.'

'Daddy, it's a guided—'

'You've guided me enough. You going to let me tell it or not?'

Phyllis held up her hands. She sighed. 'All right, Daddy. I won't pester you. It's your story. You tell it how you like.'

'Thank you, Phyll.'

'Sure, Daddy.' Her voice was cool, professional. She turned off her tablet and checked her recorder. The red light blinked, steady and passive.

Damien cleared his throat. 'I was… uh, let's see. How old was I? I was pretty young. Going to Maxwell Elementary right around here, fourth grade. I must have been eight? Nine? So I was a Black boy, eight or nine, living in Montbello. Living with Auntie Cam already—my ma had passed on. I wouldn't say my standard of living was great. Far north-east Denver for Black folks back then, we were struggling to get by.'

‡

Back before all this happened, Auntie Cam was strong. Worked construction, which meant odd hours sometimes but good pay for the two of us. Kept us afloat. I had to get myself to school and back most days. You can imagine the opportunity I saw there. There was no getting past her, though—she'd call the school and check on me—*did Damien get there? On time?* Then she'd call the apartment as soon as I was supposed to be off the bus.

I remember the first day, because it was one of those days I was getting myself to and from school alone. I'd let myself into the apartment, and there was this… thing on the floor. It was right in the dead centre of the apartment, like someone had looked at the blueprints and marked the spot. I didn't even notice it at first; I tripped over it on my way to my room.

It was about a foot tall. Smooth, and metallic. A dull gray, but with a little shine to it. I dropped my backpack. It was like nothing I'd ever seen before. Frankly, when I looked at it, the first thing I thought was that it must have been very expensive. It made me think of hospitals, of my ma in the hospital, of medical things.

I was a careful kid. I mean, my ma dying, being young and Black and a boy and poor—being just me, I guess—all of it added up to a lot of carefulness. I just watched it for a very long time. Studied it, until Auntie got home. By then I had noticed a few things, like that it was made of layers of this weird metal-that-maybe-wasn't-quite-metal, and that if you held your hand out to it, close but not touching, it was warm and it pulsed, and that it must have run on batteries because I couldn't find a cord or power source anywhere near it.

This was what you're calling First Contact, though we didn't realise that then.

So, Auntie came home. It was always strange for me, especially at that age before I really understood what life was like for her, to see her in her masculine work clothes. She had her "on the clock" clothes and her "off the clock" clothes, you know. She stepped over me, changed and washed up, and began to look off the clock, like herself again. 'What you got there?' she asked.

'It's not yours?'

'You think I'd leave it in the middle of the floor like that if it was? Where'd you get it? Looks expensive.' She looked at me careful. She had this look—this don't-bring-trouble-into-my-house look that made my spine shiver.

'It's not mine, Auntie, it was here when I came home! I didn't even touch it!'

'Good,' she said. 'Best not to mess with things that aren't yours. Leave it alone.'

She called the landlord and demanded answers, but he didn't have none. It was from him, though, that we learned that other tenants had gotten themselves injured trying to remove the "devices" from their apartments or trying to destroy them. He said we should just leave it alone. Auntie cussed him out and hung up. Then she called him back and apologised.

I scooted off then, before she could accuse me of further wrongdoing. But I lurked around while she investigated the thing, exactly as carefully as I had. It was still there the next morning, exactly in the same place, when Auntie dropped me off for school.

Everyone at school was talking about it. I mean all of us, the Black kids, the Latino kids, literally all of us. The stories were all the same. In whispers at the back of math class, at recess, at lunch, we pieced it together. We saw the staff and the teachers whispering, too, tense but not talking about it. The feeling was off all day. We figured it out soon enough: those weird metallic pulsing things, layered and delicate and stark, they'd showed up at the dead centre of wherever anyone was living. I knew a kid, Jackson was his name, and he was homeless. Good kid; sad story. He and his mama and his baby sister had to pick up and move every few days, sometimes sleeping in a shelter, sometimes doubled up with a relative. Sometimes he slept over at my place. One of those things, he said, showed up at the shelter he was staying at, dead centre in every single one of the little territories every family had marked off. Jackson, I think, was the most scared of all of us. He kept asking how it found them.

That next day, Auntie picked me up from school. I think she ducked out of her shift early, which was not like her. But then again, it was a strange day. I think a lot of folks ducked out of a lot of shifts early. As soon as we were home, we went straight to that thing in the middle of the apartment—Auntie didn't even stop to change, or make me put my school stuff away first. We had to see if it was still there, what it was doing, if it had changed. And it was still there. It had… opened up a little, is the best way I can describe it. The layers—they were like petals, or leaves, fitted tight together—they had begun to peel away slightly. But other than that, it was exactly the same. Auntie sighed and told me to put my things away and wash up. She changed. I found her looking like herself again, sitting in front of it, her chin balanced on her hand, just staring at it.

'Kids at school are saying it's aliens,' I said. She wrapped her arm around me as I sat beside her.

'I don't know about that, little man.'

'What do you think it is, Auntie?'

'I don't know. I know I don't like it. Coming into my house unannounced, like it owns the place. I don't know what's going on, Damien, but it's nothing good,' she told me. 'Stay away from that thing, OK?'

'I will, Auntie.' She gave me a look, a don't-test-me look. 'I promise,' I said.

'I'm holding you to that promise, Damien.'

'I know, Auntie.'

'OK. You got homework? Well, it's not going to do itself. Better get on it.'

‡

It was maybe a week until they told us what was going on, that they were aliens, that this was First Contact. That the devices were "interstellar biomechanical technology" we couldn't make heads nor tails of, that they were not some kind of a federal spy program, as was the circulating rumour. But that rumour never made any lick of sense anyway; reports were that the damn things had appeared in every human home, everywhere in the world. Down to the Amazon. Down to war zones. Literally everywhere you can imagine. How the American government could have pulled that off when it couldn't manage to get buses running on time in Denver alone… it would have been quite the cover, I guess.

By then, there had been all kinds of speculation on the news about what the devices might be. The government had released statements saying that they were benign, but that we shouldn't mess with them until more was known. I assume there was one in the White House. I bet some heads rolled when it showed up. I bet a million failed tests were run on that one. I wonder where the President slept that week, and the weeks after.

Auntie Cam and I took to eating dinner in front of the device instead of in front of the TV. The only thing worth watching on the TV anymore were stories about the devices anyway, and the thing itself was more interesting. Auntie just stared at it. I drew sketches of it, endless sketches. I drew a lot when I was a kid. And it made me pay attention to the details of it, and the way it changed slightly from day to day, just opening a tiny bit more each morning. It started out a tight sheath of weird, unearthly metal—pliable and iridescent—and it slowly unfolded like a little metallic flower so that you could see more and more of what was inside. What we came to learn was its biomechanics: its cabled veins, the synthetic structures, that kind of thing.

At first we just talked while we ate and watched it, but Auntie was always sharp. She was the one who noticed that it seemed to… pay attention. The way it pulsed—with a rhythm in its layers, in the heat it gave off—it crescendoed if you talked around it. So we studied it in silence. That was Auntie's rule, from the second day, always silence around the weird thing. Better safe than sorry, she'd mouth to me, and hold a finger to her lips.

About a week after it appeared, flowering day after day—one evening, it spoke to us. I wasn't there for any First Communication but that one, so I can't really talk about any other time. But that evening, Auntie and I had sat down with dinner in front of the device, just like we had done the night before. We sat in mean, careful silence. I wolfed down my food so I could start drawing—it had changed again, was more open than before.

There was a dull silver sphere sat in its centre, which I had not seen before. Then the veins running through its layers began to glow, very faintly, and it whirred; it sounded like it was powering up, but where it was drawing the power from, I couldn't say. The sphere inside glowed white and projected a hologram out into the middle of the room.

The story goes that the same thing happened to everyone, that the devices hatched holograms of an alien across the world, that the hologram spoke to the home-dweller in the home-dweller's language, and passed on the same core message however the program—maybe it was an AI? I don't know—thought it would be best received. The story goes that the devices had been gathering data on us, all of us, the whole human race, for days, to get a sense of our idiosyncrasies and habits and language and biology and technology and culture, so that the aliens could tailor their message to each individual damn member of the species. Little personal engraved invitations to the interstellar community, or whatever.

As soon as the device started acting up, Auntie Cam had her arms around me, was protecting me. She was so strong, then. She pulled a baseball bat out of nowhere. It was like it materialised in her hand. It was as strange and magical to me, that mysterious baseball bat, as the thing that was suddenly in our living room. And at nine years old, I fully believed Auntie could take on anything in the universe with a baseball bat and win. I felt safe. I just stood there, staring at the hologram of an alien in our living room.

They were so inhuman. That's what got me. In all the movies and video games and TV shows, they always looked mostly like us but just a little different, you know? Or, like white people but just a little different, really, but you know what I'm saying. But these aliens were—they were not human, not at all. I stared at it hard. It didn't make any sense to me. It looked like a… like a starfish crossed with a horse, maybe, but even that doesn't really capture it. I remember looking at it, this monstrous, foreign, completely inhuman thing, and thinking first, it's totally aliens! It's definitely aliens! And then, how in the hell did that thing fly a spaceship? Where's its hands? Hell, I couldn't even figure out where its face was until it spoke.

At first, it did to us just what we had been doing to it—it stared at us for a long, long time. Slowly, Auntie Cam reached out and slid the tip of the baseball bat through the hologram. She relaxed a little—not much, but a little. Who knew what kinds of stuff crazy starfish-horse-alien holograms could do, right? She held on to that bat tight.

It turned its long head towards us, and I realised that the glassy unblinking regions might be eyes. It opened what I guessed was a mouth, and it spoke. The sound came from the device, and it filled the room.

'Everyone needs help sometimes,' it said. It spoke perfect English. It sounded, a little, like Auntie Cam; it had her depth and tenor and cadence. Auntie had me pressed against the wall behind her. 'There's no shame in taking it. We needed help, and the Thrasks saved us. Now it's our turn. Humanity needs help and we can help you. Let us, let the Hy-Messna, let us help you.'

The image of the alien flickered once and disappeared. In less than ten seconds, the device broke apart and turned to dust before our eyes, disintegrated into a handful of metal filings.

'What the shit was that,' Auntie Cam breathed. Neither of us moved.

'It was an alien,' I said. I was terrified. I was thrilled. I was nine and all my favourite movies were coming true, but all wrong and in my living room.

Auntie wrapped an arm around me and pulled me close, and I felt like I could breathe again. 'It'll be all right. It will be. I'll make sure. What the shit. What the fuck—'

Auntie's phone rang. It was a friend, or a relative; I can't remember. But her phone rang all night. The next day, half my classmates stayed home from school. The other half of us whispered about the night before, compared stories. Our shell-shocked teachers pretended to try to teach us. Mostly, they knew we were there because we were the kids whose parents and caretakers couldn't get the day off work. Auntie's supervisor told her he didn't give a damn, that aliens or whatever had talked to his wife last night, too, but that the building still had to get built so the job was still on. It wasn't school so much, that day, as it was a daycare centre.

The story was the same for all of us, with slight variations: the devices opened everywhere each of us was living, and an image of an alien emerged and gave a message about saving humanity. It spoke Spanish to the Hispanic families. The words were slightly different family to family, but the heart of the message was the same: *we are here to help you.* And then, just like for us, the devices disintegrated, leaving frightened, bewildered people across the city to clean up alien metal dust with old brooms. Some of us were excited. Most of us were frightened.

‡

We never met them face to face. Not even President Obama, or any of the other world leaders. So who even knows if they really looked like those weird starfish-horse things they showed us in the holograms. We'll never know. I think the government reached out, but the aliens didn't want dealings with them. They only ever dealt with all of us, with all of humanity at once. They figured out we used TVs and had smartphones, figured out the internet. They infiltrated our homes first, with those devices, and then they infiltrated our communication systems. Every day, they sent out messages, videos and communiqués to the whole world, talking about why they made contact and what they could do for us and what it all meant.

They sent us puzzle-pieces of schematics for rocket ships. They sent us bits of preliminary formulations for cancer treatments, with promises of cures forthcoming—apologies for differences in biologies attached to the messages. It was wild.

The world erupted. There were two pretty solid camps: those who loved the aliens, and those who didn't trust them as far as they could throw them—and remember, you can't throw a goddamned hologram.

Auntie Cam was in the second camp. At first, I was captivated by the aliens and all the things they said they could bring us. I asked Auntie why she didn't trust them. I remember, it was one afternoon while I was doing homework at the kitchen table. She was washing up after work, scrubbing off the grit and grime of the construction site, replacing the stiff, formulaic masculinity of being on the clock with lavender bathrobes and coconut oil and private relief. Auntie Cam was herself again: protective of me, her shaved legs propped up on the coffee table, her kinky hair freed of its ties and spraying out in wide arcs. Her limbs were looser. Her face was tired, but relaxed now that it was just us and she could let herself be, that she didn't have to hide her painted toenails. I was always fascinated by the transformation, that she had this ritual and I didn't. The year before, I'd learned about butterflies and cocoons and caterpillars in school, and she'd used that to sort of explain it—that sometimes she was like a man and sometimes she was like a woman—and I asked her when I would be able to do those transformations. And she'd held me close and told me that maybe I would someday and maybe I wouldn't, but she'd love me just the same no matter what.

That afternoon, she'd had a long day already. All those days were long days. It was a strange time. She was on edge, and I was arguing with her. Having been on the other side of that now—having been an adult with adult worries on my mind, with a bright kid arguing with me—I see how she lost her temper. I was going on about how maybe they weren't bad. How sometimes we do need help, like I needed help when my mother died, and Auntie Cam was there for me. And she looked at me with this fire in her eyes. This darkness, this wild anger, but not an anger directed at me. A protective mama-bear anger directed at everyone *but* me.

'Come here,' she said, and her voice was as dark as her eyes. I didn't argue—I went right over—but my heart beat wild in my chest. She could see it on my face. 'I'm not mad at you,' she said, 'but there's things you got to learn about the world, about the universe.'

She knelt down so we could see eye to eye. She held me by the shoulders. 'What they teach you in that school, it's not going to be everything you need to know in this life. Some of it I have to teach you. You know, years ago, medical care in Alabama for poor Black country folks was hard to come by. So white government men showed up saying, "Just sign some papers and we'll help y'all out." Some of our family did; they signed those papers. They got sick, Damien. And the government men knew they were sick, and they didn't tell our family they were sick, and they didn't give them medicine or nothing. They just watched them. For years. Just to see what that sickness would do. You know what happened? They got their wives sick. Babies were born sick. Men died young and left sick wives and sick babies unable to pay for houses. All so white government men could understand a disease a little bit better. But they could have treated it, they could have made those men better. We didn't have to spend years being sick and getting our families sick just because some rich white government men were curious. They lied right to our faces. They gave us cold medicine, they set our wrists when they got twisted, but they let us waste away and get whole families sick just to see what would happen.'

'That's horrible,' I said. 'Why would they do that?'

Auntie Cam looked me hard in the eyes. 'Because we are Black, Damien. That's why. Because they're in charge. We can't trust them, you understand? Powerful people never give anything to anyone for free. They will tell you it's free, but it never is. It always comes at a price. That time, it was sick wives and sick babies. These aliens are like those government men. And I don't know what the price will be. But it will be something.'

'Then how do we find out what the price is?'

'We never know, baby,' she said. 'We never know until it's too late, and it's high time we start learning from our mistakes. We got to stop taking what's offered to us. Got to stop trusting people who aren't our people. Understand?' She hugged me tight, and I felt her tears spilling down the back of my neck. It was like a piece of her died in the telling of that horrible truth. She seemed relieved that I had listened, that I had understood, but I think part of her had never wanted to have to tell me. She had known she would have to, but she had never wanted to.

‡

The city was torn wide open. Every day the aliens were transmitting us new things, new schematics, new formulas, new promises. There were hippies here in Denver who thought they were here to save us. The government was pissed because it was useless now; and the police were scouring our neighbourhoods, coming down hard on us and taking their frustrations out on Black and Brown folks. And everything that happened in our city happened across the entire world, but on a bigger scale.

Auntie Cam and some other folks started meeting at a local church to talk things through. They went low-tech—talked the reverend into pulling all the computers, all the WiFi out of the building, and agreed amongst themselves to leave their phones at home. They started the pushback, I think. Radio Silence, they called themselves. Started marching, started protesting. Auntie took me with her. The white hippie kids always asked the same questions: "Why can't you trust them? They say they want to help us!" And Auntie Cam always had the same response: "If they want to help, then they should be brave enough to give it over in person. Don't trust what's not given to you face to face, kid." And then she'd march on.

The thing is, the police cracked down on us in our neighbourhoods, but they let us march as much as we wanted. They let us protest. They let us rail against it all. They let us destroy cell towers and chip away at the communications infrastructure the aliens were using to deliver their promises. The police stood by and watched us cause thousands of dollars of damage to public and private property.

They figured out quick that Auntie was running the show, more or less, and they left her alone in the neighbourhood. Radio Silence made cell phones useless in the city of Denver within a week, and kept them that way for three months. And Auntie Cam organised it all from our apartment, using actual written messages.

It was different in other cities. Denver was lucky, I guess; I don't know why. No one died here. In other cities, there were riots. A lot of people got hurt. Got killed. It's stupid that Denver was lucky and other place weren't. I know… I know this isn't really true, but it still feels like the reason Denver weathered that storm all right was because we had Auntie Cam looking out for us.

The whole thing was over as abruptly as it began. Even though our place was a Radio Silence household, the aliens found a way to get another device inside our apartment, just like the first one. Auntie was livid, but she was smart enough not to go messing with it. This time, it didn't need days to eavesdrop and peel apart. This time, the device opened as soon as Auntie and I were both nearby. It lit up, and a hologram filled the room of one of those hideous aliens. There was no weird staring contest. It spoke immediately.

'Humanity's response to the Hy-Messna offer of help requires Isolation procedures. According to protocol, all contact will cease. All extended information has been rescinded. No future contact or information will be forthcoming.'

The hologram blinked out. The device disintegrated. I'm told that immediately after that, all records of what the aliens gave to us—all those plans for rocket ships and potential cures for cancer and hypothetically better crops, all that magical shit—all of it was gone. Sure, there were some print-outs or what have you, but everything digital was wiped out, and they hadn't given us that much. They'd played it close to the vest, given us fragments, just tastes of what they knew. Nothing we could really do much with on our own. The only proof that any of it had happened, that it hadn't been a massive collective hallucination, were the weird piles of metallic dust on people's living room floors. That, and the carnage left over from the protests.

‡

Phyllis broke in at last, her voice throwing off Damien's train of thought. 'Can I ask just one more question?'

Damien cracked his knuckles in a flurry of impatience. He felt like he was nine years old all over again and powerless. 'Yeah, fine,' he snapped, regretting it the very same second, but pride held his apology back.

Phyllis's steely professionalism wound around her like armour. 'What did you think about Isolation?' Phyllis asked.

Damien laughed. 'I was just glad the whole damn thing was over. I'm glad it's a decision they made for us. I'm glad those creepy bastards took their toys and went home. I am.'

'But the things they gave us, the things they *could* have given us—'

'May have come at a cost. Or maybe not. We'll never know. Phyll, look, maybe those aliens were genuine. Maybe Auntie was wrong about them. I don't know. All I know is that we'll never know. And you know why we won't? Because we ruined ourselves. Spent generations brutalising each other, holding each other down. Maybe the aliens did come with open arms and Auntie couldn't see it because no one ever came with open arms for her—no one, ever, because if they didn't hate her because she was Black, then they hated her for being a "man in a dress", Phyll, and if it wasn't that, it was for being poor.

'And the white people? The rich people? How were they supposed to trust? They got where they were on our backs, and I reckon they thought the aliens were there to get someplace on their backs, that they were about to be stepped on and broken like Auntie had been her entire life. So they couldn't trust those gifts, either.

'See, we're broken, Phyll. That's what I learned from that whole damn invasion. Maybe the aliens were angels. Maybe they weren't. I don't care. And I'll tell you this, baby girl: those aliens put Isolation in place so fast, so completely, I know we're not the only ones in the universe that are this broken.'

Phyllis sighed and chewed the inside of her cheek for a long moment. 'So what do we do with that?'

'We fix ourselves, baby girl, or we die trying.'

# Glass Bones

## Kirstie Olley

Gossen was a small, densely populated town, but no matter which way Mizzy walked, she could only find children, no adults at all, let alone the sort of people who might understand her obscure request. It wasn't easy, she mused, chasing down myths made real. Most people laughed at you if you started demanding things like, 'Where's the ring's guardian?!' And Mizzy had been laughed at a lot, this past year and a half.

She glared at some kids kicking a ball against a wall, their laughter echoing between the tightly packed houses that lined the street. Maybe she should ask *them*, she wondered. It would be better than carrying on getting lost. With a sigh, she walked on—what were the chances they'd know anything anyway?

After a few turns, Mizzy glanced around and kicked at the pebbled road. She was lost again. She cursed the cobbled streets of Gossen, which started broad and open only to twist into the sorts of alleys you wouldn't want to traverse after dusk, and she was relieved she'd left fragile Bran reading in the market square. She hoped he was safe there. He should be. Surely. Her stroll turned into a stride.

The end of the alley drew into sight, bringing with it a frustratingly familiar patch of the market square. She smiled ruefully. Back where she'd started. *Again*. At least she could check on Bran.

'That's a nice set of rings there, boy,' came a voice behind her, with the mock playfulness that promised menace. Mizzy smirked.

She glanced down at the seventeen golden rings on her fingers. She only needed one more to save her brother. If this guy thought he was going to get in the way of that... well, it would be his funeral. She coolly turned to face her mugger, raising her head tall and proud.

'Really? Boy? I cut my hair short and wear trousers and that makes you ignore *these*?' Mizzy pointed to her breasts. 'Honestly, they get in the way every single time I swing my sword, and you can't even take the time to notice them?' She shifted the weight of them between her upper arms. They really did get in the way of a good swing, damn things.

The man's attention was pulled down and he stared, unashamedly, right at them, admiring her undone top button. A lopsided grin grew under his broad flat nose.

Mizzy flattened it further with a punch that knocked him off his feet. He collapsed against the stone wall of the alley and slid into a puddle of mud. Mizzy almost gagged at the reek stirred up by his landing—more likely nightsoil than mud, she reassessed. This did look like the sort of alley where housewives would empty their chamber pots.

'There you go, you like them so much, you'll have bruises that look just like them now.' She waggled her fingers so the rings glimmered, grinning over him.

He was smart. He stayed down. For a moment, Mizzy thought that was because of her, but then she looked up to see two more men approaching from the market square.

'Your friend's right, that's an impressive collection there,' came a smooth voice, from a face that was just the opposite: pocked with signs of an acne-ridden adolescence. The man smiled, shifting the craters in his cheeks. 'No need to guess why you're visiting this town.'

Mizzy's eye caught the glittering band on his finger. She smiled. No need to find her last ring bearer—he'd found *her*. 'None.'

The pock-faced man seemed to see the hunger in her. He looked at the mugger, still lying on the ground, then back to Mizzy. 'We've been watching. Will you be taking my ring by force, then?' He cracked his knuckles with a spectacular array of pops that could probably be heard in the market. His barrel-chested companion puffed himself up, trying to loom. Like an animal trying to make itself look bigger than a foe.

'We could come to an agreement,' Mizzy shrugged with a wonky smile. Her hand rested on her hip, beside the hilt of her sword.

'And how many of those rings did you get by way of *actual* agreements?'

'Not many.' She let her teeth show through her smile. Her fingers curved around the sword's hilt.

'Mizzy!' called a familiar voice, and her cocky nonchalance melted away.

Her brother hobbled down the alley towards her, one leg forever an inch longer than the other after a poorly healed break. In a flash, Mizzy shifted to cover him. She let her eyes flick over him to check for injury then turned back to the men, one arm stretching out to cover him while the other grasped her sword tighter.

'We can come to an agreement,' she repeated, the previous swagger in her tone dissolved. 'I'm as good as my word, I'll return it as soon as we come back from the gate.'

'I don't know you from sea salt.' The puffed-up man spat on

the ground. 'How're Mardon 'n me to trust you?'

'She's a Lake Maiden's champion!' cried Bran from her back.

'Great Lord, Brannory, do you have to tell everyone we meet?' Mizzy sighed, a small pang in her chest at the Lake Maiden's mention.

'Well it's true. If you'd mention it more, things might be easier.'

'Haha, a good jape, son!' laughed the big man. 'A thick-waisted girl like that, a Lake Maiden's champion?'

Mizzy drew her sword. The blade rippled in the dim light, glinting like the lake from which it had come.

The man faltered. They always did when they saw Lake Shard in her hands.

'How old are you, girl?' asked the pock-faced man.

'Eighteen.'

'Great Lord, you're barely a woman. How'd you come by such a fine blade?'

'My brother told you. I'm a Lake Maiden's champion.' Mizzy shrugged, but the urgency pounded in her veins. She needed this man's ring, now.

'That this is a gift from a Lake Maiden, I'll not deny, but you, a champion? That's harder to swallow.'

'Do or don't. Just lend me the ring.'

'Why?' The man's stance eased. He stepped closer with a new calm, clearly curious, his eyes flickering between Lake Shard and Mizzy's moon face. He gestured gently to the sword; she held the blade out and he touched it lightly. Water trickled from the metal on contact, dribbling down his fingers, dampening his cuffs.

'My brother has the curse of glass bones. They break easy and heal rough,' explained Mizzy shortly. 'No healer knows the cure and no witch, wizard, or enchanter can break the curse. Believe me, we've seen them all. I want to open Gate Eighteen. I've been told there's nothing they can't cure over there.'

'Heard the same, myself,' he replied, releasing the blade and shaking the droplets from his fingers. 'Though I've never dared cross. They say it's more dangerous than most cures are worth.'

'It's my brother's life, sir. There's nothing I won't do.'

'Now I can see the champion in you.'

Mizzy tried not to let her pride show.

'But we've a problem. I'll be wanting collateral, proof you'll come back with my ring. I need something I know you'll return for. I'd say your brother, but there's little point in crossing the gate if the one to be cured ain't there, so I'll ask for your sword instead.'

Mizzy froze. Had he seriously suggested she part with Lake Shard? She'd barely let her sword out of her sight since the Lake Maiden had forged it for her.

Her heart wrenched in her chest. This was the only piece of the Maiden she had with her. Bran touched her arm, staring up at her with big dark eyes, pleading her—but not to give over the sword. To give up on him. The one thing she would never do.

Her hand shook as she turned the handguard to the man. He corkscrewed the ring off his finger and swapped it for the blade.

'When you return, ask around for Mardon. I'll keep it safe,' he assured her, but Mizzy felt her stomach wrung out like a dish rag.

She turned, wishing she could lean on her brother without the possibility of breaking his collarbone. She felt weak-kneed without her connection to the Lake Maiden.

Her brother was still watching her as they walked away from the alley, brow creased.

'Oh, calm down,' she laughed at him through the knot in her chest. 'I just need to get a new sword and get us to the gate.' But his face told more truths than she could possibly deny.

‡

Wedged in the side of the mountain, the golden arch of the Hundred Gate was higher and wider than she'd even imagined, with space enough for a wheelhouse to pass through with ease. She marvelled to see their goal just a few steps away. A hundred different worlds could be reached from this one gate—if only you had the rings. Her stomach twirled and churned, like her little sisters were doing cartwheels inside it. She pressed one hand against it, her mind spinning too. Bran's cure, and the chance to return to her Lake Maiden. Both were tantalisingly close now.

The Keeper watched in silence as Mizzy and Bran approached him, stroking his short grey beard.

'Who comes?' he finally called, his voice a croak from lack of use.

'Mizzy—' She faltered; better to give their full names. 'Mizureleiria and Brannory Frettle. We seek passage through the Hundred Gate to the world beyond Gate Eighteen.'

'You've eighteen rings?'

'Yes, sir.' Mizzy bowed, offering up her hands. The Keeper smirked at her boldness in wearing them and removed them one by one, counting aloud as he placed them in a small basket. Mizzy assumed it was ceremony, some ancient rite or other, but she wished he would hurry up—she was too damn close to be held back now.

Her fingers lighter, Mizzy raised her head, and the Keeper indicated the hundred indents on the golden arch. 'Place the rings with care,' the old man said. 'For while any of the hundred rings may open the gate, it will not open if they are not set correctly.'

'Why?' Bran asked, tilting his head.

'A last line of defence, to prevent the unworthy from crossing to other worlds.'

'How do you know we're worthy?' Mizzy mused.

'The rings tarnish in the presence of the undeserving, the greedy, the needlessly violent. These glitter as if just polished by a jeweller.' The old man smiled, his wispy beard echoing his expression. 'I imagine some look nicer since *you've* possessed them than they did on their guardians' fingers.'

The thought baffled Mizzy, until she recalled some of the guardians they'd met during their journey. The cruel and grasping ones who'd demanded large sums of money—or other forms of bribes. Not collateral, like Mardon had taken, but things they would keep even upon the return of their rings. And while she'd duelled fairly for a few of them, one of the guardians had seemed particularly cutthroat. The stories said guardianship was passed down in families like royal titles, but Mizzy had always held onto the mythic idea that the guardians were all still essentially good. Now she wasn't so sure.

She looked at the aged Keeper, his smile turned melancholy, and tried to lift her frown. He said nothing, but turned and began to point out the specific slots for each of the rings. Several were quite high. Mizzy gulped, made her way to the arch, and scrambled up to the highest ridge in the mountain wall, gripping small protrusions in the rocks with tight, aching fingers as she drove the rings into their correct positions.

She left the lowest and easiest for last and climbed back down, patches of sweat flowering underarm by the time she reached Bran's side.

The Keeper reached into his robes and drew out two small silver rings. 'On the other side will be another Keeper. You *must* heed what they tell you. Wear these. They will translate for you.'

Mizzy gawped at them, feeling stupid. She hadn't even considered that another world might have a different language. Bran reached past her and took one of the bands, slipping it on with wide, curious eyes.

'You won't even notice them,' the Keeper said.

How handy such a ring would have been when she and Bran had travelled all the way to the Western Isles last summer, thought Mizzy. Could she find a way to keep it upon their return? Perhaps it would be able to translate the Lake Maiden's strange communication—it would be wonderful to fully understand what she meant for once, rather than just seeing images and feeling surges of emotions that weren't hers.

Still clutching the gate's last key, Mizzy took the ring from the keeper and slipped it on (she tried not to notice the way it resized itself to fit her finger), and Bran pushed his hand slowly and softly into hers. She nodded.

Mizzy carefully slotted the last ring into the lowest hole in the gate. The ground roared and rumbled beneath them. Light flashed from within the gate and she flinched from it, shifting her body over her brother's to protect him from any rocks that might fall from the mountainside.

The light faded, and Mizzy stared at the space inside the gateway. It was like looking through rippling water. There was something bright and strange on the other side, but she couldn't make it out. She stepped forward, her brother gripping her hand tight. She worried he'd stress his bones, holding on to her with such fervour: he'd once snapped a wrist merely rolling dice.

She walked up to the liquid wall and passed through, into the world on the other side of Gate Eighteen.

Beyond a sea of smooth grey stone, a metal carriage roared by, green-painted and shimmering with flecks of hidden jewels. The thick spokes of its broad wheels were black with soot, and Mizzy stared, aghast, as it left her sight faster than her eyes could process. The strangest thing, however, was the lack of horses pulling it.

The world before her was filled with the things. Some fifty or so sat stationary on flattened black ground, neatly boxed in by white markings. Others raced by, too fast to count. Heart pounding, she tore her eyes away, and they fell on the groups of people nearby who sat on small silver chairs with spindly legs, at glass-surfaced silver tables.

A woman at one of the closer tables wore blue trousers of a fabric Mizzy had never seen in all her travels, and a tight black shirt with almost no sleeves. Her hair blazed azure in streaks near her face, but the rest was coal black. She drank from a squat white cup, something that steamed, but set it down when she spotted Mizzy and Bran.

'Well, well, more visitors,' she said, sauntering over.

Mizzy could hear her brother's heavy gulp.

'Name's Sarah,' the girl said, sticking out a hand. 'I'm Keeper on this side. Which gate did you come through?'

'Eighteen.' Mizzy barely managed to push the word out, too busy staring at the woman's clothes and the carriages speeding past. She felt exposed, like a dozen strangers' eyes were on her. She heard a whirring noise and turned just in time to see huge glass doors behind her easing themselves closed. Behind them lay a palace of white stone floors, white walls, and a glass ceiling so high she wondered why it wasn't buttressed like the Great Lord's cathedral in Edrionne. There were strange rooms lining the pristine walkways, people bustling about between them in wildly colourful clothing, carrying metal-woven baskets and shiny bags. After a moment of wide-eyed staring, she realised they were stores. A palace of *stores*?

'Oh, you're from the fairytale place, cool,' Sarah was saying. 'If I could cross, that's one of the places I'd try. But first thing's first, what're you here for?'

Mizzy looked back at the girl, but couldn't focus. Numbly, her lips formed the words, explaining her brother's curse.

'Ahh, a doctor then. I've got just the guy, diagnostic genius. Some of the doctors in his centre have helped otherworlders before, but you'll be his personal first. I'll just make a call.' The girl pulled a thin black box from a pocket on her buttocks. She tapped it with a finger, lifted it to her ear and waited. 'Hello, appointments please,' she said a few seconds later.

'Uh—' Mizzy began, slightly baffled, but didn't get a chance to speak.

'Yes, I'd like to make an OW appointment with Dr. Aguta,' said Sarah. Mizzy looked around with a frown, but couldn't figure out who she was talking to. The Keeper raised her arm, looking at a bracelet on her wrist. 'Sure, ten-thirty sounds great… Oh, one sec.' She turned and met Bran's eyes. 'What's your name, sweetie?'

He blushed. 'Brannory Frettle.'

Sarah looked away again and repeated his name.

Mizzy squinted, her head spinning, but before she could react Sarah had shoved the box back into her pocket. She turned back to them at last. 'Okay, now let's get you a ride.'

She guided them across the perfectly flat stone path to where the horseless carriages flew by. She was speaking as they walked, but Mizzy couldn't hear over the rumbling in the street and her thrumming head. She looked down at her brother, who was nodding and replying to the woman. Good. At least he was listening.

Sarah raised her arm and an orange carriage swept up in front of them. A man flung open the door from inside and she leaned in to speak to him, then opened the back door and told them to get in.

'He'll take you to the doctor's. They'll run some tests and stuff. I hope they can help you. Oops, almost forgot, here—' She handed over a small green rectangle, thicker than a book page but thinner than leather. Black markings rose out of it. 'Show them this card, it should cover the costs.' She handed a wad of paper to the driver, who smiled as he leafed through it. 'Oh, and gimme the sword, you'll attract the wrong kind of attention with something like that,' she added, then snatched the sword from Mizzy's hands and slipped back out. She pushed the door shut and waved to them.

Mizzy turned the card over in her hands. It was too tiny to fit any money, but it must, somehow. How was she to open it? She sank into the soft seat inside the carriage and ran her fingers over its smooth edges.

She hardly noticed the movement at first. There was a dragging sensation that pushed her back in her seat, and then… practically nothing. No bumps, no jostling; the carriage glided over the black road.

White rooms awaited Mizzy and Bran at the doctor's lodgings, too. The large waiting room had a crisp, tangy fragrance, unlike anything Mizzy had smelled before. It was like someone had tried to mimic the scent of citrus—and yet there were other smells, poorly hidden, underneath.

A woman sat behind a tall counter. Her eyebrows rose as they entered and she stood, greeting them respectfully. She had a strange black headband perched over her blonde hair, a small arm extending from one ear to hover in front of her mouth.

'Brannory Frettle, I presume?' she asked briskly. Bran nodded. 'Medicare card?' She held out her hand, palm up.

Bran and Mizzy looked at one another with raised eyebrows. The woman gave an exasperated sigh. 'That green card.' She pointed to Mizzy's fist, which clutched the funny rectangle Sarah had given her. Mizzy handed it over.

'Take a seat,' the woman instructed, indicating several rows of lumpy seating, where people sat reading books or fidgeting with little black boxes like Sarah's. Mizzy walked over hesitantly, Bran gawking in her wake. 'Otherworlders,' sighed the woman at the desk under her breath.

As they approached the seats, Mizzy felt eyes on her again. The strangers were staring, looking over her clothes and smirking, or rolling their eyes, or squinting as if trying to figure out a puzzle. But Mizzy wouldn't be fazed. It was *they* who were dressed bizarrely, with their shirts without buttons or lacings, bearing illegible words and pictures and such bright colours.

She and Bran took seats in small but comfortable chairs. On the walls hung shockingly realistic paintings of people, words surrounding them—but it appeared the ring's translation abilities didn't extend to written language.

Time dragged by. Mizzy felt her leg begin to jiggle nervously.

Bran reached over and pulled a very slim, oddly floppy book from a low table before them. He flipped through it awkwardly, his fingers expecting something sturdier. It was filled with even more of the strange paintings, so realistic they looked like the subject might simply walk off the page. There was a painting of a woman wearing a white dress that caught Mizzy's heart in her throat. The painted woman stood in a pool with a waterfall behind her, arms outstretched, the dress and her long dark hair clinging to her skin with damp. Though her face and figure were definitely not the Lake Maiden's, the picture reminded Mizzy of her lover and her chest ached. She took the book from Bran, who protested only half-heartedly and stopped when he saw why Mizzy was grabbing it.

Her eyes misted and she blinked rapidly to hold back tears. She clutched the picture to her chest and sniffed. A woman two seats over was eyeing them up, and now whispered to her companion, 'What the hell? It's just a shampoo ad.'

Bran put a hand on his sister's arm, and she straightened up, trying to regain strength in her posture. She wiped her eyes briskly and gave him a smile that might have looked real, but sure didn't feel it.

'I know. You haven't seen her in almost two years,' he said softly, patting her arm. 'You must be worried sick.'

Mizzy almost laughed out loud. Oh, what her brother didn't know. He'd seen their first kiss, when the Lake Maiden gave Mizzy her sword in formal championhood fashion—but he hadn't been there for the others. When she looked up now, though, and saw Bran's face, she wondered at the way his brow creased, the depth of pity in his eyes. Perhaps he had an inkling.

'Brannory Frettle,' the woman at the counter called. They rushed to her side, and she led them into a small room down a corridor.

Mizzy's stomach churned as the woman closed the door behind them, shutting them in the room. A human skeleton stood in a corner, and Mizzy felt sure it might start moving at any moment. In the other corner, the perfectly preserved torso of a corpse (better than preserved, the thing was positively shining) had been opened up so you could see its glossy insides, complete with guts and lungs and—Mizzy slammed a hand over her mouth and clutched her belly, certain she would throw up.

A man was sitting on a bulky chair with tiny wheels on its sprawling legs, looking the pair over with sparkling eyes.

'Sarah wasn't lying,' he smiled, gesturing to two chairs near his desk. 'From another world… I must say, I'm excited about this one. What's the trouble?'

Mizzy fell into a seat, but couldn't open her mouth, her breakfast fighting to get past her teeth. Bran looked at her then, after a moment, began to explain. Mizzy knew he was speaking, but couldn't focus on his words. She couldn't take this world; she felt faint just sitting here. She yearned to be back home, with Lake Shard in her hands, sitting by the water and watching the Lake Maiden dance in the sunrise. She pulled that image to the front of her mind and held it there fast.

The doctor leaned forward, *hmm*ing, and edged close to Bran, looking intensely at his eyes then muttering something under his breath. 'Do either of your parents have the same condition?'

'No,' Bran replied. 'But my grandfather did. Though Mother says not half so severe as I.'

The man nodded and began a barrage of questions, which Bran amiably answered. His diet, lifestyle and childhood were discussed at length while the doctor made him flex his arms and legs, roll his wrists and ankles, follow a bright little light trapped in a smooth stick with his eyes, sit on a bench as the doctor tapped his knee—gently, at Mizzy's insistence. The man asked about their home, and then where they'd been lately, what it was like, whether the injuries had continued, and really? Your sister is a swordfighter? Mizzy prepared herself to step in and stop things from getting too personal, but the doctor at last gave a nod and sat back down in his funny rolling seat.

'Now, I could do a few tests, but they would take a while, and with your unique situation, you wouldn't have time for them. However, I'm certain I know the diagnosis. You have Osteogenesis Imperfecta.'

'What's that?' Mizzy's head rose, eyes snapping to the doctor's face.

'A genetic disorder wherein the bones are extremely fragile.'

'How do we heal him?'

The doctor hesitated, his expression tightening. 'We can't. There's no cure.'

Mizzy felt frozen for a second, then came to her feet, fists balling. 'No. This is the world beyond Gate Eighteen, there's nothing that can't be cured here.'

'I don't know what to say. Some things we just can't fix. There're lots of illnesses we can't do anything about. No world has all the cures.'

'B-but we came here. We need to heal Bran.' Mizzy's voice shook. She'd been questing for the rings for almost two years, and had spent years before that seeking cursebreakers—it couldn't end like this. She'd wanted to throw up before, but now it felt like someone had torn her stomach out.

'We could run the tests to be sure, but his height for his age, the blue tint in the whites of his eyes, the family history, and all the stories you just told me, Brannory—I can't think of *anything* else that presents these symptoms, let alone anything curable. The one upshot is that ten percent of sufferers' bones become sturdier by adulthood.'

'Percent?' Bran asked.

'Sorry, one person out of ten.'

'What shitty odds,' said Mizzy. 'C'mon Bran, let's go home.' She reached for his hand to yank him after her, but stopped herself just short, knowing her strength and his weakness were a terrible combination. She scowled all the darker for knowing how close her anger had drawn her to harming him.

She stomped to the door and yanked it open then looked

back at Bran, refusing to even acknowledge the doctor with a farewell.

Her brother gave the doctor his thanks and followed her out. He said nothing as they left the whiteness of the building, and neither did Mizzy.

'I want to look around a little longer,' Bran said firmly as they walked out to the road where the cabbie—as he had called himself—was waiting, listening to a musical box that seemed to replicate a variety of voices and instruments all at once.

'You can't, Bran, you're too fragile,' Mizzy snapped, heading for the carriage. Her head ached. *This isn't how it's supposed to go!*

'No, I'm not,' Bran snapped back. 'You keep treating me like this fragile thing, a breakable heirloom to be preserved on some out-of-reach shelf, but I still travelled all the way from the Western Isles to the Glass Mountains, from the Towers of Yon to the great city of *Edrionne*.'

'Yeah, and you broke five bones during all that travelling!'

'But it didn't stop me, did it? It didn't kill me. I'd pay that price thrice over to see all those sights again, and I don't want to miss out on seeing what else this amazing place has to offer! Do you?'

Mizzy halted.

'I… I'm sorry. I honestly thought this was it. That when we left this world, you'd be as strong as me.'

'No one's as strong as you,' laughed Bran.

'Your know, sometimes I think my feelings are more brittle than your bones.'

Her brother reached up to her. Only five years her junior, yet even on tiptoe he had to stretch to give her a hug. With painstaking care, Mizzy wrapped her arms around his slim form, wanting to squeeze him close but not daring to. Bran embraced her fiercer still, making her fret his fervour would cause a fracture.

She smiled down at her brother. 'You're right. We spent all

that time hunting down the rings; let's at least bring back a thousand tales to tell.'

‡

The cabbie drove them all over, through crowds of people so thick that Mizzy swallowed hard when the cab stopped and the mobs spilled around them. He took them to a massive building he called a museum, filled with the skeletons of monsters and marvellous machines. To a small patch of grass scattered with brightly coloured constructions, where he taught them to fly back and forth sitting on leather straps held aloft by chains, and climb a bright green ladder to woosh down a yellow chute. He laughed at their excitement more times than Mizzy could count.

He told them about his 'car radio' and named things as they drove by. They saw 'billboards' standing at the edges of roads: giant sides of brightly painted houses that were missing the other three walls, roof and floor. He took them to another 'shopping centre', slipping Mizzy some of the funny little sheets of paper Sarah had given him and telling them to buy something for themselves. Bran spent an agonising amount of time torn between some very comfortable footwear—a 'steal' at two for the price of one, according to the shopkeeper—and a thick book filled with indecipherable words and pictures of the sights they'd seen. In the end, Mizzy gave him some of her papers so he could buy both, because his smile was worth any price, and for herself bought a blouse with beadwork so fine it shamed any princess's bridal gown. To her delight, when she traded the papers for the blouse, she was returned a handful of coins—yet they were nothing like those of her world, so small, thin and shiny, printed with images wildly complex. She led Bran from the centre clutching the blouse in its 'plastic bag' tightly, imagining the look on the Lake Maiden's face when she saw her in it. Her grin was irrepressible.

The cabbie took them last to a magnificent metal arch of

a bridge that lit up with nightfall; and to a city of towers, a world of so many tall, hard rectangles built of a million glass windows, which sprouted from the ground like a concrete forest.

They returned to the gate only when their legs were leaden with exhaustion, and yet Bran's enthusiasm remained strong. He swore, as he said goodbye to Sarah, Mizzy clutching her retrieved sword, that he'd collect the rings again one day and come back to visit her. She kissed him on the forehead, saying she'd like that, and his face blazed.

Too tired to walk back to town once they found themselves home, they slept the night beside the Keeper there. Mizzy was sorry to give the translating rings back, a hard curiosity digging into her chest, but it was soon forgotten; when dawn bled colour into the world, a scowl had supplanted itself on her round face. Her brother would forever have glass bones. She *had* to find a way to protect him. But first, she needed to get Lake Shard back.

They travelled through the forest like an arrow in flight, swift and straight to their goal. As they walked, Bran practiced the tales he would tell of the world beyond Gate Eighteen. If Mizzy hadn't been with him, she would've thought him embellishing. Back in their world, she almost didn't believe her own memories.

Mizzy tried to keep her disappointment from showing too much, but couldn't help it: her mouth kept falling into a grim, flat line, her brows pushing closer and closer together. This was not what she wanted Bran to see, but each time she managed to warp her scowl into a smile—even a neutral stare—Bran's soft, piteous looks told her he saw right through it.

They'd barely been back in Gossen ten minutes, asking around for Mardon as he had requested, when a bustle of street kids found them, cheering and shrieking, dragging at their clothes. Mizzy pushed their busy hands from Bran, not bothering to fend them off her own body. Their patched, dirty trews and rough linen tunics looked dizzyingly bland in comparison to the bright colours and patterns they had been surrounded by yesterday. But it was nice, Mizzy thought, to blend in again—to not be the objects of stares.

The children dragged them with alarming purpose down bumpy streets towards a two-story house with a big blue door and, now laughing, knocked.

The pock-faced man from the alley stuck out his head, scowling.

'Off with you!' he scolded the children, but the fierceness of his voice was not in his eyes. The children did not dissipate. Mizzy shifted from one foot to the other. Her slight movement caught his attention, and his eyes widened.

'You're back?'

Mizzy ground her teeth at his surprise.

'Well, better come in then.' He opened the door wide and swept his hand inward. 'But not you lot,' he snapped at the children. 'You all go home and help with the chores.'

The kids groaned loudly, rolling their eyes and complaining with rude words or gestures, but they left as advised.

Mizzy ushered Bran inside, immediately surprised by the cleanness of the house. Then the smell hit her. Roast pork and vegetables. Oh, Great Lord, it smelled good: thick, rich, meaty. Her mouth watered, and when she saw Bran's expression of lustful hunger, she knew there was a matching look on her own face.

Mardon turned over his shoulder as he led them through the house, and laughed. 'Jave, you've some admirers of your cooking waiting,' he called out.

'I thought you said you weren't going to feed any more of those street urchins,' a deep and familiar voice called back. Mizzy tried to mask her surprise as the barrel-chested man walked through a door, wiping greasy hands on a cloth. 'Oh! Not urchins,' he rectified, his eyebrows shooting up.

'That smells real good,' Bran confessed with wide, honest eyes.

'We're only here to give the ring back.' Mizzy twisted the ring off her finger and placed it in Mardon's hand.

'You can stay for dinner, Jave always makes extra,' Mardon replied.

Mizzy cocked an eyebrow.

'You can't tell me you don't even want a taste.' The pock-faced man showed his teeth in a cheeky grin. Mizzy's stomach betrayed her with a loud rumble, and her brother gave a delighted laugh that was echoed by the men.

'Young man,' Jave asked, smiling at Bran. 'Could you help me set the table?'

'Sure,' grinned Bran.

Jave guided Bran to the kitchen to find the cutlery and plates. 'Mardon, you should give the little champion back her sword,' Jave added as he and Bran left the room.

'Of course. This way, my dear,' he said, guiding her upstairs.

The moment Mizzy saw Lake Shard, carefully placed on a decorative holder atop the mantelpiece, she nearly dropped to her knees. Then she wanted to run to the sword, grab it and hold it close. She fought both urges, not wanting to look weak in front of a man she barely knew.

'Thank you for taking good care of her.' Mizzy bowed her head.

'It would've been rude not to,' Mardon replied. He took the sword down from its display, water dripping from his fingers where he touched the blade, and handed it to Mizzy. She sheathed Lake Shard wordlessly, blinking back tears.

'I expected to see you in much better cheer.'

Mizzy's mouth twisted. Who was this guy, to judge how she felt? All she wanted was go home, to go to the lake, to curl up with the Lake Maiden and cry.

No. What she wanted was to find someone who could lift Bran's curse. Great Lord damn it, she didn't know *which* she wanted more. She blinked harder, fighting back the blurriness invading her vision.

Mardon sat, and gestured to a nearby chair. A frown curled his mouth. 'I take it all did not go as planned.'

'Well, I can safely tell you they *don't* have all the cures over there,' Mizzy spat, as if the words themselves tasted bad—which they did, curdling the saliva in her mouth like poison.

Mardon said nothing for a moment, and Mizzy glanced up. He looked stricken, and Mizzy wasn't sure he was feigning it.

'So the curse remains?' he said finally.

Mizzy nodded, closing her eyes tight to fend off the deluge.

'I wish there was something I could do. Perhaps... another world?' Mizzy opened her eyes to see him removing the ring from his finger. Her hand went to Lake Shard, clutching the blade close. 'I wouldn't need collateral this time,' he said.

'I don't think there are any worlds that have what I need.' In her head, Mizzy still heard the doctor's words. *Some things we just can't fix*. Her throat swelled.

'What will you do now? Will you stay?'

Mizzy shook her head. 'We've a family to return to, and—' Mizzy silenced herself before she said too much. 'And I have a Lake Maiden to champion.'

Mardon raised one eyebrow, the only sign he'd noticed her brief pause, then sighed. 'A pity. You'd be a force for good around here. Someone for the young girls to look up to as well. But family, I understand that. Sorry, I'd assumed you and Bran orphans. Would you mind if I ask why your parents didn't undertake this task?'

'We've five other siblings. If Mother or Father left on this journey, the others might starve.' Mizzy smirked, and thumped a bicep with her hand. 'Besides, I'm better equipped than both of them together.'

He tossed his head back in laughter. It sounded like her father laughing when she joked about her prowess. Her gut wrenched with homesickness.

'Is there anything I can do to help you home?'

'No—we did fine to get here, we can manage our return as easily.'

His brow creased again, but smoothed just as quickly. 'Well, at least stay the night after dinner.'

Mizzy nodded. This would be their last chance for a while to sleep in a proper bed.

‡

Mizzy raised her hand to knock on the chapel door. Her fingers looked strange now, without her rings. They were barely half a day's walk from the Lake Maiden, all the rings at last returned, and soon she would be home to tell her parents of yet another failed quest. She closed her eyes, sighed and knocked. An old friar opened it, smiling.

'Sanctuary, my pet?' he asked in the soft, friendly tone of most men and women of the faith.

'Yes please.' Mizzy smiled in return. It was good to see a servant of the Great Lord when times grew dark.

He guided them in, past the altar to the door of a small room filled with cheap cots. Several needed repair. She hid a small disappointment. As she'd suspected, the beds at Mardon's house had been the last comfortable ones they'd slept in for months.

'If you've a hammer and nails, I can fix those cots,' Mizzy offered, steering her brother to the best cot with a gentle hand on his lower back.

'That would be a blessing, young one. A pity we don't see more travellers like you.' The friar shuffled off for the tools, mumbling a prayer of thanks to the Great Lord for his gifts. She tried to pass him a coin when he returned with the hammer and nails, but he refused.

'Your work is more than I could ask for,' he said, his voice sombre. Mizzy waited for him to leave, and slipped the coin into the donation box.

Bran had grabbed a worn book down from a shelf along the wall. The shelf was high: he must have stood on tiptoes to reach it—and with one arm still in a sling, no less. Mizzy's pulse picked up, but she bit back her lecture. He was sitting on the bed as he'd been taught, with the book beside him rather than on his lap, so the weight wouldn't put pressure on his legs.

Mizzy dragged the broken cot pieces out into the yard so the hammering wouldn't disturb the prayers. Perhaps she'd say a prayer as well while they were here. Not that they'd done any good so far. Her brother was still cursed, still more fragile than a toy. She pounded on the nails with a ferocity she dared not embrace when fighting.

'What did that poor cot ever do to you?' asked a man behind her.

Mizzy spun around, and had to rein in the instinct to take to him with the hammer. The man stood tall, smiling softly. It was not the friar, but he wore similar robes that fluttered in the breeze.

'I'm just mad,' she confessed. 'I've done all I can, but I can't help my brother.'

'Poor child, you have the answer,' he told her, his frown piteous. 'Magic breaks curses, and you have access to a great magic.'

Mizzy sighed. The Great Lord had clearly gifted this man with the insight to help her, but she did not, this time, welcome it. 'I already asked the Maiden once, very shortly after I became her champion. Her answer was confusing—too many conflicting emotions—but she left me feeling like I'd just been given a very loving 'no'.'

'Asking won't help,' he warned.

Mizzy went cold, her skin rigid with goosebumps. His robes, she noticed then, were not the honest brown of the Great Lord's servants, but grey and faded.

'You know when those with magic in their blood are most

powerful?' he asked.

A shudder rippled through Mizzy, like a breeze shattering her reflection on the surface of a pond.

She did know.

It was when they were dying.

‡

Mizzy pressed her face into her hands. She could smell rat piss from a hole in the wall as she huddled in a corner of the church. She wished she was at the lake already, its cool comfort washing over her. And yet, what made her feel good about the lake was the very crux of her problem.

The enchanter, be he good or bad, was right. If she killed the Lake Maiden, the power released could surely break any curse. But it was a gamble. And could she do it? When the Maiden touched her, she felt safe. She found peace. Could she actually give up one love for another?

Did she have any other choice?

She walked into the small room for wayfarers and halted abruptly. The room was empty. Where was Bran?

Panic banded her chest like a too-tight corset. She couldn't breathe. Where had he gone? Was he safe? She burst from the room and through the chapel, squinting into its crevices in the darkening light. No sign of him. She tore outside, racing so fast she nearly tripped right over him where he sat on the stairs. She skidded to an awkward, hopping halt.

'There you are,' she panted, her pulse frantically throbbing still. 'Don't run off like that! What would have happened if you'd been hurt?'

He glared at her. 'I've dealt with it often enough before.'

Even as she looked down at him, knowing he was safe, Mizzy felt her lungs caged. That safe was only for now. Only for this instant.

She extended an open palm to him. 'Come with me,' she

said, her voice cracking.

Her decision was made.

‡

She held Bran's hand the entire walk to the lake.

'We never travel in the dark though,' he protested, looking up at the starry sky.

'Oh come on,' Mizzy laughed, painfully aware of how false it felt. 'As if you don't consider this just another adventure.' She knew without looking, with the stab of a bittersweet blade, that he was smiling. She focused on trying to find the flattest path by the full moon's light; after all, his broken arm had been the result of nothing more than tripping over his limp.

'Why are your hands shaking?' asked Bran.

'It's cold,' Mizzy lied, her mind too trained on what she had to do to come up with a better excuse.

She'd often imagined her homecoming to the lake: the way the Maiden would look, the relief and joy that would wash over her at the mere sight of her dearest one... Now she dreaded the familiarity of this path. The smell of the firs and camphor laurels that lined the lake's edge didn't unwind her tension as they normally did, instead ratcheting it up in intensity. When they reached the clearing, the Maiden was standing on the shore already, waiting for her. Her face held a gentle smile, drawing Mizzy closer.

She led her brother to the water's edge. The Maiden reached for her face, and the liquid that leaked from her skin dripped down Mizzy's cheeks, masking her tears.

Mizzy's body shuddered with heavy sobs, and the Lake Maiden's arms wrapped around her, soaking her clothes. Warm, wet lips kissed away each tear. Mizzy released her brother's hand so both her arms could embrace the Maiden, and at last she gave up her proud stance, sagging into her lover's liquid embrace.

The words flowed out of Mizzy's mouth as freely as water from the Lake Maiden's skin. The Maiden listened, soft fingers lingering on her arms. Mizzy told it all, even the enchanter's advice, and all the while, the Maiden shrouded Mizzy with her thoughts. She sent images of the lake; of Mizzy's home, the whole family by the fire and the smell of her mother's cooking; of practicing her swordplay while Bran read, her sisters tumbled, her father cut wood and her mother mended torn clothes; of the many embraces they'd shared. Mizzy knew the images and sensations were intended for comfort, but—not for the first time—she wished the Maiden could speak in plain words.

She didn't understand her brother and she didn't understand her lover.

She pressed her face into the smooth curve of skin between the Maiden's neck and shoulder. She had sworn never to give up—sworn it to Bran, to their parents, to herself. That left only the enchanter's advice. Mizzy shivered, and felt the Lake Maiden stiffen in reaction.

Mizzy pulled her head up and looked the Maiden in her eyes. Not to do so would be craven. Her lover didn't plead, with her eyes nor her powers. She looked sad and gentle, like she only wanted to pull Mizzy back, close to her body.

Mizzy's hand shook as she reached for Lake Shard. The Maiden gave a smile of tears. Looking over her shoulder quickly, Mizzy confirmed that Bran was still nearby, close enough to be within the explosion of power that would leave the Maiden's body. But there was confusion in his eyes, fear on his face.

'Mizzy?' His voice trembled. 'What are you doing?'

'What I have to, so you can be free.' Her words emerged through clenched teeth as she began to draw the sword.

'The only thing stopping me from being free is you!'

Mizzy froze.

'*You're* the only one who wants to swaddle me in silk and tuck me away in a chest for safekeeping.' Bran took a deep, ragged breath. 'How can you *do* this? What makes you think it would even work?'

'It has to.' Her tears were so thick she couldn't see a thing. Her hand tightened around Lake Shard's hilt until her knuckles felt as though they'd pop from the pressure.

Bran crept even closer, slowly, as if trying not to scare her away. 'I don't need to be cured, Mizzy. I need to live my life, to see the world. You've already shown me so much of it, without even realising: every witch and wizard we sought for a curse-breaker, this journey to collect the rings and go through Gate Eighteen. I don't think you ever understood why I was there with you this whole time. Didn't you ever wonder why *I* never gave up?' He paused again, swallowing hard. 'I've known all along there was no magic cure. I came with you to see the *world*, and everything you were chasing. And there's still so much more out there. I want to see it all. But you have to stop this.'

Hesitation held her. A violent tremble began to take over and her mind rebelled, baffled and hurt.

A damp hand touched her shoulder. She felt the Lake Maiden's love wrapping around her, rubbing away the hard edges of her confusion and pain.

'I want to be free to see the sights, free to break, free to live.' Bran's voice was quiet, but in the eerie silence it felt as though it could have been heard across the lake.

Tears in her eyes, Mizzy let the sword splash to the shallow of the pool.

'I—I'm sorry,' Mizzy choked the words out. 'I've been failing you all along.'

Bran's laughter echoed out to the stars. 'You haven't been failing me. You've given me everything I wanted. Do you get it now, finally?'

'Great Lord, I think so. Yes. Maybe. I don't know.' The trembles came back. 'You want to go back out into the world, don't you?' Mizzy asked. Bran nodded. 'I—I don't think I want to. I want to stay here, with the Lake Maiden.' She reached to her shoulder and held the Maiden's hand there. 'But I understand.

You have to go.' With a small smile, she met his eyes. 'You're going to be amazing.'

Bran beamed brighter than all the light in the sky above them. It was infectious.

Mizzy turned carefully to look at her beloved. The Lake Maiden's arms opened like a flower, and she fell into them. She clutched to the Maiden with a ferocity she never dared with her brother.

'I'm such an idiot,' Mizzy half laughed, tears still gushing, as the Lake Maiden stroked her hair. 'Can you forgive me for even considering hurting you?'

The wave of love she felt was a tsunami.

Mizzy basked in the warmth, and slowly let her mouth form a smile. It was strange and terrifying to think of Bran out there on his own, and almost as strange to think that—even if only for now—she was trading her own adventures for a chance to settle down. She could still feel the tingle of protective panic for him, even as the Lake Maiden embraced her; but, she thought, as the Maiden's waters careened over her skin, if she held him back from adventure now, how could he ever find a love of his own half as great as hers?

# Unnecessary Risks

## Abigail Rosenhart

'I assume you know who I am,' she said as she reached my table.

I nodded, and gestured for her to take a seat. *Everyone* knew who she was. From the moment she had entered the tavern, every eye had been upon her. Those who had reason to fear her shifted in their seats, their hands inching towards their weapons; those who had lived relatively blameless lives—or simply didn't believe all the stories—were murmuring quietly amongst themselves and pointing her out to one another.

'Good,' she said, and slumped down opposite me. A barboy placed a pitcher of wine between us, and she gestured for him to fill our glasses. The last few months had been scarce in good wine, and the sight of the deep, red liquid made my mouth water. This was not the cheap stuff.

'You will forgive me,' I said, watching her closely, 'if I swap our glasses?' She nodded, the corner of her mouth twitching up in a distant relative of a smile.

'You've been burnt before?'

'No,' I said, taking a sip that turned into a few deep gulps. Wonderful wine. Earthy: tobacco, oak and plum. Probably vintage. 'But you don't get as old as I am without being cautious.' I smiled. The cup was emptied in three more gulps, and the barboy refilled it immediately. An excellent arrangement.

'No, I suppose not,' Mathilda said. 'I understand. Your job is to document. You can't take unnecessary risks.'

'Was,' I said. 'My job *was* to document. I am retired now.'

She studied me over the rim of her beaker.

'I have a proposition for you, Scribe Eckhart.' She loosened something from her sword-belt with her left hand, and placed a small leather purse on the table. She tipped it over: a few gold fellens and a silver don slid across the rough wood. There were more of those beauties glinting inside. I picked up a fellen and weighed it in my hand. It was a long time since I had last seen one. A good month of modest living, it would get me. Or I could go back to Bergendahl and spend a week in one of those inns by the river…

'You come out of retirement for one night,' she continued, interrupting my train of thought, 'and I will leave this purse on the table. There are at least seven and a half fellens in there. You can count them, if you wish.' I gathered the coins from the table and slid them back in the purse without looking. Those alone would have bought a king a month of service—I wasn't going to break the Scribe's honorary code for a single night's work.

'I most graciously accept. Let's meet back here tomorrow eve—'

'No!' she interrupted. 'It has to be now.'

Her face gave nothing away, but it was then that I noticed an unpleasant smell reeking from her. I sighed inwardly. These mercenary types: they put so much pride in the execution of their jobs, but I had yet to meet a single one who presented themselves with the same care. As these things went, Mathilda was way ahead of the curve—stunning, even—except for the smell. Granted, her age had rendered certain features less prominent than they once were, and her boiled leather armour was marked by heavy use, but she carried herself with such poise that you could, in passing, mistake her for a queen. Her long braids still had a whisper of red running through the grey, and her wrinkles contoured every emotion that flew across her face. Even her armour, with its polished rivets, bloodstain shadows, and obvious nicks and tears, was beautiful—in its own terrifying way.

'I'm afraid I don't have my kit with me,' I said, keeping my face carefully in check. I had just sold my kit for drinking money—and where would I find the necessary equipment at this time of night?

'It has been arranged for,' she said. 'Do you accept the terms? One night of writing for the purse.'

I spun this around in my head a couple of times.

'You'll leave the purse with the money still inside it?'

The look she gave me would have left a younger man weeping on the floor.

'I'm sorry, Milady,' I said. 'An old man needs to take his precautions.'

'I will leave the purse with the money inside it.'

'Then we have reached an agreement,' I said. She sent a small nod to the barboy, who returned moments later with a fully equipped writing kit and another bottle of wine.

'Leave us,' she said, and he placed himself next to the bar, ready to spring forward at the slightest sign of thirst.

I spread the thick parchment out in front of me and dipped the pen. Two tentative strokes… Yes, excellent tip and good ink. Satisfactory indeed. I took a few sips of the wine. Still wonderful. I cracked my knuckles and wriggled my fingers. One more sip of wine.

'I am ready.'

She took a deep breath and closed her eyes. She looked old

and worn now; she reminded me of my younger sister in the way she hunched over. When she started to speak, however, she straightened up, and the last trace of that tired soul vanished.

'I am not in the habit of listening to idle gossip,' she said, 'but I do assume you have heard some of the stories about me. Tonight, I only want to fill in the gaps, and clarify some misunderstandings. Make sure everything is remembered the right way. I need you to take down what I say, just the way I say it. Is that understood?'

I stared at her, feeling the wine and the project slowly turning my body warm and excited. Mathilda had long been called "the last true hero" by those who adored her, and the Braided Menace by those who did not; there were dozens of songs written about her adventures, and I knew of at least four dirty rhymes praising her physical attributes as well. Yet, she had somehow remained a bit of a mystery.

I nodded. I would take down her every word and gesture exactly. Oh, to be the one who knew the truth about the Braided Menace!

'The next thing I want you to do,' she said, 'is to stop me when you realise who I am.'

'Excuse me, Milady?'

'I am going to be talking through some important parts of my story. When you realise who I am, you stop me.'

'But I know who you are! Everyone does, Milady. You are *Mathilda*, the hero of Bergendahl! Mathilda, the champion of Fjellstad! You are Leader of the Hulds. Uhm… You are the Braided Menace!' I attempted a little grin to cover my awkwardness. I could feel my own age in that moment. I was no more than ten—maybe fifteen—years older than her, and yet my creaking body seemed dry and ancient compared to hers; now my memory was failing me, too. Four years ago, before I retired, I am sure I could have called up a dozen more of Mathilda's titles. But these would do.

'Yes,' she conceded, 'but I am more. When you figure it out, you stop me. Are you ready?'

I nodded.

'These days, most people know about me. They know I am the strongest Jarl the Hulds have ever had. They know I brought them out of obscurity. Of course, now, the Hulds are the best of the best; anyone with money and a need for protection would rather have a Huld than anyone else. But the part of the story that *isn't* told,' she said, awkwardly loosening the buckle on her right shoulder plate, 'is that before I became their leader, they were well on their way to becoming nothing more than common assassins. Their previous Jarl—her name was Audrey, I believe—she joined for the money, and stayed for the violence. She had no finesse, no moral code.

'I joined when I was seventeen because I didn't have a choice. I was strong, used to wielding weapons, and I had made a considerable mark in their territory after that whole business in Fjellstad. I had started taking on mercenary contracts, and sometimes assassinations, if I believed the victim had it coming. So Audrey, or Anita, or whatever her name was, invited me to join them with a knife to my neck. I gratefully accepted, with a knife through hers.

'The Hulds weren't organised—nor interested—enough to avenge her. They flapped about like a brood of headless chickens, waiting for someone to step into action. So I did.'

Mathilda was a thoughtful storyteller. Her tempo was slow enough for me to follow, and she would occasionally pause to let me catch up. All the while, she kept our glasses full, but I noticed that she only ever moved her left arm.

'May I ask,' I interrupted, 'are you injured?'

She gave me a brief nod. 'It's just a flesh wound. Don't worry about it.'

I could see the contours of a rose of blood right under her arm. Now that her buckle was loosened, it had spread out through the padding underneath. It was not fresh. But blood does not bother me anymore, fresh nor old. I have taken down the last words of many a wounded soldier in my day. It always happens: people think they see their final hour approaching, and want to make sure they're not forgotten.

'I simply raised my voice,' Mathilda continued, 'and asked, "Does anyone object to my claim to her position?"

'They all looked at each other, and although I'm sure many would have *liked* to object, they were just individuals back then. There was no Huld family to speak of, no loyalty, no sense of belonging. None stepped forward, for none could trust their comrades' support.

'This huge tower of a man walked up to me. His sword was drawn, and I was unsure if I would be able to take him if it came to a duel. It took every ounce of willpower I could muster not to shy away from him. His long black curls, his impressive beard… I realised this was a man I had heard of. This was Beorn the Champion.' She stopped and smiled; my frail old heart skipped a couple of beats, and I couldn't help but let out a thin squeal of excitement. Mathilda and Beorn were legendary. Probably the most infamous duo of our age. But I had never heard told the story of how they had met—and here I was, hearing it straight from the source.

'Beorn had been travelling with the Hulds for some time, but was as unimpressed with the leadership as I was. He had wanted her dead for years, he told me later, but he was a very clever man; he knew he'd be safer next to the leading horse than upon it. He knelt before me and planted his sword. "Jarl," he said, and I could hear the title echo through the camp. And that was it. I was Jarl of the Hulds, and I had a Champion as my hirdman.

'I reviewed the current contracts, and refused several of them. There were murmurs when I started returning seal money and refusing business with some of the Hulds' regular clients. But I didn't want my Hulds to be lawless.

'Some in our ranks had been picked from the streets. They were nothing more than promoted scoundrels and thugs. Some were retired soldiers: warriors who didn't fit the royal ranks, but could still wield a sword. I steered them all in a new direction—but I let each of them decide if they wanted to stay. Not everyone did. I let most of them leave honourably. You see, everyone who'd joined the Hulds had done so voluntarily—even if their only other option was death. Now, they were free to leave and start their own lives, if they so wished. I even gave many of them a small severance for loyal service. However, there *were* those we didn't see fit to stay with us, yet didn't want to let loose in the world. Perhaps you remember the Eftmund twins?' She gestured for the barboy to bring another bottle of wine.

I searched through my memory and came across a fragment from a song. It had to be at least thirty years since I'd heard it last:

*'The Eftmund twins did swing their axes*
*whispering, whinnying through the air,*
*They severed the head of the one who did taxes*
*from his shimmering, shining hair,*
*Hey! Drink! Raise your mugs!*
*Severed his head from his hair—Drink!—and shoulders.'*

I croaked out these lines and chuckled. She smiled. A man just a few years younger than me kept the song going in a corner. It had been very popular back then.

'The very ones,' Mathilda said. 'They had a frail truce with the Hulds. They travelled with them, didn't harm them, and in return, the Hulds turned a blind eye to the twins' insubordination and bloodthirst. To be frank with you,' she said, grimacing a little as she loosened the buckle on her shoulder another notch or two, 'for the Hulds, I think it was mostly a case of wanting to keep the added dread the twins evoked as part of their company. But I had a vision for what the Hulds could become, and the twins didn't fit anywhere within it. It was one of my first decisions as Jarl to have them executed.

'So, as you see, I did not, in fact, bring the Hulds out of

obscurity. I brought them out of infamy.'

The sentence hung in the air and quelled some of the noise around us. Mathilda's low voice didn't carry across the room, but her words seemed to pass from man to man.

'The next thing I would like to clarify is my relationship with Beorn. I have heard many versions of it retold by others. None tell the truth.' She seemed to drift off in thought for a moment, and I stopped to stretch my fingers. My arm had already started throbbing gently. I had truly let myself go since retirement.

Not to worry. The purse on the table was calling to me. Tomorrow, I would leave this town the Gods forgot. I would go back to the city, find a beautiful young prostitute who wouldn't mind playing house for a week or two. Generously, I would offer her a whole fellen for her work. Or perhaps just a don—still, much more than she'd normally get, even with the new guild rates. Perhaps I could even write a book on Mathilda: combine these unknown stories with what I already knew. I could make the money grow. I could drink in the best inns, read from my book and spend the rest of my retirement in a comfortable daze.

'Do you need anything?' I asked her, eager to continue. She surfaced from her line of thought slowly, and shook her head.

'Beorn and I were never lovers. We weren't secretly married. Beorn was not my brother, nor cousin, and I did not kill him during a lover's spat. I do not think he expected me to be a good leader, but even that first evening, as I went through the contracts and sent out my orders, I could tell his respect for me grew.

'When I ordered the execution of the twins, Beorn was the one who swung the axe. There were two attempts on my life during those first few months, and although I dealt with them swiftly, I noticed both times that Beorn was right there, ready to run into action. I don't doubt that he would have saved my life, had any of those dumb youngsters caught me off guard or sleeping.

'And then... came Bergendahl,' she said, and I felt a shivering silence spread through the inn. Everyone was listening, except the old man in the corner, who was still trying to remember the rest of the lyrics to the song about the Eftmund twins. 'The fact that we were in Bergendahl at all was just a coincidence. Beorn and I had travelled there to negotiate a contract with some Duke from Geatland. We were on our way to meet him when a royal guard fell from a balcony above us with an arrow sticking out of her back.

'Not even in Bergendahl do these things happen so often that it isn't a bit of a shock to your system. I looked up, and two green-clad Southmen flew over our heads and disappeared onto the balcony above us. Their white skin was still a bit of a surprise to us back then; we hadn't met many Southmen before. Beorn swore the oath of the Gods under his breath, claiming he'd seen a ghost. That's how rare they were to see...' A flash of a smile shot over her lips, but she became serious again as she continued.

'The guard by our feet was spitting blood. She was so young... probably not more than eighteen. Just a year or so younger than me. I crouched down to grant her mercy, but she grasped my sword, stared me straight in the eye and sputtered, "The King. The King."'

The people around us were listening so attentively now that a young pickpocket—I had been watching him in action earlier in the evening—was having the most successful night of his life.

'I nodded to the guard that I understood, and her grip on my sword fell away with her life.

'"At least two more just flew past," Beorn mumbled when I had closed her eyes.

'I asked: "Assassins or Mercenaries, do you think?"

'"Assassins," he said.

'"Piss and thunder. Can you get me up there?" I nodded to the balcony. He stretched his arms and looked around for something to step on.

'"Maybe, if you spring hard," he said. We had practiced this move several times. I would climb his body and balance in his hands, then he would toss me into the air, and I would jump at the last second. We'd used it to reach high windows a couple of times, on assassination contracts. People rarely expect intruders through the second-floor window. Gives you a bit of an edge.

'He tossed me with a roar. I leapt, and caught the lower edge of the banister with my fingertips. I fastened my grip and pulled myself up. Behind me, there was an odd cawing sound, followed by a thump. Another Greencoat had leapt from the roof opposite and been slung to the ground by one of Beorn's axes.

'"Watch your back, you cursed braided menace!" he called to me. I heard him kicking down the door on the ground level.

'The balcony led into what looked like an empty bedroom. I pulled my swords, and stepped swiftly through the opening and to the side. One stab to the gut, and the guard lurking there was taken out.' Mathilda's dark skin was practically glowing now; she was emphasising words with her able hand, changing the intonations of her voice to make it more exciting. I was struggling to keep up.

'I could hear downstairs that Beorn had run into problems of his own, but I kept moving. I took down another assassin and ran towards a heart-wrenching scream. It led me to a large, luxurious bedroom, decorated with utter chaos.

'Assassins and kingsmen were shedding each other's blood. Two beautiful, naked women lay on the bed, one screaming her heart out and one split open like a slaughtered lamb. Behind a shivering young guard in the corner stood the King, undressed and unhappy. This was a losing battle for his men.

'I quickly took out two of the pale-faced fighters. Beorn came thundering up to join me. We fought back to back and, after just a minute of dancing, two minutes of creative dodging and a couple of minutes of sticky, bloody war, Beorn picked me up and threw me across the room. I took out the last assassin as I leapt through the air.

'There were many dead Greencoats. Eleven of them in the bedroom, three downstairs, the two I killed on my way in and the one Beorn axed down from the sky. I'm sure the guards had taken down a couple, too. They lost six of their own men, so I surely hope so. But rumour quickly spread across the city that two Champions from the Hulds had singlehandedly saved the King from a full troop of Southmen assassins.

'We were invited to court to tell our story, under strict instruction not to mention the sordid nature of the king's visit to the house. It was there, when Beorn repeated his lines from outside, that the name "Braided Menace" took root. It grew like a weed, and spread its branches far and wide. People think it offends me. But every time I hear it mentioned, I think about Beorn, and the way we fought together.

'They said we had celebrated our victory with a kiss. They said the assassins had come tumbling in through our bedroom window. The rumours grew wild and took on impossible shapes. We celebrated by kissing, that's true—just not each other. Beorn kissed the King's niece, and I, the King's wife.' She laughed. Her eyes had a light to them now, and she had spoken herself flushed and glistening. I could easily imagine what she had looked like thirty years ago, swinging her swords, her braids whipping through the air.

'Are you all right, Milady? Do you wish to take a break?'

She looked at the almost-empty wine bottle in front of us and signalled for the barboy to open and pour the next one. She seemed to study my face for a moment before she continued.

'I did not murder Beorn. That is another myth I wish to dispel. I do blame myself for his death, and for that reason I have never corrected the impression, but I did not personally extract his life from him. It is true, however,' she said, rubbing her shoulder absentmindedly, 'that we fought that day. Even throughout the battle that killed him. Beorn had come to me with a concern: he felt it was time for the Hulds to break up into smaller groups and spread out. I disagreed. He suggested I was getting drunk on power, and I called him a simple thug. I likened him to the things that grow on slimy walls by the rivers of Bergendahl. I accused him of wanting my jarldom.

'After many attempts to have me see reason, he started repaying me with the same coin. He shouted that I was no better than a royal whore who charged just two coppers from a king who offered me gold. That's when we were ambushed by mercenaries from the Tusses. Funnily enough, the Tusses were one of the many reasons I had wanted to keep the Hulds strong and together—they had been trying to make a dent in our ranks for months.

'There were only four of them, and we had six Hulds just a few minutes behind us, so we didn't even pay much attention to the fight. We slaughtered them while yelling at each other, arguing about the Hulds' future, giving no regards to our own.

'The four fell quickly. Beorn was walking around, giving them all a thrust through the neck, just to make sure. He kept thundering abuse at me, and I trailed after him, roaring abuse right back.

'"You bawdy dog-fucking scoundrel! You're not fit to lead the Hulds—you're barely fit for feeding the wolves!" he shouted.

'And I yelled back. "You watch your back, Beorn! I'd sooner see you dead than listen to these base court insults. You're nothing but a hedge-born, dimwitted whoreson!" He opened his mouth to reply, but no sound escaped. He looked so confused, so hurt, and bewildered.

'I began to apologise. We had… an unspoken agreement, not to touch upon his mother's profession. But he just looked slowly down, and I followed his gaze. An arrow was buried deep under a seam in his breast plate, nothing but the feathering poking out.

'The cursed Tusse at his feet had a crossbow. She had shot

straight up through Beorn's armour. A crude shot, but it did the job. She was spitting blood and grinning at me. I yelled in fury and drove my sword through the mongrel's eye, taking pleasure in the crack and gargle. Beorn fell to his knees, and I tried to steady him.

'"Don't you dare, you filthy son of a scold!" I shouted. "I will kill you myself if you even *try* to die on me!" I was... surprised by the anger I could hear in my voice. He looked at me, his face empty.

'"I think," he croaked, swaying unsteadily from side to side, "I'll have to take your word for that..." He coughed once. "You reeking shrew..." He coughed again. "My braided menace..." And then he fell forward.

'I screamed. The sound came from a place I didn't know I carried inside me. I could feel such a tremendous rage driving through my body—so much sadness, so much... I didn't even notice myself plunging my sword into him. "You're a lousy, deceiving troll, Beorn!" I howled at him. "I hope your corpse is picked apart by ravens and scattered by dogs!" My voice scared the forest quiet. I even scared myself.

'This is what the Hulds who were following us came upon: the Champion Beorn lying flat on his face with my sword buried deep in his back, and me, emptying myself of every horrible word I could remember—in between the waves of bile that kept pushing their way up from my stomach, out over the body of my best friend.'

The bar was quiet. Even the young pickpocket had frozen in his tracks. Pipes had burned out, and no one was tending the fire. There were tears on Mathilda's chin and they sparkled with a thousand facets, giving each and every one of us a glimpse of someone from our own past we thought we didn't miss any longer. She cleared her throat.

'As you well know, I have led the Hulds a good fifteen years since Beorn died. But I miss him every day. I've had plenty of lovers, all of them women. I've had some friends, mostly men;

but no other person in my life has been for me what Beorn was. He was my family, and he was my friend. He held my heart because he didn't want it. I held his for the same reason. I still ask his advice sometimes…' She unbuckled the strap on her shoulder plate completely and readjusted the blood-soaked padding. 'I seem to have less time than I thought,' she smiled, 'so let us move on.'

I nodded, ignoring the intense pain in my forearm as I frantically tried to get down every word.

'There is one part of my life in particular that is little known. Before I joined the Hulds, I had already made quite the reputation for myself. I think it is fair to say I started making an impression on the land from the moment I stepped out of a cart in Bergendahl. I was a hard-boiled soul with a blood-stained dress. I was a warrior, right from the start.

'The blood on my dress had been drawn from a man named Dirt. And when I stood there in Bergendahl, at seventeen, Dirt had been my owner for the past seven years. He took me from a burned-down village when I was just a child, and I had travelled with him and his bandits ever since.' She locked me with her gaze. Seemed to brace herself for the story she was about to tell.

'In the beginning, I was their assistant. On jobs, they had me climb through narrow windows and toss them whatever valuables I could find. They had me make them food, and dance for them at night. They beat me when I disobeyed, and sometimes when I didn't. All had their fun leaving bruises on my face—but I belonged to Dirt, and he let them know it.

'When I grew just a little older, he started to satisfy his most unholy needs with my undeveloped body. He was a cruel and vicious man; he did not see me as a child, nor as a girl, nor as a woman. He saw me as a toy. A possession. A pet.

'I hated him. I hated them all—but they kept me chained up most of the time, and I didn't have anywhere else to go. So for years, I clenched my jaw shut, closed my eyes, and waited for another day.

'Dirt was not a popular man. He would frequently get into fights with the others. This escalated over the years, and they started loathing him as much as I did. Then, one drunken night, he accused them all of theft, and he threatened Gaup's wife with a knife.

'They left us behind that night. I was awake when it happened, and I begged Gaup to bring me with them. But I was chained to Dirt's tent, and they didn't want to wake him, so they turned their backs on me and left. As they trotted out of the camp, the elder, Jerv, dropped a bag of supplies from his horse. He turned and gave me the briefest smile of kindness. It fuelled me.

'I ended Dirt's life without hesitation. I took his purse and his sword, unchained myself and left. He had left countless scars on my body, and I left him dead. After seven years in captivity, I felt the deal was fair. I got on a coach headed for Bergendahl, and you know my story from there… But there is one more part you don't know.' She loosened every buckle that ran down her right side, wincing a little as she did so.

'Are you sure you would not prefer to take a break for tomorrow morning?' I suggested, thinking as much of my own swollen fingers as of her health.

'I will not make it 'til the morning,' she said matter-of-factly. I believed her. Her brown skin was paler now, and she looked tired, drawn. Her eyes were like dark marbles. She took a couple of deep sips of wine and pressed on.

'I grew up in a village in the North Country. It was called Oorskof,' she said, rubbing her eyes the way we old people do. 'Have you heard of it?'

'Can't say that I have, Milady,' I said. She looked at me, studied her hands. Sighed.

'So you've never been there?' she asked again. I shook my head apologetically.

'It was a beautiful little village, right at the edge of the great river. I was the oldest of three sisters. We used to play…' She winced and clutched her side. Took a couple of deep breaths. She pushed ahead.

'I had a loving mother who would dye our black hair red, and braid it with ribbons and feathers. I had a doting father who brought us small presents he found in the forest: nuts, berries, pebbles and fossils. I loved my family, and I watched as they were all slaughtered in front of me.

'I was already hiding under the bed when the raiders came through the town. My sisters and I were playing hide and seek, but instead of being found I saw my sisters impaled, my mother raped and strangled, my father tortured and killed. I didn't say a word, and I didn't close my eyes. Some things will force open the windows of the soul and fight their way through. That's just how it is.

'They set our village on fire. I held my breath until it hurt, and then again, and again, until I could no longer see through the smoke. Then I pushed my way out of the door and in through the flames. Everywhere was hot. There were flames and smoke… I couldn't find a safe place, so I ran out of the town into the forest. I didn't go back, because I didn't know if the raiders were still there. All night, I watched the light of the village dim from bright yellow flames to dark, glowing embers. There was nothing left standing in the morning. There was no one left.

'I hid in the forest, keeping an eye on the road. I had heard stories about how bandits often came in the wake of raiders, picking the rubble clean of jewellery and valuables. Everyone knew bandits ate children, or sold them to witches, or made them disappear. I was ten years old, a terrified child, and I hid from the sun and the wind and every crack in the forest. On the third day, a single man came riding towards me. He didn't look like a bandit, and when he came up to the village, he simply walked around, writing notes. I ran out to him.

'"The raiders came," was all I said. I was a little shy, and I didn't really know how to approach him.

'"I see," he said, scribbling fiercely. "Were there many survivors?"

'"Only me," I said, with tears welling up in my eyes.

'He said he was a documenter from the University in Heimsborg. I had to tell him everything I remembered. He asked for all the details I was trying to forget, and he never once looked at me, just at his parchment.

'"You've been very brave to hide for so long," he told me as he got back up onto his horse. "Good luck!"

'I screamed. "No! Let me come with you!"

'"I can't do that. The roads around here are dangerous already. There are bandits around, and I have to move quickly. I am doing an important job, you see. My job is to document. So I cannot take unnecessary risks." He rode away without turning back.'

My chest was tight, my heart racing as if it were trying to beat me back in time. I remembered now, as she talked. Somewhere in the deepest hidden chambers of my mind, I remembered a dark-skinned child with dyed red hair, braided with ribbons and feathers. She was begging me to take her away from a pile of ashes that used to be a village. I cleared my throat and tried to blink away the image.

'You remember now,' she said. 'I'm glad. That night was so cold, I crawled down to the village to see if I could find any spots that were still warm. I was caught by Dirt and his men that morning, and that was the beginning of me.'

I swallowed. 'I'm sorry, I… I was young, I…' I tried, but I could not find the words.

'It's okay. We're even now,' she says. She opened the coin purse and let a small glass vial roll out onto the table. I recognised it right away. Dawnslight's milk.

'But, but…' I stuttered. 'You drank the wine as well!'

She stood in front of me, pulling down the padding under her open armour. I gasped. The smell protruding from her was not, as I had thought, uncleanliness. Her wound was infected, oozing, full of pus. She was rotting, and had been for a while, by the looks of it.

'I have chosen a better death for myself than what fate had in store for me. I like choosing for myself. You might have noticed that, from my stories.'

She refastened her armour and stretched her legs. 'You should still have a couple of hours. Maybe three,' she said, and headed for the bar. 'I suggest you put your affairs in order.'

I looked at the purse of money on the table. I felt old. I finished writing her story, but there was much more I wanted to say of my own. I arranged for the papers to be sent to my granddaughter, and hoped she would forgive me.

Mathilda sat by the bar, drinking the finest wine and eating grilled chicken. A heavyset woman kissed her cheek and sat down next to her, arm around her waist. I left them to it. Everyone gave them peace. There was a whisper of history running through the bar. We were grateful for the story she had told. A single gold fellen I brought to my room, together with a local girl who would make my last few hours worth it all. The rest of the money, I left behind, along with the dreams of all I should have spent it on.

# Nothing Good to Say

E H Timms

'Rumour says you—'

'I know what rumour says.' Cuss leans forward, bracing his hands on the guildmaster's desk to take some of the weight off his injured leg. 'And I say there's too many raiders. The walls won't hold.'

The guildmaster glares back with weary exasperation. 'You're *supposed* to be recuperating. What were you doing walking the walls?'

'Recuperating and *teaching*.' She's the nearest he has to a friend here, so Cuss corrects her with only matching exasperation, not anger. 'I had to show the trainees something. Anyway, this comes under teaching. Assess your enemy. Know when to attack and when to run. And I say they have to run. For safety.'

'Isn't that for me to say?' One black eyebrow lifts towards a fuzzy hairline as she turns the challenge back on him.

'Guildmaster Sarai—' Cuss begins, and shakes away memories of a raider-burned guildhouse, and blood, and sand. 'Oh fine,' he snarls. 'You decide, if you can see the future better than I can. But all I see is death.' Death on a raider's blade for most of them; death in the arena, later, for any captured children. Doesn't matter. He's been there. It's still death, either way.

The guildmaster glides to her feet and leans forward to match him. The single thin braid that marks her as a guild warrior drops from her temple, swinging against her jaw as she moves. Her voice turns to steel as she counters, 'Your death or mine?'

His eyes flick to her braid, reading the signs for duty and skill. He shrugs the shoulder on his good side. 'Everyone's.'

She harrumphs. 'I've heard a lot about you. Seems some of it is even true.' The guildmaster points to a chair opposite her desk. 'No. I don't see your fate. I don't know mine either—apart from my birth chant, of course. Now sit down before you make that leg or those bruised ribs worse.'

'I don't have time to waste on fardling about,' Cuss mutters, but he limps over to the chair anyway and drops into it.

Guildmaster Sarai takes her own seat again. 'The way you talk, you'd think the rumour you have a stone for a heart was true.'

Cuss shrugs again. 'There's a seed of truth there.' He heard that one again only yesterday, whispered behind his back as he taught map-work to the older warrior trainees—along with the one that says he's more sword than human. 'And I enforce it. Nobody should get close to someone like me.'

'Why not?'

'I wind up in too many fights.'

The guildmaster rolls her eyes. 'Is *that* how you get wounded?'

'Sometimes. But I don't start the fights.' He straightens, as much as he can. 'Listen to me, or don't. Doesn't matter. I'll be down at the gatehouse, buying you time. Use it well.'

'But—' She scowls. 'Why you?'

'Why not me? I can't run with this leg. I'd be last out of

here anyway, I might as well play rearguard.' He limps quickly across the office, and is out of the door before the guildmaster can call him back and drown him in memories that taste like blood.

He used to start fights. He used to have to. Bright sun, white sand, gladiator's silver shackle on his wrist, stone wall all around and the crowd chanting the fatelines of the favourite. His own lines, often enough, pounded into him until they became his heartbeat. *I am the curse upon the wind…* The words bound him to the strings of the crowd's desire. Bound him to a fate of tearing through other people's lives and never looking back. He'd danced to the chant again and again, a blade as his partner and death in his smile, until he escaped the sands in a trail of blood. Once free, he'd fled to the warrior's guild for shelter. But even the guild couldn't shelter him from rumour.

‡

Rumour trails after him as he scowls his way down the corridor to his assigned room.

'*—flirting and he didn't even notice—*'

'*—you know what they say, cursed birth day means a cursed child—*'

'*—can't even love himself, let alone someone else—*'

'*—don't let him break your heart, or your life—*'

'*—gets things done, I guess, but the way he does them—*'

'*—wears two braids, but that's just bragging, no one's that deadly—*'

He sifts through it with half an ear but catches nothing new.

He's never bothered to deny the whispers. They keep him safe, free and uncaged. Better for would-be lovers to be put off by rumour than for him to have to spurn them in person. Besides, he reckons rumour's almost right about some things. He *doesn't* notice flirting, any more than he responds to any other language he doesn't speak: he's aromantic as they come and asexual as his blades. But it isn't a curse—more of a blessing. At least, he reckons, if he has to tear through lives like a blade though butter, he isn't going to leave a string of kids and broken hearts behind him.

Rumour can preach all it wants that there is nothing good about him, not even his name, but he knows better. And while rumour may come close on some accounts, it's very wrong on others.

He doesn't fall in love. It doesn't mean he doesn't care.

He doesn't start fights any more. *Not again,* he swore when he escaped the gladiator cages, *never again.* But he does wade in to finish them. And as always, what rumour remembers is the fight, not the reason.

‡

The reason: there were three of them, apprentices, beating on a younger kid who looked at least part raider. The warrior's guild gatehouse was right there, but he didn't stop to ask permission. He just grabbed the kid and shoved the battered body to safety. Then he bouldered towards the other three and flattened them.

The guard on the gate gave him a sour look. 'Kid'll need looking after. Who's paying?'

'Add it to my tithe.'

'And you are?'

'Cuss.' It was a usename, not a full name, and they both knew it, but the guard wrote it down anyway.

Kid was battered, but still standing, raider-blue eyes on Cuss. He shrugged off the gaze, turned carelessly away and left for his courier duties before the bullies woke. He was seventeen, and he'd already learned not to look back. Looking back meant losing time on the road and losing the fight. He couldn't afford either, with two fates weighing on him.

That was the first.

There were other times since, when he'd intervened to take another's fate on his own shoulders. Two starveling brats huddled together for warmth; he set down some travel bars, tightened his belt and moved on while they still slept. A series of runaways seeking various guilds who he pointed brusquely towards the nearest ones. A girl with no home or family left, hauled from under a tree, who followed doggedly after him until he shoved her exhausted body under a guildhouse gate and fled before she woke. A pair of elopers, absurdly young. He saw them safe along the worst of the bandit-riddled roads. A gaunt thief-child, no more than ten years, trying to raid Cuss's pack one night. He dragged the child to a large town and turned him over to the local thief-prince with a glare.

'Kid's your duty,' he told the prince in disgust. 'Do it better next time.'

‡

The candle clock flickers in the draught as he enters his room. He turns his back to it and eases into his armour, contorting and cursing as he stretches to fasten the buckles. His fingers brush against someone else's reaching hand, and he whips round. 'What?' he snaps, but it's only a lanky trainee. One from his class, he decides—the face seems familiar.

'Nothing.' Sullen eyes meet his for a moment, then drop away. 'I can see what I'm doing, is all.'

'I don't need help. You should be off to the tunnels until the raid's over.'

The trainee yanks his shoulder straps into place and buckles them down. 'I know,' she snaps. 'You don't help, you don't wait, you just get things done.'

His scowl deepens but he doesn't waste more time arguing, fastening the more easily accessible straps as the trainee fastens the rest. As long as she knows, there's no danger.

She finishes with the armour, gives him a long look and a scowl fit to match his own, and leaves.

Cuss slides the double harness for his swords over his armour.

The lower belt for crossbow, dagger and bolt-case settles around his waist. He sits on a stool to let his swords jut down behind him and winds an extra supportive bandage around his knee, then glances at the candle. Time is burning away.

‡

He was there when the inn went up in flames; came running out of it with his pack over one shoulder and a child over the other. He joined the bucket lines, muttering curses and swearing as the fire found the ice-wine. It was his hands that grabbed the child's father and stopped him charging into the alcohol-fuelled inferno to search for her, and his hands again that punched the man out when he wouldn't stop fighting. He dragged him clear of the fire and dumped him beside the child. No one else tried to enter.

They remember the punch, and the face set like stone. The child might remember hard hands lifting her to the safety of his shoulder, and a harsh voice reassuring her the danger would be over soon, but she was only three years old. *She'd forget soon enough,* he had reckoned.

‡

He shakes his head as his memory twists and the child's face becomes that of the lanky trainee. *Of course.* Obviously she hasn't forgotten, even twelve years later. He grimaces and stands, shifting his weight to test whether his leg will hold him. Not ideal, but good enough. He'll manage. He claps a metal cap on his head and walks slowly, stiff-legged, to the gatehouse. Kids race past him from different directions, heading for the entrance to the tunnels, while the last adults from the village trickle in through the gate behind them. Nobody spares Cuss a glance. He smiles slowly. At least the guildmaster took him at his word. At least she trusts him to get this done more than she trusts the rumour that says he's a worthless good-for-nothing.

Down in the gatehouse, he slips his cap off and braids the hair at each temple, tying them off with a grey thread pulled from a frayed cuff. He replaces the cap and makes sure his braids are visible below it. Anyone who can read braids can read the danger they face in him. It's a small warning, perhaps, but that's all he plans to give them. He rolls his head on his neck, then his shoulders, warming the muscles gently. He loads his crossbow and hooks it to his belt. He loosens his swords, checks the blades and how close they reach to the gatehouse walls, and slides them lightly home again. He paces restlessly between the first and second portcullises, counting steps from the centre of the arch to each of the portcullis levers, and back. For now both ends of the arched gatehouse tunnel remain open, but a swift yank on a lever can change that. His steps echo back to him.

‡

Just one of many scuffles saw a battered kid, a warrior trainee, staring at him like they'd met before.

The trainee caught him afterwards at supper. 'Why did you do it? *Why?*'

He looked up. His eyebrows climbed his forehead over the muddy brown of his eyes. He said nothing for a moment, but took another spoonful of soup and considered his words. There was no give in him, no softness. He never cushioned his words, or offered his own memories in explanation. 'It seemed like a fun fight,' is all he said, and he shrugged.

He saw the trainee flinch at his words, and the hurt in the mouth that clamped tightly shut. He saw the fire in the raider-blue eyes and the trainee's determination to prove he wasn't worthless, but Cuss added nothing more. There was nothing else to say that could change things, and he had a job to do. He couldn't bind himself to one place or one person. That way lay a cage, and he could not bear the idea of being captive once more. He needed to fly free. He needed to leave, and to be able to leave. He was a curse, carried on the wind, and he refused to inflict that on anyone.

'Good,' said the hurt little voice opposite him. 'They want another try at it.'

His eyes narrowed. His mouth tightened. 'At you or at me?'

'You.'

'Fine. They'll get it. One way or the other.' He finished his meal down to the last crumb and stood. For a moment, their gaze connected, but then Cuss was out of the door.

There was a brief stunned silence behind him, then running feet as he loped over to the gatehouse. He stepped outside the gate arch, clasped his hands behind him and waited.

The trainee grabbed his arm. 'What are you doing?'

'I have an early start tomorrow.' Cuss twitched his arm free. 'If they want me, here I am.'

'But—'

Cuss turned his head and gave the trainee a long look, his face set as hard as stone. The trainee broke the gaze, and Cuss turned to face forward again. There was a crowd gathering, and he could almost feel the strands of history twisting around him too, as he saw the bullies, once young apprentices, now adult journeymen, in the crowd.

'What are you waiting for?' one of the bullies yelled.

'I don't *start* fights.'

'Are you a coward, then?'

He didn't even bother answering that. He gave them only stillness, though he could feel the thrill of the impending fight rolling through his body.

The bullies shouldered their way out of the crowd, and the trainee fled to lean against the wall of the gatehouse. The three stared at Cuss, waiting. Then one of them threw a punch at his unprotected belly. Cuss's arm swept around, grabbed the punching arm, twisted and pulled.

The bully hit the ground. The other two separated and

lunged from opposite sides, trying to get at Cuss's back. He slammed an elbow back to wind one, then a fist forward to knock out the other. The first bully scrambled back into the fight, and this time Cuss wasn't gentle. He kicked him in the groin with a booted toe, broke his nose, knocked him out and spun to do the same to the third.

That one was just getting his breath back, and had sense enough to back away with his hands up.

'It's only a raider kid, nothing worth fighting over…' he pleaded.

Cuss grimaced. He'd been one of those kids not worth fighting over, once—cursed rather than raider-blooded, but still. He looked over the crowd and the bullies, then turned on his heel and walked back inside.

‡

He turns now at the sounds of hoofs. By the time the raiders turn the corner, he's composed and apparently calm, his hands clasped lightly behind him.

They draw up in a long line on their horses and face him. He doesn't twitch. He just stands in the precise centre of the gate's arch, alone. His braids swing lightly and openly against his jaw.

The raiders laugh, and one nudges his horse forward. 'Move,' he orders Cuss.

'No.'

'You are one. We are many. Move.'

Cuss's hand moves sideways. He tilts the crossbow up and around, and fires. As the raider slumps from the saddle, Cuss repeats flatly, 'No.' There's no time to reload. He lets the crossbow fall and draws his swords instead. His lips curl upwards to bare his teeth in a mirthless smile. 'Come and meet me,' he tells them. He speaks the first lines in the chant of his fate softly, listening to it echo and resonate around him as the dance begins once more. 'I am the curse upon the wind. I am the corpse that's flayed and skinned. I am the wraith burned down to bone. I am the life that's swiftly flown…' His fate is another weapon in his hand. He chants it with every death. It greeted his first breath as it will greet his last and remind his soul of its destiny. He knows what he is and how to use his fate, and he delights to see the question on their lips, the doubt in their eyes.

'Come,' he tells them again. 'Come and meet me.'

And then they do. Singly at first. He parries, thrusts upwards under the ribs, snatches the sword out again as they fall, and the horses balk and circle back to the raiders' own lines.

Then faster and more frequent they come, until a mounted raider raises a sword too high and jars it against the underside of the tunnel so hard he drops it. Cuss grins and raises his voice so that the chant fills the air, just like the baying of an arena crowd. On foot he isn't limited by the height of the arch, and he makes the most of that advantage.

Then they dismount, some to catch the riderless horses circling uncertainly, others advancing to crowd him in. One on his left thrusts a spear to skewer him, but Cuss ghosts just out of reach and the spear pierces the raider on Cuss's right instead. The pierced man drops his sword and doubles over, bile and vomit flying from his mouth. After that, the raiders attack more cautiously. Cuss dances among them, blades spinning with careless precision.

A blow smacks against the side of his cap, driving it into his brow. Others slide and strike on his armour, and he snarls as his bruised ribs protest. He flicks his blades out low and high as he rides the adrenaline thrill, and they bite into legs and faces. He uses the thrill to block the pain of the blows he can't avoid and retreats deep into himself to let his ingrained instincts take over.

His swords dance faster and wind around him like a moving shield of silver and red. The raiders recoil a little and he follows the movement without thinking. A grazing strike on his arm pulls him back to himself, and he stops just before he steps out of the gatehouse tunnel. His eyes flicker over the raiders, the bloodied ground and bloodied blades, the road and the gatehouse. Then he retreats to his starting position.

He flicks the worst of the blood off his swords. The movement pulls at his wounded arm and he grimaces. 'I don't move so easily. The gate is mine to hold.'

'Yours to lose. We *will* take it.'

'You *might*. But it will cost you. Might cost you everything. I'm willing to pay that price. Are you?' He hears death singing in the back of his head, like a lark soaring into a cloudless sky, and he breathes deeply. His head lifts to the beauty of the song and he smiles.

The nearest raider gets a good look at the smile and shrinks back. Something akin to terror and horror uncoils in the spattered dust between Cuss and the raiders, and suddenly none of them will meet his eyes. They glance away or down—or up at the walls—and he can tell that they're assessing the area; looking for ways around him.

Fate cannot be beaten any more than death can, but he takes one more chance at slowing them. 'It's a beautiful day to die,' he taunts, 'and there's only one of me to kill. Why are you waiting?'

Six of them charge him on foot.

He leaps sideways as they lunge beneath the outer gate, tries to strike the first lever with his wrist. His leg buckles as he lands, and two more dash through to him before he can launch himself up again. He catches the lever on the second try. The outer portcullis drops behind them and he charges to meet the eight of them; a wraith of grime and dust, wrapped in blades. Their swords slice into him as his own cut through them, but in the end, he is the one left standing.

He wipes his blades on their corpses, gives the raiders beyond the gate a mocking salute, and sheathes his swords. He uses the gatehouse wall for support as he backs clear, then pulls another lever so that the inner portcullis drops too.

Turning a corner out of their sight, he stumbles a few paces and stops. He waits with gritted teeth as the thrill fades and the pain grows, then cradles his wounded arm against his body and staggers on. Blood streaks down from his temple where the cap has dug in and split the skin. His left braid is only red now, no longer brown tied with grey. Red for heart overriding grey for duty. His body is spattered with blood, vomit and bile, each streak marking a blow in the fight. His armour is scored, slashed and dented. As he draws close to the tunnel entrance, he hears the shocked voices of the villagers ahead of him, but clings to his focus. If he stops, if he loses that focus, he'll fall. He doubts he could get up again.

Strong hands grab him and haul him the last stretch up the slope to the emergency cave and its tunnels. The guildmaster's voice asks urgently, 'Did you stop them?'

He shakes his head to clear his vision. 'Slowed. Delayed. Too many to stop. The kids?'

'Safe.'

'You listened, then.'

'How much did you pay for it?' The hands fumble with the buckles of his harness and lift the swords away, then shove him to a seat against a stone wall.

He lifts his good hand and eases off his cap. 'Swords stay with me. Always.'

'Fine. They're right here, beside you. And you aren't going any further until the healer's looked at you.'

Cuss sighs, leans his head back for just a moment and closes his eyes. 'If you must.' The song is fading from his ears as a new set of hands claws at him, and darkness claims him.

‡

He dreams: his back is hard against a rough stone wall. He's been here before, will be again. A dagger juts from his right shoulder, putting his arm out of action. Blood streams down his face from a cut on his brow. He still holds his left sword as the attackers stalk closer across the arena sands, and he sees the faces of everyone he has fought before. Behind them, crouched atop the wall, others wait for his permission to join the fight.

He shakes his head. He won't let them risk their lives for his, for these are the children of his heart. Every kid he has rescued stands here in his memory like a brightness across his shadowed life. But with that denial, he hears their massed voices lifted in the arena chant, cheering him on in the fight that no one can win forever. His name is Damoneltya, his name is *Cuss*, and rumour is wrong for the last time. He has no kith, he has no kin, but he has a kid in every town. They don't forget him. He will never, can never, forget them.

'Come,' he whispers to the ones he's yet to meet, as death's song soars in his mind and he rises on its wings to face life once more. 'Come to me...'

# From Dust 'til Dawn

Helle Reiersen

The sun pushed down on my shoulders like a white-hot weight, pressing me into a sweaty lump in my saddle. Even my familiar seemed beaten into unconsciousness, its serpent-like body hanging in heavy coils about my waist. Every joint and muscle ached with the camel's jerking gait, but I held on. For forty burning days and forty freezing nights, I'd held on. The rest of the caravan stretched for miles behind us, each camel tied to the one in front and their masters leading the way.

As we crawled along, the desert fell and rose in wind-carved dunes and sandstorms; I'd passed cities lost to ruins aeons ago, and seen mirages, calling out to me, of people I would never see again. With every dip of the sun behind the waves of sand, we drew closer to the lost temple of the Red Desert, the Temple al-Sharasa.

The place where I was going to die.

I drew a sharp breath, my dusty throat stinging, and grabbed onto the front pommel of the saddle.

A hand lightly touched my arm. 'Shafiqa, are you all right?'

I tried to blink away the sweat running into my eyes—sweat that had nothing to do with the heat. The caravan's guide looked at me with concern, her familiar flitting about over her head. A many-faced, blue hummingbird, each face pointing in a cardinal direction.

'I'm fine,' I lied, resisting the urge to reach under my veil and scratch at the stubble on my chin—the itchy result of days without proper grooming—but judging from the sceptical quirk of her brow, she could tell I was afraid. Then again, anyone travelling the Red Desert with an elite entourage of the Sons of Daylight had to be afraid of something. But these proud sentries weren't leading *this* maiden away from danger; they were escorting me right into the bowels of it.

My guard was spread around me in a circle, the soft, scorching sand swallowing their feet; their once-white-and-gold armours dulled with dust; their sabres hanging heavy at their sides, *just in case*. Not that they would use them, even if I did try to escape, even if I had anywhere to run. They didn't exactly have human sacrifices to spare.

'You're shaking,' Guide said, passing a scrutinising look over the parts of my skin she could see—which, with the veil, the robe and the hand wrappings, admittedly weren't many. 'You should drink.'

I pulled a waterskin out of my satchel, hesitating only a second as my mind whispered something lame about 'rationing', and took a deep drink. The rush itched, then scratched, then burned in the back of my throat. I doubled over, choking down the water and coughs that threatened to spill out. My familiar tightened its grip around my stomach.

'Remember that the next time you try to chug down the whole thing in one go,' came a voice, a little too jovially.

It seemed that the youngest of my guard, one Latiif ibn al-Shams, had deigned to break formation and was casually strolling—well, trudging—alongside us like we were all old friends. How *wonderful*.

'I'm sorry, I'll strive not to die until it's *convenient* for you,' I bit back, and his smile faltered.

I felt a tiny pang of guilt. He *was* the only one of the guards who had said more than a few sentences to me the whole journey. He almost seemed… genuinely nice. But he wasn't *supposed* to be nice. Not to me. The Daughters of Night had told me all my life that the Sons weren't to be trusted. They were the opposite of everything I'd been taught to believe in. I mean, what kind of cult cut away their men's own familiars, as if half their soul was a burden to be shed?

Even now, there was something uncanny about Latiif's carefree presence, and the distinct *non*-presence of his supposed-to-be-eternal companion. Like he'd been hollowed out.

I shivered.

'Guide, I've been meaning to ask,' Latiif spoke up, ignorant of the tension in the air or, possibly, trying to dissolve it, 'Why is this place called the Red Desert, exactly? The sand doesn't look redder here than any other place.'

'It's not a description, more of a… reminder,' she started hesitantly. 'It comes from an old tale of my people.'

'Let's hear it, then,' Latiif said.

I perked up a little at that, I must admit. It wasn't every day I got to hear a story from a land so many leagues from home.

Guide gave a small, crooked smile and, in a ceremonious tone, she began: 'My people tell of this desert's tragedy so that those lost may be remembered, and we who live may never forget.

'A thousand years ago, this land was plagued by an alkabus, a god-like being of chaos and destruction, whose storms ground mountains into dust and tore the heavens so that darkness bled across the world. Every great kingdom in the east was crushed to sand.'

Oh no. My stomach twisted. I couldn't look at her, could

only keep my gaze straight ahead to the horizon. I knew where this tale led. Every word pulled me one step closer to a precipice, one I knew well from my nightmares, the ending looming far, far below.

'The eight sultanates in the West summoned their armies in a last, desperate effort to save their lands. And this is where the war between man and god was waged. Over one hundred and one nights, the humans were massacred, without mercy. Down to the last man.' She paused, letting the gravity of their deaths, their failure, fill the silence.

I was at the edge now, staring into the abyss of all the fear and despair that I yet refused to face. The lightest of breaths could have pushed me over, bringing the horror into reality.

'In the end, there was only the desert, soaked red with their blood, and the alkabus, that mighty and cruel creature named—'

I took the last step and plunged. 'Sharasa,' I whispered.

Guide halted, confused and perhaps a little disappointed. 'You already know this story?'

'Parts of it,' Latiif conceded. I kept my gaze ahead. 'And then the first High Sorceress and Her guild of sorceresses defeated the alkabus and imprisoned it in the desert, where it has slept ever since,' Latiif finished in a matter-of-fact tone, his optimism long gone.

I fidgeted in my seat, wishing the guards would let me Craft, just to keep my hands busy. Some of our fellow travellers, the nomads and merchants crossing the desert to sell their wares in the east, were knitting blankets, using loose tufts of hair that they picked free of the camels as yarn. I tried to keep my eyes on the intricate symmetry in the woven patterns, tried to keep my mind from looking back to that night in the Academy, were the Daughters of Night, resided. My home.

'Sharasa has awakened.'

My forehead was pressed to the floor of the council's audience hall. Massive pillars had surrounded me, carved monsters clawing over each other towards the domed ceiling. The elders bore down on me, their faces cut deep with age as they calmly explained how they were throwing me to the lions to save their own hides.

'We fear it wants revenge on the guild that entrapped it in the lost temple. If the alkabus unleashes its wrath on us, none of the Daughters—in the entire land—will survive. We are to give it what it wants. A sacrifice from among us.'

Silence had fallen as I waited for the order, and they in turn waited for me to make the offer.

'Shafiqa, we trust you will do your duty,' one councilwoman had said, so damn smug and satisfied it still made me sick. 'After all, we cannot be expected to give the life of a *real* Daughter.'

Sheer indignation had echoed through me, beating at the walls of my mind until it broke free, 'I will *not* just let it kill me!'

They had laughed, of course. What chance did a "half-woman" of an acolyte have against a god?

That same night, I'd been led out by my guardsmen, leaving the Academy for the first time since I'd first set foot there, a starving bag of bones begging for scraps. I had changed a lot since then.

Rage of past and present pushed back against my fear. I would not beg for my life. No, this time I was going to fight. If I had to die, I was going to take Sharasa with me.

I took another drink from my waterskin, the searing sting of it making me gag and my familiar flex its coils. I didn't feel any braver, but I figured it was hard to be fearless after weeks of anticipating every single way a monster might kill me.

‡

As the sun slowly drowned behind waves of red, our caravan reached an oasis in which to set up camp—miles of sand giving way to dirt in a sudden burst of life, shy plants clinging to the water banks. A resting point that had been used by caravaners for centuries, Guide told me. With some ten camels to every person, the stars were peeking out by the time we had finished unloading. I stretched my limbs until they ached.

Under a shining moon, I sat by the embers of our fire pits with Guide, her familiar perching on her head and mine with its head in my lap. She stirred a pot of stew as I undid the wrappings around my hands and feet, digging my toes into the cooling sand with a sigh. I reached under my veil to loosen the bindings and my fingers brushed over the coarse hairs again. I halted. No, I'd leave the veil on. I didn't feel like dealing with intrusive questions right now.

'You have very beautiful tattoos,' Guide said, gesturing to my hands.

'You think so?' I pulled up my sleeves, revealing the swirling lines that crawled from the tips of my fingers and up my arm like vines. Black against the amber glow of my skin in the firelight, the patterns outlined a mosaic of leering faces. 'They're not meant to be decorative—' I stopped myself as Latiif appeared, nodded and sat down. My familiar jerked its head up and hissed.

'How can you stand it?' I blurted out. Latiif looked at me, surprised, I think. It somehow made me angrier. 'Having your familiar cut away. How can you stand having your soul cut down like that?'

He blinked. Then he started laughing. 'You think—because I don't have one of those things, an ashbahi *pet*...' he managed to choke out. 'All they do is tempt us into evil.'

'My familiar makes me stronger,' I snapped. 'It protects me from sickness—trust me, if *you* ever swallow poison you're going to wish you had one—and it's what enables me to Craft. Here you are, leading me to my death—who are you to think that everything you do is right and good, when you're only half of what you're supposed to be?!'

Latiif didn't look even slightly amused anymore. 'You don't

get to decide what makes anyone human. I'm just as capable of right or wrongdoing as you, even without a familiar. So don't you dare tell me I'm broken. I am *not* half a person.'

Whatever I was about to say died on my tongue.

Guide started handing out stew. Latiif sat silent, staring into his bowl. 'So,' she said after a while, 'you can Craft? Can you... tell me how it works?'

I nodded slowly. 'Most ashbah are shapeshifters, but their faces are like masks. If you can form the mask of one and bind it by its name, its power becomes yours. That's where the ability to Craft comes from.' I raised my arm, indicating my tattoos. 'You can bind an ashbahi to anything: a sculpture, a painting, a carving—or a tattoo.'

Guide's eyes widened. 'Wait, you keep them inside of you?' She reached out her hand, tracing over the markings on my skin, something like awe glinting in her eyes.

'It's not natural,' Latiif said, still looking into his bowl. 'The human body contains iron, right, so why don't bound ashbah die, or at least get sick?'

A loud whine pierced the night.

We shot to our feet. More groans vibrated through the air—a cacophony of grumblings.

'It's coming from the camels,' Guide cried. 'It might be bandits!'

I ran for the water, Latiif passing me like a shadow. At the bank, I could just make out the silver-lit outlines of the mass of camels, stomping around and whining while their handlers tried to calm them.

Something was moving in the sky, blotting out the stars above for just a fraction of a moment. And then, more. Shadows swarmed the air, bouncing on the camels' humps and pulling at their hair as if trying to ride them.

I called my familiar, and immediately I felt its snake-like body meld into mine. Heat coursed through my muscles, washing away the aches and pains of the day. I could see clearly now, down to the grains of dust being kicked into the air in the panic. And I saw the ashbah, their ever-shifting bodies glowing with inner fire.

One of them peered down at me, its mask almost curious. Instinctively, I kept my eyes trained on it—a mistake, as it now seemed to realise that I, unlike the others, could see it. It lashed out towards me with an arching wave of energy. I pushed Latiif away with the strength of my familiar and leapt to the side. The wave sliced at the ground, and the open space between us erupted in heat and sand. A flash of pain shot up my left arm and I jerked back, pressing it to my chest, wet warmth seeping through my robes.

I gritted my teeth, my familiar already working to dull the pain and knit the flesh back together, and cast a glance at Latiif, who stood with his sabre drawn, apparently unharmed. Moonlight glinted along the blade and, with my familiar's senses, I could see the fragments of iron worked into the metal. The attacking ashbahi had seen the ominous glowing grains as well; perhaps it was reconsidering its odds against this prey.

I wanted to laugh—the creature had no idea what it was facing. I could do far more than just see it. I had spent days and months and years drawing these tattoos across my body, capturing ashbah inside me and making their power mine to control. I only had to think a name, *Aniif*, and an eight-legged equine creature erupted from the tattooed seal on my shoulder, its body armoured with stone plates, its face covered by a one-eyed mask with long, sharp horns. I sent Aniif ramming straight into the ashbahi, piercing its shifting body on a horn. It writhed and cried out as Aniif slammed it to the ground, and the ashbahi disappeared in cinder and smoke.

At the noise, the wild ashbah soared towards us like a furious cloud. I steered Aniif to meet them head-on but the ashbah pushed back, the air itself quaking upon impact. Some had torn themselves away and were heading for me, their skin glowing brighter as they neared.

I summoned more of my ashbah just as a wild one released a blast of flame. I turned the energy outwards and concentrated it on my skin; the fire hit, deflected off my shield and sprayed over the ground. Steam thrust up before me as the glowing sand melted into glass. I fired a few shots of my own, exploding several masks, but more ashbah always replaced them.

*Rhyb*, I called out. A long, thick trunk of intertwining tentacles shot up like a tree behind me. Its body shuddered as attacking ashbah slammed into it. Rhyb grabbed them with several of its limbs and started tearing chunks off the raging things, while other ashbah were smacked away by its writhing tendrils.

'Shafiqa!'

I shot a glance over my shoulder. Latiif stood a hundred paces away, his legs slightly bent and sabre raised, searching blindly around himself for the enemy. Fear of the iron must have kept most of the ashbah away from him, but now I could see some circling closer.

*They don't yet know that he can't see them*, I realised, and cried back, 'Up from your left!'

Latiif spun and sliced his blade diagonally upwards. The iron bit into an ashbahi and it jerked back, bleeding fire.

'With me!' I yelled, running over, and he broke out in a dance, swinging his sabre wildly and sending frightened ashbah away in panic.

The mass of ashbah that had clung to Aniif launched into the air like disturbed crows. Aniif was in tatters, limbs missing, mask cracked and wounds leaking red smoke. Shards of masks glittered about its remaining hooves. Above us, the ashbah gathered, spiralling up high in the shimmering, crackling air. I pulled Latiif as close as I could and called for my ashbah again. Rhyb rose up before us while Aniif limped in our direction, more pieces of its body breaking off with every step.

Rhyb's massive bulk covered us as the ashbah swarmed. Fear spread through me like acid.

*I can't die here!* my mind screamed.

The sky burst into light and fell. Rhyb collapsed against the blast, crushing us under its weight. I heard bones snapping and a scream, maybe my own. I gasped for breath. Then the pressure on my lungs eased. Rhyb was pushing back, rising just enough to avoid flattening us into paste. Little black dots swarmed the edges of my vision. I tried to focus, summoning every speck of power within me, forcing it all into a single point: the need to survive.

I reached out through the hot, crushing pain and pulled desperately at any energy I could find. And then I pushed. The power surged through Rhyb's body, turning it to dust, and clashed into the ashbah's spell circle. They struck back and I pushed harder, until all my remaining bound ashbah ruptured out of me in a red cloud of limbs; until a white light burned behind my closed eyes and a crash of thunder filled my ears.

The thick pressure snapped and scorched air rushed into my lungs. Burning light faded into starlight—and the cloud of twisted masks. I squeezed my eyes shut, dread, despair or hopelessness blossoming in my stomach. They weren't all dead. I'd given it all I had and the beasts still wouldn't die.

I lay hollow on the ground, my exhausted familiar like a leaden weight. I had nothing left. I barely registered the pair of arms pulling me to my feet. I looked desperately to Aniif just as its broken body scattered like sand. I sucked in a breath.

The space in front of me exploded in a geyser of sand, a single shadow coming straight at me through the haze.

My eyes widened but I couldn't move. Too slow, too tired. It was too close.

A glint of silver flashed across my sight. The ashbahi froze in the air, a curved edge of steel springing through the centre of its mask. I shifted my head to see Latiif, holding me up with one arm and burying his sabre in the ashbahi's skull with his other.

Latiif pulled his blade free as the ashbahi fell apart. 'I—I hit it?'

Struck dumb with disbelief, I just nodded. Above us, the last ashbah hung in the air, one of them beginning to flare with power. I grabbed Latiif's sword-arm and raised it towards them, the iron misted by the dead ashbahi's essence. I grinned coldly. *Have at me, then, you bastards.*

The flaring ashbahi hovered, burning and ready for the final assault. It cocked its face at me and I tightened my grip on Latiif, sweat stinging my brow. Then—like blowing out a candle flame—the ashbahi turned and flew off into the night with the rest of the creatures.

My knees gave, and Latiif dropped his sabre to hoist me up, half-dragging, half-carrying me back to camp. Caravaners emerged from their hiding spots to check on their camels and merchandise, my own guard—*now, that's a laugh*—heading towards us, looking stern.

'Where were you?' I wheezed, cutting in before the captain could open his mouth.

He glowered down at me. 'Looking for *you* until it started raining hellfire. Was this your doing? Explain yourself.'

If I'd had the strength, I'd have jumped on him and clawed out his eyes. As if reading my mind, Latiif tightened his arms around me.

'We were attacked by ashbah, sir, but Shafiqa managed to drive them off,' Latiif said, sounding only a little less exhausted than I was. 'I'd be dead if it weren't for her.'

The captain looked about to respond when a voice cried my name and Guide came running to my side, looking sick with worry.

'You're bleeding! By the pits, Shafiqa, we need to get you to the healer's tent. Now.' Without sparing the Sons a glance, she grabbed hold of my arm, and she and Latiif hauled me away. Surprisingly, the captain didn't protest, though his eyes were disapproving enough.

I turned slightly to meet Latiif's eyes. He'd fought with me and saved my life—whether just to protect the prisoner or for his own survival, I wasn't sure—and he'd just defended me against his own captain. I felt like I might drop dead at any moment, and yet I had to know. 'Why?'

He squeezed my arm like I was one of his fellow soldiers, and smiled. 'I'm duty-bound to protect the innocent, and despite what the circumstances might make you out to be, you're not evil. And you saved me first.' Then he blinked, suddenly looking worried.

They left me with the nomads' healer, and my barely conscious mind snapped back to attention when she moved to undo my robes. Instinctively, I clutched her wrists, but she simply looked at me with the sad sympathy of someone trying to coax a wounded animal out of its hole. I forced myself to release her and lay back, tense, waiting for a gasp or a curse or a sigh of pity, but the woman said nothing. Swathed in her silence, I soon fell asleep.

I woke up—covered in bruises and stitches, but otherwise in travelling condition—to the muted farewells of our fellow travellers as the Sons packed up our supplies. The caravan wouldn't take us much further into the desert than this, so we'd have to make our own way, meaning I'd be stuck with nothing but the Sons for company for *literally* the last days of my life. I couldn't wait.

The only one I was truly sorry to leave behind was Guide. She didn't bother masking her sadness when her smaller hands clutched at mine in goodbye. She said no farewell, but before letting me go, she traced the pattern of an eye in my right palm. A symbol of protection. I said nothing in return, but held my right hand tight to my body, where it has stayed ever since we left her.

The next few days of our journey each fell heavier than the last, every step a battle against the most primal desire within me: *I want to live.*

I'd been ready to fight before, sure, but without any delusion as to the outcome. I'd imagined fighting out of spite—against the alkabus, the elders, the world—not for my life. But now... I had faced death and defeated it, and my heartbeat sang in triumph. I felt like howling at the stars, jumping to the moon.

But the cost of that victory... All my ashbah. All my power. Gone. Only my soul companion remained, my familiar, too weak now to even manifest outside my body. A deep ache settled in my stomach. Begrudgingly, I took another stinging gulp from my waterskin.

‡

At last, we arrived at the temple. It wasn't very impressive. Hundreds of spiked stones stuck out of the sand, a single square platform at their centre. We left behind the few camels we'd kept with us and walked up to the slab of rock.

I stood on the platform, surrounded by the soldiers and the rows upon rows of stones. It felt strange to have such solid ground under my feet again. The captain raised his arms and stared out over the wasteland.

'Sharasa!' he bellowed. 'On behalf of the His Holy Grace, the Sultan of the forth sultanate, the Sons of Daylight humbly offer you this gift as a token of peace.'

Silence, and a ripple passed over the sand. A low buzzing sent trembles up my legs, and a harsh quake almost knocked me off my feet. Latiif grabbed my shoulder to keep his balance. The sand all around us began to spiral in, churning around the platform on which we stood. The desert drained into itself before our very eyes, quicker and quicker, dragging with it the camels, which whined desperately before being crushed under the endless sandfall.

As the sand sank away, the stone spikes became the crowns of hundreds of towers, striking upwards from miles below, our little platform now grown into the top of an obelisk. Steps cut into the rock reached down into the depths of the temple entrance—a hole in the very bedrock of the desert. The temple's gaping mouth grinned up at us.

'After you,' I told the captain.

We made our cautious way down the narrow steps; down, down, down, past the mangled heaps of our camels and supplies, and into the darkness below. Hands grabbed elbows and shoulders as we descended. Shivers passed through us like vibrations on a string. Finally, our feet hit open floor, and fires flickered to life over our heads.

We were in a cleansing chamber, I realised, the same kind I'd used so often back home before entering the holy halls. The tub in the centre of the room was filled, steam pooling out over the edges. What a strange—what a *laughable*—thing to find in the den of a monster, as if I needed to purify my flesh to be worthy of Sharasa *eating* me.

Still, my muscles ached, my skin was caked in sweat and dust, and to the pits with it if that bath didn't look like the most inviting embrace I'd ever seen. I tore off my clothes, wrappings and veil, and was half across the room when I felt the pinpricks of their eyes on my back. I halted and turned around.

The guards stared at me, propriety be damned, the captain's eyes frozen on my body.

'You're… but you're not…' The captain fumbled, and then his jaw tightened. 'What have you done? The alkabus wanted a *Daughter*, not…' he trailed off, making vague gesticulations at me.

'And I am here, just as ordered,' I snapped, but they didn't hear me; they just kept glaring at whatever it was they *thought* they were seeing: a woman who looked like a man, or a man who looked like a woman, with a body shaped a little like both and therefore, in their eyes, never enough to be either.

They stared in shocked silence. I couldn't help hating them for it, because hate is such a warmer feeling than fear, and fear was something I was used to feeling under the scrutiny of others. In skin like mine, you learned early how small the human mind was. Unwilling to accept that which was in between, to even give it a name, the mind would reduce even another human to nothing.

'She's a freak.'

'Disgusting.'

'Sharasa is going to be furious.'

'How could they let this happen?'

The insults were too old to hurt, but what I heard beneath them stung. *They* felt cheated? *They* were afraid to die? They thought *they* had a right to be angry?

My eyes met Latiif's: the only one still silent, still staring at me with confusion—and not just staring at my face, either. I had seen that look many times before: the eyes crawling over me, searching for the bits that weren't there or weren't shaped right. Never finding what they wanted to find. The eyes of those who'd tossed me into the streets, the elders, these "guardians"—to them, I was always half of a whole, less than human.

They didn't see that I had never been less of anything.

'You fool!' the captain yelled. 'Our only chance to make peace with Sharasa, and you and your council throw it away for some sick joke!' He grappled at the hilt of his sabre.

Instinctively, I reached inwards to summon my ashbah, only to grasp at smoke. I was empty and, worse, I was defenceless. Tension gripped my body like a vice. My heart was beating so hard it hurt. I was naked and alone, and faced with tempered steel and men with betrayal in their eyes.

And I was going to die.

The thought was a lightning strike of clarity. Yes, I was going to die. But not here, not like this, at their hands. There was something I needed to do, damnit. And they needed me, whether they liked it or not.

'Enough.' I was surprised at how steady my voice came out. 'Whatever else you think I am, I am still a Daughter of Night. Nothing has changed,' I said through gritted teeth. 'But fine, beat me or kill me or whatever. And then what? You'll have no prize for Sharasa and a snubbed god on your hands, and everything we have all been through will have been for nothing. And personally, I don't feel like rolling over and dying for the sake of *your hurt feelings!*'

I looked at Latiif, imploring him to listen. 'I can do this. I'm enough as I am—*I* am not half a person!'

Latiif took a step forward. Then another. His hand was resting at the hilt of his sabre, ready to—

'Captain, I want to finish our mission,' he said, turning back towards his leader.

Before the captain could respond, the floor lurched, knocking my feet from under me, and I fell, and fell, and fell, way down past where I should have hit the ground. My stomach flipped. Nausea pushed at the back of my throat. Then, with a stumble, my feet caught something hard.

A hot blast of air brushed over my skin and I looked up.

The groaning voices of the Sons were sucked into the dark that stared down at me. In that black surface, I could just make out the phantom image of a naked woman, pale and frightened, and I realised it was me; a tiny soul reflected in the endless pools of several enormous eyes. Eyes that grew and swallowed everything—the puff of my breath, the beat in my chest—until the whole world seemed to have drowned in their depths.

AND WHAT IS THIS?

The voice shook the walls and echoed back to beat against my body. I took an involuntary step backwards and slipped. My hand shot out but my fingers skidded across the flawless surface and I lay sprawled on the floor, not daring to raise my head lest I be pulled in again to the creature's gaze. Was this it? I'd been prepared to fight until my last breath—and I succumbed this easily?

COULD THIS BE THE LITTLE OFFERING? STAND UP, DAUGHTER OF THE NIGHT—OR DID THEY BRING ME A DEAD ONE?

There was more amusement than curiosity in its tone. I took a deep breath and moved into a crouch. I turned my head to get a grip on my environment—anything to avoid looking at *it* again. I was in a huge chamber of dark glass. My gaze trailed the great expanse of the floor to the far-off wall, which twisted and folded in glass reliefs, elaborate and glowing.

This was no ordinary artisan's work. This had been Crafted. I followed the wall higher and higher to the ceiling, and saw a thousand shapes and faces of glass. Ashbah were held here; I could feel the thrum of their ancient power, the energy that had kept Sharasa captive for so many centuries.

The shadow of the alkabus filled my vision, seeping into every crack of the immense hall, and all thought fled my mind like birds before a thunderstorm.

THE LITTLE ONE IS PLAYING COY. THE DAUGHTER THINKS SHE IS SO ABOVE ME THAT SHE WILL NOT EVEN GIVE HER NAME.

Another voice answered before I had a chance to. 'This is the Sultan's offering, mighty one,' said the captain from somewhere above me. 'A... Daughter of Night.'

I gritted my teeth at the hesitation. A spark of old defiance flared under my skin. 'My name is Shafiqa,' I said, my voice only slightly unsteady, and forced myself to look up.

Four diamond eyes dominated its face, pointing out from the centre, so huge I could see how the fibres in its multicoloured irises pulled at the edges of its pupils. Its black-blue skin shone as if touched by moonlight. Sprouting from its torso were dozens of arms. From its shoulders, its back, its stomach, limbs shot forth and melted in, sometimes thin, sometimes thicker than the pillars in the Academy's great halls—and sometimes one arm split into two or five or hundreds of new ones, stretching out in all directions, pushing against the floor, the walls, the ceiling. A giant cave spider, eagerly stalking its prey.

I AM SHARASA.

From somewhere in the dark, the captain spoke again, 'Mighty Sharasa, do you accept this pact of peace for the mutual benefit of yourself and our people?'

The alkabus's face bulged. A tiny crack appeared between its eyes before sinking in again.

I AM... GRATEFUL... FOR THEIR GIFT.

A wisp of air zipped past my face like a bug. There was a sudden cry from behind me and the sound of something heavy slamming into a hard surface. I whipped around, trying to see what had happened, but found only darkness and shadow. There were gasps, and the unmistakable chink of sabres pulled from their sheaths. I called my familiar and gave a frustrated cry when I realised it was useless.

Voices speared the darkness.

'What happened? I can't see.'

'H-he's dead. We've been betrayed, we—'

'It's that she-man's fault!'

'We should have just killed her!'

'Those old bats tricked us!'

'What are you doing?' the captain yelled, louder and braver than the others.

Thunderous laughter rolled over me. Two giant arms shot out across the chamber and closed around something in the blackness. A wet crunch. Hunched on the floor, I saw—but couldn't understand—the blood pooling between its immense fingers and pouring, wet and echoing, to the floor; more blood than I thought a human could contain.

I heaved, tasting acid.

The captain's glinting sabre struck through the alkabus's hand, the skin around the puncture sizzling. The smell of rotting seaweed filled my nostrils.

WHAT'S WRONG, WARRIORS? AREN'T WE HAVING *FUN?*

At the last word, Sharasa swiped one of its arms to the side, shoving the human shadows into the wall so hard that they hung there, groaning, impaled on the Crafted glasswork. A soldier choked and spluttered as one of Sharasa's other arms forced its way down his throat, his body jerking wildly until it suddenly stilled.

'Stop!' I yelled weakly, shaking off some of my shock. Another Son was hauled into the air. Countless hands grabbed at his arms and legs. 'Please, stop!' I screamed, horrified.

The hands pulled. Joints snapped. Tendons tore. And the crying, limbless form fell to the ground with a thud, only to be squashed by a giant hand, like an insect.

THE DAUGHTER SHOWS CONCERN FOR *THEM?* INTERESTING.

I watched helplessly as Sharasa picked up another Son in its fist. My heart stopped when I saw who it was, his face barely illuminated by the shine of the alkabus's skin. Latiif.

Desperately, he drove his sabre into the hand again and again, but to no apparent effect. Sharasa lifted him up to its bulging face. The slit at its centre opened and grew wider until its face opened like a flower, revealing a gaping gullet. Tongues of flame leapt up at the boy from within.

'No, wait! Why are you doing this?' It was me who was supposed to die here, so why in the pits was I still breathing? Was Sharasa just saving me for last?

Latiif hung, still struggling, over the chasm. To my surprise, the beast paused, turning one of its eyes towards me.

AND NOW SHE BEGS FOR THE LIFE OF THIS ONE. MAYBE SHE WILL EVEN TRY TO BARGAIN—IF I WILL LISTEN.

I blinked, shaking and drenched in sweat. Bargain? What could I possibly bargain for Latiif's life with? I'd been thrown out of my home, the council wanted me dead and my ashbah were gone. There was nothing left for me to give.

Tears welled up in my eyes, turning the alkabus into a blur of moonshine and biting fires. Latiif gave a cry of pain.

I sprang to my feet. 'Stop it! Leave him alone, you—' *Wait. No.*

I blinked hard through the tears. My eyes had to be deceiving me, they *had* to. The flames that flitted through the air were dancing, growing and shrinking, pulling at Latiif's clothes as if playing a game. Masks. They were ashbah made of fire.

I wiped my eyes with a furious hand. These ashbah were the same as the ones from the oasis—I'd bet my own heart on it. This was where they'd come from. From Sharasa. But why try to stop us from reaching the temple? Didn't it want its prize?

I clenched my fists, nails digging into skin. It was Sharasa's fault I'd lost my ashbah. It had cut me down for itself, robbed me of what little I had left in this world, and yet now it wanted to *bargain* with me? For what?

'That's it!' I froze, almost knocked over by just how stupid everyone had been. It didn't want something I *had*. It wanted something I could *do*. 'You need me.' It was a bold thing, a stupid thing, to challenge Sharasa like this, but still. It hadn't eaten me yet. 'You can't escape on your own.'

I could feel the magic of the ashbah trapped here, and the power of the Craft of the High Sorceress and her Daughters of old. That power had kept Sharasa bound for a thousand years and, even if it had now waned enough for the alkabus to awaken, it would be another thousand before those chains could break. Sharasa needed a way out.

*A sorceress would have sensed this*, I thought angrily, *if only one had been allowed to deal with Sharasa before now.*

THE DAUGHTER WILL BRING ME TO FREEDOM BY HER OWN FLESH AND BONE.

'You need a vessel.' The cold reality washed over me. I could barely keep my voice from trembling. Those fools on the council. The alkabus didn't want revenge or a feast—it wanted a sorceress to seal it inside their own body and simply walk it out the tomb unhindered. I cursed the elders with every vile plague I could think of. They'd been so afraid of the alkabus exacting retribution that they'd gladly handed over its only means of escape.

'Shafiqa, run!' Latiif's desperate call was cut off by a long groan as Sharasa's fist clenched, crushing his ribs. I yelled out again and Sharasa eased its grip, leaving Latiif gasping in pain on the chamber floor.

SHE WILL GIVE HER BODY OVER TO ME?

'Yes, I will,' I said without hesitation, without thinking twice.

I let out a short breath of relief as the alkabus's face closed back over the fire-spitting gorge. It turned to me, its four eyes twisted in an expression that might have been a grin. Its form grew hazy, like I was seeing it through a creeping fog that blurred its edges into shadow.

The shapeless darkness surged towards me and Sharasa enveloped me, blocking out the light of the ancient magic. Like needles pressing into my skin from every direction, the alkabus dug down through flesh and tissue and bone, drilling towards my centre.

A scream pushed at the back of my throat, but it was choked to silence by the slow stabs of pain in my chest, neck and face. Sharasa was compressing itself into the nooks and crannies of my body. Muscles grew leaden, veins engorged, my heart strained with every beat. I gasped desperately for breath as I drowned in the alkabus's essence.

But somewhere deep inside my mind, where the pain hadn't yet pulled me under, cowered a weak thought. The alkabus was scraping at the door. Just before the pain could tear my mind asunder, I let the thought slip out of its cage, an enfeebled command.

*Now.*

The scoring pain of the needles came to a quivering halt and a new burning came alight in my stomach. The searing heat stung as it washed through me, like pouring ice-cold water on a fresh burn. A scream of pain and confusion and rage roared from within me—and yet, it was not mine. I had never heard a more satisfying sound in my life.

WHAT IS THIS—AAARGH!

"This" was the pure, concentrated iron in my stomach being released into my blood by whatever shreds of my familiar remained. Iron that I had been ingesting for days, mixed in my waterskin, and which my familiar had strained to keep from being digested lest we both die from its poison. The amount of iron in a human might not even itch a alkabus, but sealing itself inside a body containing *this* much was bound to do more than just hurt.

And here, I'd thought I'd have to trick Sharasa into possessing me.

'This is your death, Sharasa.'

Sharasa's form convulsed, inside and outside of me, and it howled. It writhed against my body, trying to twist away, but enough of the alkabus had been sown into my flesh to bind it fast.

My mind was still against the pain, like a pond undisturbed by a raging storm. I felt myself suspended in the air, tossed around by Sharasa's tantrum like a leaf in the wind, spasms jerking at my body.

STOP! SHE MUST STOP IT NOW—GAAH—OR I'LL KILL HER!

My mind shattered its restraints, and our joined bodies of fire and flesh loomed over Latiif, his expression of terror beyond anything I'd ever seen. Before I could intervene, flames were consuming his body. His face contorted in pain, eyes sinking in, skin charring black until only ashes trickled from our grip. I hadn't saved him, hadn't even had time to try.

Sharasa screamed in rage, and suddenly it flung our huge, twisted body towards the chamber entrance. We ran through rooms and hallways that hadn't been there before, growing weaker as we went, and then we were at the bottom of the obelisk's steps.

I'LL KILL THEM ALL! EVERYONE, DOES SHE HEAR?!

The caravan. Guide. My sisters.

*No! You're not going anywhere!*

I fought to wrestle control over our body. I screamed curses at it. I threw all my will into beating at its dying essence. Still we slowly ascended, crawling and gripping at the steps, the iron eating away at us both and ancient magic trying to pull the monster back into the chamber's mouth. But our merging was snapping the old bonds' hold on the alkabus, and it pulled us out of the hole, breaking the last chain of its leash. I felt a glimmer of its triumph before we collapsed on the stone steps.

*So this is it, then.* And then I repeated what my mind had been whispering since the oasis. 'I still don't want to die.'

THEN DON'T. SAVE US BOTH, SHE KNOWS HOW.

I did know how. The alkabus *possessing* a body filled with iron might be enough to kill it—and me, without my familiar—but if I Crafted a proper seal for it, its power would be mine. I could use it, to heal myself and save both of us. But was saving myself worth letting Sharasa live—and live inside me?

I CAN SEE HER PAST. SEE HOW THEY SACRIFICED HER, TREATED HER AS LESSER. WHAT DOES SHE OWE THEM?

Something hard and warm covered my face. Its smooth mask fitted awkwardly over my features. I ran my hands over its surface.

WE COULD MAKE THEM PAY.

The skin moulded like clay in my fingers. The raw power of Sharasa thrummed in my veins. No, I wouldn't destroy them. They had only done what they thought was best, cowardly as it may have been. But I could show them what a mistake they'd made; how great I could have become if they'd only given me the chance.

SHE WOULD BE THE GREATEST DAUGHTER SINCE THE FIRST HIGH SORCERESS.

The ground beneath me rumbled. I dug my fingers into the face over mine until my nails bit into my own skin. What if I wasn't strong enough? Could I risk setting Sharasa loose on the world?

*But I am strong.* I'd survived the streets and struggled for years to perfect my Craft, no matter every scornful face that told me I wasn't worthy. I'd fought the ashbah and won, I'd accepted my own death, I'd even tricked a god. *Yes, I am strong enough. Stronger than you, Sharasa.*

The rumble grew louder. Streams of sand came cascading down the edges of the pit. The hole in the desert was caving in.

Needles pricked my face, and wet trails fell down my cheeks and chin. I couldn't trust it, I knew that, but I could control it.

The walls of the hole gave, exploding in a torrent of sand that came rushing in to bury us in the belly of the desert. The moon blinked out of sight as darkness surged down to meet us.

'THEN LET US STAY TOGETHER FOREVER.'

‡

I opened my eyes to crisp night air, tendrils of sand falling from my shoulders and retreating to the ground. I lifted a hand to my face. It felt clean, familiar, but not quite mine. A breeze brushed over the sand, faint silver clouds dancing across the dune. There was no trace of the temple or the battle that had been, only untouched mounds of sand.

*I am free.* I smiled. No longer chained down by anything or anyone, I was free. And out there was a whole world, just waiting for me. To the north, I could see the tail of a caravan snaking away through the desert, to lands I'd never seen. I felt a pull there, but I couldn't remember why. And to the south: the Academy, the elders, those who had trapped me. I wanted to—no, I would not return home.

*This one is strong,* I thought, and let the pull take me away, my feet not leaving the slightest impression on the sand. *Soon, the world will know true power once more.*

# Acknowledgments

This anthology has been a labour of love, and has come about through buckets of blood, sweat and tears. There are many people who deserve thanks, starting with all our Kickstarter backers. This simply couldn't have been done without you, and we are humbled and grateful for the amount of support, signal boosting and encouragement we received throughout the campaign.

A huge thank you to all of our authors. We are eternally grateful for your patience, humour and willingness to carry on making small changes, right up to the finish line. We love each and every one of you, and hope to work with you again.

Thank you to our sensitivity readers for your help bringing these stories into the world. We value your input immensely.

Thank you to everyone who tweeted, wrote about and talked about our campaign. We owe you one!

Thank you to Dr Wheeler, our champion—the vial of tears is on its way—and thank you to all our friends and family for backing us up throughout this project.

We would both like to thank each other for picking up the slack when one of us wavered.

And thank you to you for reading this anthology. You're the reason we did this in the first place.

Amelia and Antonica
Manager and head editor
Ink & Locket Press

68276268R00139

Made in the USA
Charleston, SC
04 March 2017